D1240682

Guardian

WITHDRAWN

GUARDIAN

A NOVEL

Natasha Deen

GREAT PLAINS
TEEN FICTION

Copyright ©2014 Natasha Deen

Great Plains Teen Fiction
(an imprint of Great Plains Publications)
1173 Wolseley Avenue
Winnipeg, MB R3G 1H1
www.greatplains.mb.ca

All rights reserved. No part of this publication may be reproduced or transmitted
in any form or in any means, or stored in a database and retrieval system, without
the prior written permission of Great Plains Publications, or, in the case of photo-
copying or other reprographic copying, a license from Access Copyright (Canadian
Copyright Licensing Agency), 1 Yonge Street, Suite 1900, Toronto, Ontario,
Canada, M5E 1E5.

Great Plains Publications gratefully acknowledges the financial support provided
for its publishing program by the Government of Canada through the Canada Book
Fund; the Canada Council for the Arts; the Province of Manitoba through the Book
Publishing Tax Credit and the Book Publisher Marketing Assistance Program; and
the Manitoba Arts Council.

Design & Typography by Relish New Brand Experience
Printed in Canada by Friesens
Second printing, 2019

LIBRARY AND ARCHIVES CANADA CATALOGUING IN PUBLICATION

Deen, Natasha, author
    Guardian / Natasha Deen.

Issued in print and electronic formats.
ISBN 978-1-927855-09-6 (pbk.).--ISBN 978-1-927855-10-2 (epub).--
ISBN 978-1-927855-11-9 (mobi)

    1. Title.

PS8607.E444G83 2014   JC813'.6   C2014-903353-2
                                       C2014-903354-0

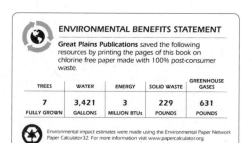

ENVIRONMENTAL BENEFITS STATEMENT

Great Plains Publications saved the following
resources by printing the pages of this book on
chlorine free paper made with 100% post-consumer
waste.

TREES	WATER	ENERGY	SOLID WASTE	GREENHOUSE GASES
7	3,421	3	229	631
FULLY GROWN	GALLONS	MILLION BTUs	POUNDS	POUNDS

Environmental impact estimates were made using the Environmental Paper Network
Paper Calculator 3.2. For more information visit www.papercalculator.org.

FSC
www.fsc.org
MIX
Paper from
responsible sources
FSC® C016245

For Cyril

When your dad owns one of the few funeral parlours in your town, you get used to seeing dead bodies, but when the dearly departed is in the trunk of your car, curled up where the spare tire should be, it's a little different. Especially when the corpse belongs to the late but unlamented Serge Popov, the biggest bully and dumbest jock ever to set foot in Dead Falls, Alberta.

My canvas messenger bag slithered along my leg and dropped to the asphalt with a dull thud. Blowing on my fingers to warm them up, I peered at the shadowy form of his body. The smell of his cologne— orange blossom, coriander, and amber—wafted past, and filled the cold night with tangy, sweet scents. Years of helping my dad prepare bodies for burial meant I didn't scare easy but seeing Serge was like seeing a dead rattler. You knew it couldn't hurt you, but you remembered the venom. My breath condensed in the frigid air, grey smoke against the dark shadows of my car trunk. I peered inside, hoping to find...*anything*, but in the dim light of the library parking lot, it was hard to make out much.

I dug into my coat pocket, pulled out my phone, and lit up the flashlight. The hard angles of Serge's face glowed blue-white. There were no marks on his skin, and I didn't smell blood, vomit, or human waste. I glanced around his body but there was no vapour or fog. That was some good news.

His scarf was bunched around his neck. I didn't want to disturb his clothing or the scene. I blew on my hands again and put my palm to his face. Ice-cold but not freezing. Then I held my fingers in front of his nose.

Nothing.

He'd been dead long enough for his temperature to drop, but not long enough for all his body's warmth to evaporate. After a quick double check to verify the empty bottle of pills in his hand, I had enough information to phone the cops.

I put my hands on the trunk lid. My exhalation streamed out in a long, thick plume.

Crap.

I hated the guy, but I was sorry he was dead. Seventeen is young to off yourself. And I was super creeped out that he'd decided to do it in my car. But that was Serge. He always had to be the last to give you the finger—even from the grave. I flipped my cell around and phoned my dad.

He picked up on the third ring. "Hey, baby girl, what is it?"

The sound of his voice—soft and gentle—soothed me. My whole life, it's never been anything but me and my dad, which made us both seriously over-protective of each other. I went for a casual tone and said, "Hey, Dad, I got a problem here." Through the phone lines, I felt him stiffen.

"Yeah?" There was an edge to his voice, like he was ready to put on a military uniform and turn our beat-up minivan into a Sherman tank.

"Nothing like that—well, a bit like—Dad, Serge's body's in my trunk."

There was a stunned pause. "Maggie, what did you do?"

"What! Nothing—!" Okay, maybe I deserved that. One day, I'd live down the sausage incident but right now, I was staring at the cadaver of my six-foot-three-inch tormentor. It didn't seem like the time to argue over the past. "He killed himself...in my car."

There was a worried, processing silence on the other end. "You sure?"

"I think I know a dead body when I see it."

"No, I mean about him killing himself. You sure someone didn't dump him in your car?"

Well, thanks a lot daddio. That just added a whole new level of creep-me-out to the October night. "I don't know," I said, my sudden drop of confidence reflected in my tone. I leaned over his body again.

Serge jerked suddenly, rearing up and reaching for me.

I screamed, dropped the phone, stumbled backwards, and fell on my butt. Pain shot from my tailbone to my teeth. Jagged pebbles dug into the palm of my hands.

He jumped out of the trunk, laughing. "Awesome! So worth freezing my butt off!" He reached behind his neck and pulled out his cell. "Downloading fresh and live to all the viewers of the Serge Network." He cackled and said in a falsetto, "I think I know a dead body when I see it." His voice dropped back to its usual guttural bass. "Stick to books, Deadhead. You suck as a cop."

"Dickhead!" That one might get me grounded if Dad heard. He didn't like me swearing. I kicked at Serge's legs but he dodged out of the way.

"Loser!" He turned his back to me.

"Where's my spare?"

He just laughed and swaggered out of the library parking lot.

Cussing, I got to my feet and grabbed my phone. "Dad?"

"I heard," he said, his voice tight. "All of it. We'll talk about your language, later."

In the background was the metallic *clink* of keys slapping together. He may not be in army fatigues, but he was definitely about to test the limits of our van.

"I'm going to call Nancy."

"Don't," I sighed. "The sheriff can't do anything and I don't need the extra attention."

"What's this about your spare?" The dull thud of a door closing preceded the growl of the van coming to life.

"He must have slashed my tire. That's why I went into the trunk in the first place, to get the spare, but God knows what he did with it."

"Stay there, I'll come get you. We'll fix the tire tomorrow."

"Thanks." The phone beeped. "I'll see you in five."

He hung up and I flipped to the other line.

"Maggie—I just got a video in my inbox—"

I cut Nell off. "Yeah, Serge strikes again."

"I wish he really had offed himself."

"Me too."

"Maggie...he sent it to the whole school."

My heart cramped and my intestines followed with a double-twist. "That's fine," I said, talking big to hide the tears. "Let him and his buddies make fun of me."

"Didn't you—y'know, notice any *stuff* to tell you he was really alive?"

I sighed. "No. The shock of seeing his Easter Island face in my trunk undid my usual keen observational skills."

"Your *woo-woo* failed you?"

The left side of my mouth lifted at Nell's code to describe my skills. "No. No *woo-woo*."

The tapping of her fingers on the keyboard clicked over the phone line as she said, "It's not so bad—I don't think—I mean—"

It was worse than I thought. My half-smile fell off my face. When Nell runs out of words, it just hasn't hit the fan, it's propelled its way up into the upper atmosphere. "Listen, my dad's going to be here in a bit, so…"

"Yeah, okay. I'd say 'call me later' but I know you. You're going to turtle."

I didn't argue.

"I'll see you tomorrow?"

I nodded, then remembered I was on the phone. "Yeah, tomorrow." I hung up and checked the doors of my vehicle. Breaking into a 1952 Ford A Convertible with soft-top roof was something a drunk monkey could do—which explained how Serge was able to manage it. But that car had been in my family since the day it rolled off the assembly line and the stunt was trademark Serge. It was one thing for him to mock me, but screwing with my car…that was crossing the line.

A little voice in my head pondered the sanity of valuing a car above my own person, but it was ten o'clock and I figured a philosophical debate could wait till morning—or my deathbed. I locked the car up as best as I could, then took a seat on the library steps and waited for Dad.

He arrived a few minutes later.

I look nothing like him—except our height. We're both tall, but he's well built, filled out without being heavy. I look like a stick, and the only bumps on me are my knobby knees. Sometimes—a lot of times—I wonder if I look like my mother, but Dad never kept any photos of her. I understand his motivation, but sometimes—a lot of times—I wish he'd kept just *one* snapshot.

"Why didn't you wait inside the library?" he asked as I climbed into the van.

"Didn't want to let the car out of my sight." I turned the heating vents my way and let the warm, dry air blast my face.

He gave me a look that once again had me wondering why an inanimate object ranked higher in priority than my person and said, "It's cold—didn't you notice?"

"Fantasizing about killing Serge kept me warm."

Dad shook his head. "If he doesn't die in some bar fight, your tax dollars will be paying for his stints in prison."

I smiled. "Yeah. Should upset me, but the idea of him in a cage and having to pee in front of other men makes me happy."

My dad snorted. "It's Serge. He's been peeing in front of people since he was four."

"Oh." My fantasy lost its fuzzy, warm edge.

"Of course, there are always cavity searches."

Hope buoyed me once again. I grinned. "Thanks."

He chuckled. "Any time."

We drove in silence for a little while. "Dad...when I phoned, did I—"

"No, you didn't."

"Are you sure?"

The passing light of the streetlamps revealed his grimace. "I heard what that little dung heap said, and I checked your inbox while we were talking. The video's clean."

Most kids wouldn't like their parents checking their emails, but Dad and I had a different kind of relationship. We looked out for each other—partners against the world, and teammates in the game of life. "Okay," I said, feeling a small weight lift off my chest. "Thanks."

We arrived home about ten minutes later. The buttered lights of our duplex warmed the dark night. I caught sight of the police cruiser in the driveway. "Couldn't help yourself, could you?"

"Thought she should know. That kid's a menace."

Dad phoning Nancy Machio had more to do with his hormones than fatherly outrage, but I didn't say anything. He hasn't dated since Mom left us seventeen years ago and he needs a woman.

Heck, I needed a woman.

Until Nancy came into our lives, I didn't realize steak came in versions other than "charred black" and there was more to spicing meat than salt. She introduced us to exotic spices like black pepper. If Dad wasn't man enough ask her out, I'd start dating her.

We got out of the car and headed inside. The door opened and she was there, all curves and steel, arms open, an expression between fury and sympathy on her face. I took the hug. She smelled like gun oil and photocopier toner, gardenia flowers and bread.

"If I could lock up that little creep, I would."

"I know," I muttered into her thick, blond braid.

"If I could have him disappear down a lonely stretch of road, I would."

"I know."

Nancy had been coming over for a few months, and she wasn't just securing room in my dad's heart, but mine as well.

"Thanks." I pulled away so I didn't start bawling about Serge, my absent mother, and my total lack of cool.

"I brought you some cannelloni and meatballs."

Geez, I love this woman. She's Italian and thinks what can't be solved by food can be solved with a gun, handcuffs, and an alibi. "Marry me, Nancy."

She blushed and looked at my dad. It was a sweet, wistful expression and when I glanced at him, I saw the same look on his face. It took years off of him, made his blue eyes sparkle. When my dad's eyes start sparkling, that's my cue to leave.

I hung my coat up in the closet and turned towards the steps that led to the living room. Grey fog seeped out of the kitchen, curling as it rolled along the floor, tumbled down the short staircase, and spilled over the banister railings.

Great. Just what I *didn't* need: the confused dead. Unzipping my hoodie, I went up the steps to the main area and entered the tomato-scented embrace of the kitchen.

It was an old-school set-up. Cupboards on the left and the counters underneath separated the dining table from the rest of the kitchen. On the right was another row of counters and cupboards, and in the middle was the window, above the sink. This wasn't the house for espresso machines or four-slice toasters. No floating islands or granite countertops, no food processors. We don't even have a blender. We didn't need any of those things. With Dad's cooking, all we really needed were the takeout menus on the fridge and the fire extinguisher for his yearly attempt to make Christmas dinner.

There was a cobalt-blue plate on the white counter, half of it filled with pasta, the other half with Caesar salad and garlic-buttered bread. My stomach growled and my mouth watered.

A woman rose from the table and came to me. Fog poured off her purple Vera Wang shift dress. She gave me an uncertain smile. "I'm afraid I'm a little out of sorts, here," she said with an Alabama drawl. "My name's Annabelle. I was meetin' some friends for drinks and I tripped." Her water lily-blue-eyed gaze surveyed the room. "The next thing I know is I'm standin' here with the most *awful* headache."

"Take a seat, toots," said a man with a rock-and-gravel voice who sat at the table. He was all slits and folds, a fleshy, beefy chunk of meat with stubby fingers and bushy eyebrows. "I got here first, and the lady's helping me."

"Well, yes." The Southern woman was all etiquette and genteel grace. "I don't mean to interrupt...But"—she cast a helpless glance my way—"why am *I* here?"

The guy laughed, though it sounded like a death rattle. He ran a hand over his shiny palette. "I'll let you figure it out." Focusing his dark eyes my way, he said, "What now?"

I turned away and went to the fridge.

"Need something, honey?"

"No thanks, Nancy. Just some milk." I pulled the carton out. "I got it."

The cop moved past the woman, brushing against her bare shoulder and went to the cupboard.

Annabelle blinked. Her lower lip trembled.

"I could charge him with disturbing the peace," continued Nancy.

"No one was around. It was just Serge and me."

She puffed out an angry breath.

Tears filled Annabelle's eyes. "Oh." She looked down as dark bruises began to form on her fair skin. "Oh, *nuts*."

Nancy walked through her. "I'll check. That little turd had to violate something—"

I took the glass she offered.

Annabelle gingerly touched the back of her head. When she pulled her hand away, a bright layer of blood dripped off her fingers. The tears came down. "*Darn it*. I'd just gotten promoted." She turned to the other ghost. "*Promoted*! Do you know how hard that is?"

"Hey," he grunted. "In my line of work, if you're not moving up, you're moving down. Six feet down, you know what I'm sayin'?"

She shook her head then wailed. "I'm dead and you're talking to me about gardening!"

He blinked then gave me a bemused look.

"You volunteered a lot at church, didn't you?" he asked Annabelle.

She sniffed. "What? Yes. So?"

He was up and around the table, pulling her into his arms. "It's okay, Doll face. Let Gio take care of you." He looked over at me and winking, pointed at Annabelle—specifically, her butt—and made a thrusting gesture his fist.

Oh boy. Whatever killed this guy I bet a high dose of Viagra or Cialis was involved.

Nancy caught my gaze. Her eyes widened and she gave me a brilliant smile. "Breaking and entering." Light infused her face and made her pupils glitter. "I knew I'd get that little bastard."

I swiped an extra piece of bread from the pan. "Remind me never to get on your bad side."

But she was already pulling out her cell and dialling. "Roger. Pick up Serge Popov. Breaking and entering"—she gave me a thumb's up gesture—"and destruction of private property."

"That dame—" The man moved Annabelle's hair out of his face and flicked away the blood on his hands. "She's like a Rottweiler." A smile lifted the side of his mouth. "It's sexy. She your ma?"

"Stay away," I told him around a mouthful of food.

"Huh?" Nancy looked up.

"A-Okay. You go get 'em."

"You know it, sweet cakes."

I looked over at Dad and gave a subtle nod in the direction of the mobster and the Sunday school teacher. "I'm going to my room."

"Feeling foggy?"

"Times two."

He grunted. "Good luck."

I nodded. Grabbing my food, I headed up the steps to my bedroom. It had lavender walls, black furniture, and a white duvet. Well, mostly white duvet. I glanced at the two mounds of black fur on my bed.

"Normal animals," I told them, "greet their owners with joy and wild abandon."

Buddha's response was to give me a yawn wide enough to make his mastiff jowls jiggle. Ebony opened a green eye, watched me, stretched out her claws and went back to sleep.

The mobster and Annabelle had followed me to the bedroom. Pine and evergreen scents preceded them, carried by the fog. I shut the door with my heel and said, "You just have to let go."

Annabelle blinked. "Let go of what?"

"Life."

"That can't be it—"

"That can't be it." Gio echoed. He lifted his hands and glanced around like he was looking for a band of supporters. "*Let go*."

"Yeah. You're dead. That's it. Stop hanging on and go." Usually, I'm a lot more comforting and patient. But I was hungry, humiliated, and didn't have time for chitchat.

Annabelle pulled at her hair, like if she yanked hard enough, she'd wake up and this would all be a dream.

I sighed and reminded myself that while I'd been dealing with the dead all of my seventeen years, this poor woman had not. "You just died, right? Less than twenty-four hours ago?"

Her brows pulled together. "I don't...maybe."

"Trust me. You smell like evergreen trees. You just died."

She swallowed. "Oh," she said softly. "Okay."

"And there's a lot to deal with—all the dreams you won't get to fulfill, all the things you'll never get to do."

Her eyes misted.

"But this isn't the end."

"It isn't?"

I shook my head and nibbled on the bread.

"Are you sure?"

"Almost a hundred percent."

She flinched. "*Almost?*"

"Look, all I know is this: life continues and being dead isn't…well, being dead. I don't know exactly what happens after—"

"What kinda psychic are you?" asked Gio.

"Listen, your pipes are going. You gonna call an electrician or a plumber?"

"Plumber."

"It's the same thing with those who see the dead. We're like contractors—each with our own specialty. I can see the dead who need to transition, but if the dead come back to visit loved ones, they go to someone else." I shrugged. "All I can tell you is that there's nothing to fear on the other side"—I turned my gaze from Annabelle to Gio—"for her. For you, I don't know."

Annabelle plucked at her dress. "It's not scary, you promise?"

My breath froze. I glanced at the radio. "Uh, for you. No, not scary."

She reached out to me. "Will you hold my hand?"

I grasped her fingers. One day, I'd figure out why the dead are as solid to me as the living.

She took a breath and began to whisper, "It's okay to let go. It's okay to let go." When she opened her eyes, her pupils had disappeared. Her eyes were silver orbs, catching the light and reflecting white-blue hues. "Oh. You're right—" She gave a soft cry. "Cupcake! Hey, pretty girl! How's mommy's princess?"

Annabelle vanished, slowly, gradually.

I couldn't see what she saw, but the joy she felt radiated from her face and made the air hum with a soft, warm energy.

Her form turned transparent. The weight of her hand in mine lessened, lightened, until all I felt was the memory of where she used to be.

I turned to Gio.

"Not me." He held up his hands. "We both know what's on the other side for me."

"So...what are you going to do?"

"Can I wander?"

I frowned. "Yes, but the longer you wait, the harder it is to cross over."

He scrubbed the underside of his jaw. "I'm okay with that." He looked around. "How do I get outta here?"

"Just think of where you'd rather be."

He gave me a wicked grin and I knew he was thinking of his favourite strip joint. Gio laughed, deep and growling, and faded from my view.

I gave it a moment, to see if he'd come back, but obviously a G-string wearing pole dancer took precedence over his immortal soul. Eyeing a spot between the furry ones, I moved to the bed and wiggled my way onto the firm mattress. Buddha grumbled but grudgingly gave up some room. Ebony—typical cat—refused to budge. I set the milk down and, giving her a glare, said, "Don't even think about it."

She closed her eyes slowly, deliberately. A sure sign of feline dismissal.

I inhaled dinner and shared the leftover cheese from the cannelloni. After I had given myself enough time to calm my inner hysteria, I went to my computer and called up the video. I grabbed a bottle of the pink stuff, just in case what I saw gave me indigestion, and hit the play button.

It was horrific, for sure. I looked and sounded like a total idiot, and the only thing good thing was the darkness hid my non-photogenic nature. But dad had been right. I didn't say anything that could really get me in trouble. I cussed out Serge again, then shut down the computer.

I turned on the television and tried not to think of Serge or Nell. Or Craig. I *especially* tried not to think of him. Instead, I reminded myself that I only had ten months left, if my university application was accepted, and I'd be out of this town and away from Serge.

I went to my bathroom and had a quick shower. When I came out a guy was standing in front of my television. He was skinny but well built, with dark hair, blue lips, and, apparently, a fondness for white briefs.

"How did I get here?" He rubbed his arms. "Did they leave my clothes?"

"They?"

"My frat brothers." He glanced around the room. "Is this Omega house?"

I wrapped my ratty grey bathrobe around me. "It's kind of your Alpha *and* Omega house." I pointed to the blanket on my bed. "You wanna use it?"

"Uh—" He blinked. "No…is this part of the rush?"

"Oh, boy, have I got good news and bad news. Good news is that whatever frat house you were rushing, you've made it."

He smiled.

"Bad news: it'll be posthumously."

His face went blank.

"Let me guess—as part of Rush Week, you were locked in the trunk of a car without any clothes or a cell, right?"

Slowly, he nodded.

"They forgot you were there."

"What? No—they wouldn't—" He stopped, sniffed the air. "You smell bread baking? Smells like the kind my Nana used to make."

"You should check it out."

"You—" His eyes did the same thing as Annabelle's: turned to metallic silver orbs. "Nana?" He gave a soft laugh. "No kidding…"

I took a breath and he was gone. Glancing at the animals, I said, "Too bad I can't have that effect on Serge."

Buddha chuffed.

I pulled the sheets down, doffed my robe, and climbed into the cool bed. Closing my eyes, I pretended that I could handle the mockery that would come tomorrow. Ebony curled on my chest and started purring. Buddha took a spot by my feet and he was out for the night. I took a breath and told myself that even if I couldn't handle what happened tomorrow, at least I'd have my home and family.

And home schooling, if it became necessary.

And Nancy to hide me if I decided to go Italian and take out Serge.

CHAPTER TWO

I didn't sleep well. Coupled with having to wake up extra early so I could walk the dog before heading out to fix the flat tire, my Friday morning started with all the bang of a wet firecracker. I picked Nell up and headed to school.

"Here." She handed me Jackie-O sunglasses.

I glanced at her then at back at the road. "What are these for?"

"Because I know you and know that behind that brave front you're totally mortified. You can hide the circles under your eyes so no one knows you lost sleep over that jackass."

I snorted. "That's just going to draw attention to...everything."

"C'mon." She jiggled them at me. "I brought them especially for you—they looked fine on me. They'll look fine on you."

We crested a hill and came to a stoplight. I turned and looked at her. "Of course they look fine on you. You're all blond and dewy." I turned my head and gave her my profile. "See this?" I pointed by my ear. "Side burns, okay? I'm dark and ethnic and I'm pretty sure if I don't get these under control, I'll be able to go as Blackbeard the pirate for Halloween."

Her response was the irritated sound she always made when she thought I was being difficult. "You're built like a model."

I snorted. "Model. For what? The latest two-by-fours? I'm not going to hide behind anything. Last night was more about Serge's character than mine." Hallmark and after-school-special words that did nothing but empty my lungs.

She reached out and squeezed my hand. "We're early. Let's grab a Timmy's."

I took a left at the lights and headed to the Tim Hortons by the gas station. A large double-double for me, a bagel for her—both Nell's treats. We sat in the crowded parking lot, the scent of coffee and cream cheese intertwining with the toasted heat coming from the car vents. Too soon, the food was gone and I had no choice but to head to school. I tried to take my time and go slow, but sooner rather than later I was pulling into a spot in the student parking lot.

"Well," I shut off the engine and glanced at the too-curious faces looking back at me. "We're here."

Nell checked her lipstick and flipped the visor up. "I don't know why you're worried. If I could do what you do, I'd walk in there like a queen bee."

"You already walk around the school like a queen bee," I said wryly.

She grinned. "You should own it, rock it. It's a great talent—"

She could say that; she'd never been confronted by the ghost of a woman hanged for being a witch. and had to listen to the torture she'd endured.

"—you just worry too much."

I raised my right eyebrow. "I've been in Dead Falls for four years and it's the first place I can *remotely* claim as friendly. I don't want to lose anything."

She shrugged. "That's you. I think the best defense is a good offense."

Of course she thought so. Nell was the resident genius and head cheerleader with a pixie face, small body, naturally curly hair, and an hourglass figure that would get her the centerfold spread in any magazine. She'd never be on the defensive and the only thing she offended was my sense of fair play because God had decided to give her a double share of boobs.

"Hurry up!" She was out the door and waiting, the wind making her blond hair sweep across her face.

I sighed but followed. The smell of school—stale cigarette smoke and the despair unique to the teenage life—turned the air grey. We walked towards the main entrance. I tried to project a "don't care" attitude, but last night had permanently undone any hope that I would ever be kissed before I was eighty. My shoulders slumped and my head seemed in a permanent downward dog position.

We got inside just as first bell rang. Usually, between the banging of locker doors and the yelling of kids and teachers, it was hard to hear anything in the hallways. But this morning, the voices dropped as we walked by.

No one would say anything to my face, but that was the shadow Serge cast: few kids wanted to look like they were choosing my side.

I went to my locker then headed to visual arts class. Tammy and Ben, two of the exceptions to the don't-question-Serge rule, were there.

"I saw," said Ben. "Want me to try and drown him during practice?"

I smiled. "Thanks, but he's not worth the prison time."

"I was thinking about it last night. Maybe"—Tammy tentatively reached out—"he likes you and doesn't know how to express it."

That's Tammy. What she doesn't have in academics, she makes up for with optimism and a belief in happy endings so devout, she makes Walt Disney look like a fatalist.

"He's not secretly crushing," I said.

"Are you sure? I saw a movie last night—"

Trademark Tammy. Life according to romantic comedies. I glanced at Ben.

He shrugged.

Telling Tammy the hard facts of life is like telling a four-year-old there's no Santa Claus. "Trust me on this."

Serge came into the room, his girlfriend Amber Sinclair on his arm.

My stomach clenched. That bastard was responsible for my burgeoning ulcer and if I'd weighed more than a wet rag, I would have gone up there and decked him.

He met my stare with a sneer. What I wouldn't give for a blistering line. But I was the kind of person who thought of the great retort three days later, when no one remembered the slight but me. My mind was eagerly working a scorching one-liner that called his manhood into question and included a dirty twist on car trunks, but then Craig walked into the room, and the only thing I remembered to do was breathe.

His folks had moved to Dead Falls this year, and that meant he knew nothing about my non-reputation reputation, and I still had a chance to wow him into a relationship before I fell into the "one of the guys" or "weird" category. He was the tall and lean captain of the water polo team, with brown eyes and a smile that made me willing to undergo sixty-three days of vomiting and fat ankles if that meant one day I'd marry him and have his kids.

Craig saw me and smiled as he dropped into the seat beside me. He grabbed my hand and said, "I saw. You okay?"

I smiled weakly because his hand was warm and his fingers long, and I was embarrassingly close to swooning. The fact that I didn't say anything made him frown. He squeezed harder and I grew weaker.

"Maggie?"

I tightened my hold on his fingers, gave myself a quick second to memorize how he felt and said, "I'm good. Honest. I'm used to it by now."

Behind the black frames of his glasses, his eyes clouded. "You shouldn't have to be used to any of it."

He hadn't let go and all I could hear was the pounding of my heart. I nodded.

"Whoa, MacGregor, holding hands with the deadhead? Always thought you were gay." Serge pushed in between us, breaking our hold. He glanced back at me. "Always figured you were asexual—like a worm."

I stared him down. "You really want to admit to thinking about me and sex when your girlfriend's around?" It wasn't much of a retort, but it was the best I had.

Serge's jaw worked up and down. He clenched his fist.

"Don't even think about it," said Craig. "There's still time to pull you from the game."

Serge shrugged. "What do I care? I'll just drink and bang, right?" He turned on Amber and grabbed her breast.

She slapped his hand away, her cheeks burned scarlet.

He laughed and walked off.

Amber turned to me. "I'm so sorry—I saw what he did. When he said—"

"Yo! Get over here!"

She jerked at her boyfriend's bellow and scurried after him.

"Why does she stay with him?" Ben shook his head.

"Low self-esteem?" I offered.

"Penance for sins in a previous life," he countered.

"Maybe—"

We looked at Tammy, waiting for an answer worthy of rainbows, talking fawns, and meeting lost loves on top of the Empire State Building. She studied Amber then shook her head. "I got nothing."

Craig shot me a meaningful look.

The audio-visual teacher came in. He did the usual: took attendance, shushed us. Mr. Parks scanned the room as he asked for volunteers to talk about their class project. Serge's hand shot in the air, and my heart dropped to my toes. I knew, I just *knew* yesterday's fiasco would feature in his video.

He strutted to the front of the class, DVD in hand.

"Tell us about your project," said Mr. Parks. "How did you capture the essence of life?"

"I took a different approach and did a case study of one particular life, and how this person deals with death."

He started the video.

I watched, my jaw clenching so tight I thought I'd crack my teeth.

I didn't dare look at Craig, but the muffled laughter of the kids made my eardrums sizzle. Even Tammy couldn't help but laugh at the confidence in my "I know a dead body when I see it" followed by my squealing like a two-year-old when he jumped out of the car.

Mr. Parks's rubber-soled shoes squeaked in the dark. The screen went black. Then the lights flared on. Craig didn't look at me and I couldn't read the meaning behind his tight, frozen posture.

Mr. Parks cleared his throat. "Good camera angles," he said.

Yeah, thanks for sticking up for me, teach.

"But the night footage was grainy. You should have included extra light." He looked at me. "Maggie, why don't you go?"

Nice. The school bully pranking me didn't elicit a word. I sighed and moved from my seat. "Um—I was at an art gallery in Edmonton once, and the artist had displayed photos of people from the morgue—"

There was an audible inhalation of disgust and shock.

"No—no, it wasn't like he had shots of dead bodies. It was just parts of them." Good one, Maggie, because that was *way* less creepy.

I was too freaked to do anything but talk to my shoes. "Um, anyway, I thought it was interesting, and I thought I'd do something similar."

"Did you get permission to for those pictures or did you just sneak into the morgue when your dad wasn't watching?" asked Serge.

I glanced at Mr. Parks. "I have permission for all the images used." He nodded.

I slid the video in and went back to my seat. Mr. Parks shut off the lights and blessed darkness fell. For music I'd used Pachelbel's Canon in D because everyone had it in their wedding processional. I'd wanted to put the song in a different context. I had put this together to confront the seeming creepiness of being an undertaker's daughter, and I'd thought, "People already see me as a freak. What could it hurt?" But I sat there in the darkened room, watching the images of the dead next to the living, I realized it could hurt a lot.

The music ended and Mr. Parks flipped the lights, saying, "Very sensitive. Class? Any thoughts?"

A few kids raised their hands and said noncommittal things like good framing and nice use of contrasting colour. I took it for what it was, an olive branch offered by people too afraid to offer the tree. Short of my four friends, no one was brave enough to put themselves in Serge's crosshairs.

Craig went after me. He did his video with the theme of life as a game and had a stadium rock soundtrack and images of sports battles and victorious players, their faces bloody, their teeth missing, but in their broken fingers, the trophy. Tammy, of course, did an ode to love as the essence of life, and Bruce had taken the project instructions literally. He'd done a five-minute video on one-celled creatures and their evolution into complex animals. A few more kids went and then class ended.

"Don't let him get to you," said Craig.

"Easy for you to say," I told him.

His lips twisted to one side. "We all have embarrassing moments. If you let him get to you then you're not the kick-butt chick I thought you were."

My mouth went dry. He thought I was kick butt? "You thought I was—"

But he was on to other things. "Are you coming to the game?"

He was looking at the group, which dashed my hope he was subtly asking me out.

Tammy nodded. "Wouldn't miss it."

We dodged kids in the hallway on the way to the next class and talked loudly to be heard above the noise.

"Would you really have benched Serge?" I asked Craig.

He grimaced. "McNally's a threat and he knows it. If we want to get to regionals he has to play."

I nodded.

He looked over. "I'm sorry. I would if—"

"Naw." I brushed him off. "My wounded ego isn't bigger than the school's need to get a trophy." If we didn't start placing soon, funding would be cut. And if funding was cut then I would no longer get to see Craig wearing nothing but a pair of Speedos and a smile. A bigger tragedy I couldn't think of.

"What are you doing tomorrow?"

I waited for someone else to answer him but then I looked up and realized he was talking to me. Only me. "Uh, nothing."

"Will you come to practice?"

I blinked. "Um—"

"I think something's wrong with my technique," he said. "We video the practices, but I need someone who'll watch only me and tell me what I'm doing wrong."

Holy crap. He wanted me to stare at his mostly-naked body. Somebody in the Great Locker Room in the sky really loved me. I nodded because I was drooling too much to talk.

"Great." He grinned and headed down the hallway. I stood, watched, and thanked every chromosome and DNA strand that made up his firm butt. Too soon, the crowd of kids milling in the hallway swallowed him.

"Keep that up and you'll turn the hallway into a pool." Nell came up behind me.

"I don't care. Mr. Parks says we're supposed to take in and appreciate all forms of beauty."

She snorted. "I think it's a bit more than his beauty you want to take inside you."

"I wish." I was too chicken to have sex. Let's face it, I worshipped the ground Craig walked on, but he was still a seventeen-year-old boy and I don't give them any credit for being able to put a condom on right or keeping their mouths shut. I didn't need my virgin lovemaking moves being the top story in the locker room and I wasn't keen to be known as the "undertaker's pregnant teenager."

"I'm not a big fan of Speedos," I said, "but on that boy, I'd take a thong."

Nell grimaced. "Thongs aren't meant for the male anatomy. They're barely meant for female anatomies. I always feel like an underweight sumo wrestler when I wear one."

"But on him, wouldn't you want to see it, just once?" My vision went blurry as my fantasies sharpened. "Something in red, or zebra print."

Nell choked on her bottle of water.

"You're right," I said. "Nix the zebra print. That would just be tacky." I paused. "Leopard."

She looked at me, her eyebrows went up.

"I'll be Jane. He'd be Tarzan."

She shook her head. "And which vine would you be swinging from?"

I grinned. "His."

"Yeah, right. You'd never do it."

She had me there. I punched her on the arm, then turned and headed to my next class, hoping I wouldn't have to deal with Serge for the rest of the week. Of course, knowing my luck and his immense jerk factor, I was pretty sure it was a vain hope.

CHAPTER THREE

The next day, when practice came, I was on the front lines of the pool, so close my toes were practically in the water.

"Hey, Maggie."

I turned and saw Craig coming out of the locker room. He'd ducked under the shower before heading out. Beads of water slid down his skin, highlighting every bump and ridge of his abs and chest.

"Thanks for doing this."

I nodded, my mouth wetter than the pool beside me.

"Don't hold back. You've been to all our games, you know what I should be doing."

"My eyes will be glued to your form, promise."

He grinned. "Excellent. Thanks." He held up his towel. "Do you mind holding this for me?"

I must have been beyond good in my previous life. I must have been a freakin' saint. Not only was I going to watch my personal Adonis, but I was going to be the first one he came to after practice, when his muscles were bulging from exercise and he was breathing hard. I snatched the towel out of his hand. "No problem. I got this."

He went to join his teammates and I took a spot on the retractable bleachers.

The coach blew the whistle and the guys dove in. He led them through a serious workout of laps and drills. Craig's arms pistoned in the water, churning the waves into froth and making me wish I was a drop of water in the pool. The team broke into groups and the practice started. I was so entranced by Craig that I didn't even care about Serge's half-naked body occasionally coming into my line of view.

"Miss Johnson."

I turned and stood. "Hello, Reverend Popov, Mrs. Popov."

Neither of them moved. The Popovs made me seriously uncomfortable—they always had—and not for the obvious reason of being Serge's parents. No matter what perfume Mrs. Popov wore, the scent of fermented apples followed her everywhere. And the reverend always wore a blood-red handkerchief in his blazer pocket. There was something about it—maybe the colour, maybe the too shiny, too slippery look of the silk—that left me feeling nauseous.

"I heard what he did to you," he said, his watery blue eyes seemed to look through me, to a distant point behind my head. His face held a stony expression. "I apologize for his behaviour."

It didn't sound like an apology. It sounded like he was annoyed his kid was alive and even sorrier that I was, as well.

Mrs. Popov's skinny, bony hands flapped towards me. "He can be a handful—he was always an over-active child—"

"Your excuses are why the boy's as bad as he is." The reverend spoke the words quietly, but the venom in his tone made me flinch.

It reminded me of another reason I'd never liked him—he was a bully, like his son.

Mrs. Popov's eyes darted from me to her husband, and an apologetic smile trembled on her thin mouth. "I am so sorry he embarrassed you like he did. His practical jokes sometimes go too far—"

"There you go again," said the reverend. He turned his rattlesnake gaze on her. "Excusing him." He gripped her by the arm. The movement wasn't hard but it was possessive. "Your son's behaviour is shameful."

He gave her a look that was lost on me but made her swallow and drop her gaze. Strands of her brown-turning-grey hair fell in front of her face.

"This family," he said quietly to her, "carries enough shame."

Her cheeks turned red.

I moved reflexively and took Mrs. Popov by the arm, tugging gently so her husband had no choice but to let go. "I accept your apology," I told her.

Reverend Popov tried to stare me down, but I wasn't in the mood to be intimidated.

She gave me a grateful smile.

He gave his wife a contemptuous glance.

My father may have taught me to respect authority, but this guy just pissed me off.

I glanced over at the pool. Craig was in the net, but Serge was watching us. He caught my gaze and looked away.

"Is this how you respect our marriage and the decisions I make?" asked the reverend.

His wife flinched.

"That's enough," I said. "You've apologized and I accepted—"

His nostrils flared; his lips curled back. "This is a private conversation, Miss Johnson. I apologized for Serge's behaviour. Who will apologize for yours?"

The heat in my cheeks spread to my neck, and the pounding of my heart filled my ears. My eyebrows jerked to my hairline. I wanted to cuss him out, but contrary to what the reverend thought, I *did* know the consequences of my actions. And telling off a man of the cloth would get me in serious hot water with my father. I gave Mrs. Popov a tight smile and walked away. Taking a spot closer to the coach, I glanced over at where Serge was. Our gazes connected and the fury in his eyes left me trembling.

CHAPTER FOUR

"That family is twisted." Craig wiped his face with his white towel. We looked over to where they stood in a huddle, pressed to the side of the tiled walls like hieroglyphics coming to life. Mrs. Popov's beige cardigan swallowed her thin frame. Her arms crossed her chest, held her tight and pulled the worn, wool fibres against her shoulders. The only colour on her came from the—fake, I was sure—peridot and ruby bracelet hanging from her fragile wrist. Serge stood in between his parents, water dripping off his body and pooling on the cement floor. His back was to us, the muscles tight, rigid.

"Do you think Reverend Popov beats them?" I asked.

Craig shrugged. "Abuse can be more than physical." He turned his warm chocolate gaze on me. "What did they say to you?"

"I have no idea," I said. "It started off like an apology then ended up with a warning I was going to go to hell." I kept my gaze on the family, trying to see more, trying to sense...anything. But between the naked demi-god beside me and the terrifying guy in front of me, my emotions would only zip between lust and fear. "The whole thing's weird. What are they doing here, anyway?" I turned to Craig. "Coming to his practice? That's not their style."

"Mrs. Popov comes occasionally, but the reverend..." Craig paused. "The whole thing's weird."

His tone made my skin prickle and I waited for him to say more.

He smiled, shook his head. "I know you were probably too pissed off to notice anything after they came in, but did you see anything off in the way I played tonight?"

"Sorry," I sighed. Until the Popovs had come, I'd been fixating on a more sexy focus and hadn't noticed anything. "To be honest, you looked perfect to me."

He smiled, but worry robbed its brilliance. "Thanks. I hope I'm just as perfect at next week's game."

"Come on. Go shower and I'll treat you to pizza." It wasn't exactly asking him out for a date, but it was close.

He sighed and rubbed his hair with the towel.

My eyes lingered on his abs. Reluctant to reveal myself as the lech I really was, I dragged my gaze back to his face.

"I'd love to, but it's my mom and dad's date night. I'm babysitting Zianna."

It was plausible, believable, but the rejection stung. And it reminded me that given the opportunity to confide in me about the Popovs, he'd chosen silence. "Oh, right, sure." I went for a nonchalant shrug. "Another time."

His full lips pulled back to show teeth that—I swear—were designed for nipping my neck.

"Promise." He pivoted for the showers. "Maybe tomorrow, after the game?"

Excitement made me hold my breath. "Yeah."

"Cool. We'll grab the gang."

Great. I was getting a too-clear idea of how much alone time he really wanted, but I forced a smile. "The gang. Sure."

He left.

I turned back to the Popovs. His parents had gone, but Serge stared at the ground like he wanted to beat the tiles until they were dust.

He looked up and his gaze honed on me.

I tripped over my sneakers as I ran for the exit. Serge came at me, hard and fast. His iron fingers clamped onto my shoulder and dug into the muscle. I winced as a moan of pain betrayed me. My knees buckled.

Serge wrenched me upright, spun me around, and grabbing me by the throat, backed me against the wall. I peered past his shoulder, but the place was empty.

The water cut and reflected the lights of the pool, casting forks of yellow and white that danced and rippled along the ceiling. There was no sound, not even the sound of my breathing or of Serge's. My lack of inhalation, I understood, but the fact that *he* wasn't breathing...that was terrifying.

Trying to force air into my lungs, I turned my focus to the boy whose thumb dug into my carotid.

Every crooked edge of his freckles was highlighted by the white fury that mottled his face. "What did they say?" The question came out quiet, hushed.

The hairs on the back of my neck prickled. "I—I can't rememb—"

The dry heat of his body radiated into my flesh and the smell of pepper filled the air as his fist brushed my cheek. I heard the sick *crunch* of bone hitting tile. Warm, wet spatters of blood hit my cheek but I was too freaked out to wipe them away.

"I asked you, what did they say?" His voice went quieter, almost a whisper.

He asked the question with a casual tone that set my teeth on edge, sucked the marrow from my bones. "I don't know—I don't remember."

He pushed his face close to mine.

The chlorine evaporating off his body made my nose burn and my eyes water. "I promise—God—I swear!" I could barely push the words past the terror clogging my throat.

"Good—"

His breath was hot, moist, and smelled of stale beer.

"If anyone asks, that's *exactly* what you tell them." He leaned in, so close his freckles blurred into a blob. "I'm apologizing, you hear me?"

I nodded.

His fingers squeezed tight. "You hear me?"

I wheezed my answer. "Y-yeah, I hear you."

"Good. My parents ask and I was truly sorry, hear?"

I grunted, my mouth too dry to speak.

He let go then jabbed me in the chest, hard enough to bring tears to my eyes. "You say different, you tell anyone about our conversation, and next time, it'll be you in that trunk." He spun on his heel and stomped away.

CHAPTER FIVE

I sat on the cold tile so long that the chill spread from my butt to my hips, but I was too freaked to move. Serge was a crazy bastard. However, I'd never counted on him being so close to the line of murdering psychopath. I didn't know if he was planning on revisiting our talk, maybe adding in some physical persuasion, and figured the best thing to do was wait until he left. Of course, short of going into the boys' locker room I had no way to find out if he'd gone. The smart thing: wait.

Sixty minutes came and went. I wrapped my arms around my chest and gave him an extra half-hour, just in case he'd decided to blow dry his hair. I'm not a coward, but I'm not stupid either. A hundred and fifteen pounds of freaked-out girl is no match for two hundred and thirty pounds of lunatic. From the boys' change room, I heard the sound of locker stalls being opened and closed.

Then I heard the footsteps.

I swallowed.

They were coming my way.

I tried not to hyperventilate and to think of three deadly things I could do to protect myself. Unfortunately, I didn't think smacking Serge with the paddleboard would render him unconscious or powerless. Nor did I know how to make a proper fist. On the plus, my long hair was pulled back in a braid that reached my waist, and I'd seen a Kung-Fu movie where a girl had used her braid like a whip. I jumped to my feet and did a practice head-whip. Instead of helping me find a useful defensive move, it gave me a head rush and whiplash. I winced in pain and grabbed my neck.

A figure appeared.

Fear made my vision blur, but the height difference between this person and my tormentor assured me it wasn't Serge.

"Maggie?"

The sudden rush of relief left me swooning. I grabbed hold of the wall to stabilize myself. "Oh, hi, Mr. Donalds."

"What are you doing here?" He had a soft, high voice that suited his delicate bone structure and hairless, round face.

"I was watching the practice."

He looked at his watch. The overhead lights cut through his thin, blond hair and shone off his pink scalp. "It's been over for a few hours."

"Oh. I guess I was watching the water. Very calming." I pushed my shoulders back, thinking that would work out the kink in my neck. Pain shot down my back and made me grimace.

He frowned and set the mop and bucket on the floor. "Are you okay?"

I nodded and reinjured myself.

His frown deepened. "Are you sure?" He came over. "Can I help?"

The only way he could help me with Serge was if he threw himself in front of the bully and offered himself as fodder while I ran.

"Did you hurt yourself?"

"I twisted my neck."

He blinked. His gaze ran from one end of the pool to the other, searching the barren walls and randomly scattered paddleboards, probably trying to figure out how I could have injured myself in an empty room. "Why are you here so late?"

"Oh." I glanced—gingerly—down at my watch. It was nine o'clock. "I guess I lost track of time. Um, is the school empty?"

He nodded. "Yeah, everyone cleared out."

That should have made me feel safe, but it didn't. Visions of Serge lying in wait by my car gave me the heebie-jeebies.

From behind his bifocals, he peered at me. "You sure you're okay?"

"Yeah, I'm good. It's—"

"Serge."

"How did you—?"

"I saw the video."

Man, even people I barely knew were aware of Serge's grudge.

He gave me a small smile and patted my shoulder. "Why don't I walk you out?"

We walked to my car and after I'd climbed in and locked the doors, he went back inside.

I started the ignition and let the vehicle warm up. The night was cold and frosty—a typical fall evening where my breath came in thick clouds and steamed the windshield. I checked my watch. Nine-fifteen. I didn't have to be home for another hour and a half.

Nancy was probably over, and since it was Friday I knew freshly made bread was waiting. But I didn't want to head home. Dad could read me too well, and I didn't want to relive the subtle rejection from Craig or the not-so-subtle threat from Serge. I had three-quarters of a tank and nowhere to be.

After a stop to grab a burger and shake at The Tin Shack—Dead Falls's answer to fast food—I drove to Widow's Peak. Then I remembered it was Friday and every couple went to that hill to make out. Seeing rocking cars was going to take the taste out of my chocolate shake. The road was too narrow to do a U-turn, so I had to crest the hill before I could turn around. I didn't pay attention to the cars until I saw a too-familiar hatchback. Craig's car. And it was rocking hard enough to need new shocks.

"Babysitting. Yeah, right," I muttered as I drove by and repressed the urge to rear-end his car. I swung my vehicle around and left Craig to the rear-ending business. At the bottom of the hill, I idled by the stop sign and watched frost and fog creep along the road while I wondered why I'd believed Craig could ever see me as girlfriend material.

I debated turning on the radio. Dead Falls is too small to have a proper radio station and too far away from any of the bigger towns to borrow theirs. Instead, we have Harriet the Heat—a sixty-year-old camp cook who broadcasts music from her iPod and waxes philosophical about hot flashes, bioidentical hormones, and a thousand uses for cream of mushroom soup.

Nancy said listening to Harriet had helped her to lose fifteen pounds. "Believe me," she'd said, "after listening to that woman talk about vaginal creams—their textures, prices, and applications—the last thing I wanted to do was eat."

I eyed the dial as though it were a snake waiting to bite. The radio could be mindless company. It could also be my psychic undoing.

As if it heard my thoughts, the radio clicked on.

My mouth went dry, my skin tightened, and my heart felt as though paddles had been applied.

On the other side of the radio wasn't Harriet with her smoked-unfiltered-cigarettes-since-the-womb gravel voice. Instead, it was the static—the weird, whispering kind that made my intestines twist and tighten.

"*Maggie.*"

The voice crawled along every vertebra on my spine and left it tingling.

My clumsy fingers flipped the switch.

It didn't work.

Of course not. It never worked. When The Voice came through, there was nothing to stop it.

"*Maggie.*"

A normal person would have run. A normal person would have launched themselves from the seat and raced for help.

I wasn't a normal person, and The Voice did more than freak me out. It had weight, this whispery, silvery murmur, and it held me shackled and imprisoned. I had no more ability to free myself from the driver's seat than I'd had of escaping Serge at the pool.

The Voice went silent. It filled the space.

I flicked on the signal light. Home was on the right. I went straight on Miller's Avenue.

I did a U-turn.

The voice disapproved and punished me by pressing its damp weight on my chest. "*Maggie. He's coming.*"

I grunted but pushed on. If I could make it home…if only I could make it home. I passed the turnoff for Widow's Peak, and pressed the accelerator to the floor.

"*He's coming for you. Maggie. Ohhh, Maggie.*"

The shakes started next. They rocked me from side to side, made my abdominals clench and my teeth chatter. My fingers lost heat, turned ice-cold.

Still, I drove. The pressure increased until it felt as though a giant was standing on my chest. My hands went numb. To control the steering wheel, I had to use my forearms. The nausea hit. Whatever it was that controlled this side of me did not want me going home.

I pulled to the side of the road and wiped the sweat off my face. Fumbling in the dark, I found my cell and called Dad. "Hey," I wheezed, letting my voice shake because there was no point in lying. "My chest hurts."

There was a sharp pause. Then, "How does it hurt?"

In the background, I heard Nancy say, "Who's hurt?"

"Giant on my chest hurt."

The silence grew pointed ridges. "Where are you?"

"It's not where I am—it's where I should be."

"Is that Maggie?" Nancy asked, her voice tense. "Is she hurt? Did someone hurt her?"

"No," Dad's voice moved away from the phone. "She's fine."

"Then why are you asking her if she's hurt?"

I smiled despite the stomach pain that cut me in half. Trademark Nancy. A cop, interrogator, and nurturer, combined.

Dad ignored her and said, "Tell me where you are, I'll come get you."

Muffled rasping filled my ears. Nancy's voice came over the line. "Maggie. What's going on?"

She didn't know about me—not this. "I think my milkshake was old, or maybe I'm coming down with something."

"I knew it!" She turned from the phone.

I couldn't hear what she said, but I got the general tone, and sent up a prayer for Dad.

"Where are you? I'm coming."

"Um—"

"Maggie." Concern mixed with cop Don't-Screw-With-Me attitude.

Now what? If it had been Dad, I'd have told him I was heading to the old lumber mill and he would have known. What was I supposed to tell Nancy? And if she came with Dad to the mill, how would I explain any weird discovery made?

"Maggie! Answer me!"

Roll in pain and vomit, or face the unknown? I hate the taste of a milkshake coming up instead of going down. "I'm by the lumber mill."

"We'll be there, soon."

"Okay." I ended the call.

As soon as I turned the car around, the pressure eased. My car rumbled to the mill, and with every passing kilometer the pain in my abdomen lifted. Heat and warmth returned to my fingers, my muscles turned from hard cement to pliable tissue, and my lungs found space to breathe again.

I turned left off the road. The barren trees creaked in the wind, leafless skeletons of the branches butted and rubbed together, and clattered like bones. There was only a pickup in the lot, though even if it had been packed full, I still would have known this was the vehicle I was destined to find. It glowed, an angry orange-red only I could see, and spewed raw-edged flames skyward.

The psychic fire burned so bright and hot that I didn't realize who the vehicle belonged to until I was right beside it.

Then the sick, nauseous feeling returned.

Serge.

I pulled my car next to his. My tires crunched on the gravel. I put my head on the steering wheel and hoped if I clicked my heels this would all turn out to be a dream. There was only one thing I could do.

I shut the engine off, pocketed the keys, and got out of the car. "Serge? Can you hear me?"

Of course not. Purple fog rolled from the jambs of the door. "Serge?" Yeah, because calling his name slower and louder would *really* help. The tips of my ears went cold and frosted air broke the barrier of my jeans. I crossed to the driver's side. A darkened shaped slumped in the seat.

I pulled the sleeves of my jacket over my fingers and tried the door. It opened and the interior light came on. Serge's half-naked body fell out the door. The purple vapour swirled into the air. I put my jacket to my mouth, tried to breathe through the stink of vomit and human fluids seeping down his jeans. Gingerly, I reached out and felt for a pulse.

I may have been wrong before, but this time there was no mistake. Serge was dead.

CHAPTER SIX

Through my spot in the back seat of the sheriff's black SUV, I got a view of the dashboard, cut into tiny squares by the metal grill that separated the front and rear sections of the vehicle, and the occasional shadow cast by the emergency personnel. Breathing in air made mouldy with stale coffee and listening to the hiss of the dispatch radio did nothing for my nerves. I climbed out.

The air, sharp with the bite of the coming winter, nipped my skin and devoured the lingering sheen of sweat from my forehead. I headed to the rear of the vehicle. I crawled in and wrapped the grey blanket around my shoulders.

From my vantage point, I saw Dad off to the sidelines, waiting behind the crime tape for someone to question me so he could take me home. The red and blue lights of the emergency vehicles turned in slow, silent rotation, bathing the ground and the faces of the emergency crew in alternating shadows of black and blood.

The entire force—all three cops—bagged evidence and took photos. Systematic and slow, they didn't move as much as they seemed to dance. One cop pirouetted and stretched toward the windshield. Another twisted forward and leaned inside the vehicle. Elegant despite the bulky coats, lithe with the grace and synchronicity born of years of working together, they arced and lunged, turned and sidestepped, with the occasional flash of the camera serving as a spotlight to their quiet choreography.

The paramedics leaned against the side of the white ambulance. They'd long since come to the same conclusion as I had: Serge was dead and no amount of needles, drugs, or CPR was going to save him. They talked to each other in hushed tones, waiting for the moment Nancy gave them the nod. Then they would put Serge's body in a black bag and take him to the morgue.

Rory, one of the only two tow truck drivers in town, was our coroner. Though I couldn't see his face, I knew the squat, round body standing by the EMTs was his. The red glow of his cigarette flared in the dark and disappeared. His job was administrative—thank God. Rory was many things, but that guy couldn't tell a heart from a hiney. He'd arrange for a medical examiner to come up from Edmonton and perform an autopsy—typical procedure for anyone who didn't die of natural causes, and I knew nothing natural had taken Serge out.

Nancy came over. The night had dusted her cheeks red and her nose had a glow that would make Rudolph jealous. She stamped her feet. The action caused blond curls to fall from her hat and bounce about her face. She folded her arms across her chest. "Are you sure you don't want to wait inside the car—where you can't see...?"

I nodded.

Her brows pulled together.

"My dad's an undertaker," I said. "I've probably seen more dead bodies than you have."

She put her hand on my shoulder. "I know, sugar, but this isn't like old lady Singh popping off in her sleep."

I didn't bother to tell her that I helped to prepare the bodies of guys who'd died on the rigs and in highway accidents, and Serge was downright pretty in comparison.

She took my silence for mourning, because she said, "I know it's hard. He was a jerk, but it's never easy to see someone you know in such a state."

His state was exactly what I was worried about and I prayed he'd gone into the great hereafter without a backward look.

"It'll be over, soon." She sighed, pained and sad, and I knew she was more upset about his death than I was. "The M.E. will have to do an autopsy, but it's pretty obvious he died of alcohol poisoning."

I shook my head. "I don't understand—Serge only drank beer. The truck reeks of...well, I dunno, but it's not beer."

"Tequila." She grimaced. "You get drunk on that stuff once and you never forget the smell."

"Who left him here?"

She said nothing.

"You know this isn't normal—"

"Honey—"

"His shirt was off. He wasn't here alone. Besides, tequila wasn't his drink. I heard enough about his weekend partying to know that. Someone killed him."

"It could still have been accidental."

"You think he decided to shuck his shirt off in the middle of minus-ten weather and chug tequila?"

"No. We'll have to clear up some details," she said. Her forehead wrinkled. "It's a police investigation and I can't talk about the specifics. The boys—they think he was having some alone time, but there's no way that kid would be here by himself. It's so…"

"Un-Serge-like."

She nodded. "But this may be a death from misadventure. It could be an accident."

"We—uh—I mean, you need to figure out who he was with." I paused, then added, "And why they left him here."

"Maybe they went to get help. Cell reception isn't that great out here."

"How long has he been dead? Do you know—exactly?"

She shrugged. "That's hard to determine. We know, because of the polo game, that it had to be within the last three to four hours." Her face scrunched together. "They always make it look so easy on television. Just take the liver temperature and there's your time of death, but the human body is so much more delicate than that."

I didn't say anything.

"He was in a vehicle, and Lord knows if the engine had been running when he died. If he'd had the heater going that's going to screw up his TOD—Time of Death. Add in the cloth seats, the cold weather, and open windows…"

"I don't think this was accidental. I think someone did this to him on purpose." Actually, the red-orange fire had assured me of that, but I couldn't offer psychic visions as proof.

"No, sweetie—" She sounded sad. "I don't think it was an accident, either."

"It doesn't take four hours to walk into town from here. If someone had been with him and he'd drunk too much, they would have reached a phone by now." I waited. "Someone left him out here on purpose, Nancy."

"I know," she said softly. "And it breaks my heart on so many levels, I can't even begin to tell you...he was a prick, but leaving someone to die? That's cruelty that even he wasn't capable of." She put her arm around my shoulder. "I sure am sorry you're the one who found him."

Me too.

"But good thing you did." She glanced at me, concerned. "How's your stomach, anyway?"

I shook my head. "Seeing Serge and everything—it kinda made the whole nausea disappear." I couldn't have been more truthful—more specific, but not more truthful.

She hugged me close. "It'll be over, soon."

"Did you call his parents?"

"This is the kind of news," she said, her voice strained and tight, "that you want to give in person."

I nodded.

"I know it isn't easy, honey, but can you go over the night for me, one more time?"

I told her the same story as I'd told her when she first arrived, about watching the game, Serge's parents showing up at practice, his fight with me, and my driving around town. I didn't add in the part about Widow's Peak. The way I figured it, seeing Craig's car was personal information and not necessary to their investigation.

"Was there anything unusual—anything that may have caused him to drink too much?"

I snorted. "Serge lived for drinking. He didn't need an excuse. Did you guys see anything unusual?"

"There's nothing." She drummed her fingers on my shoulder. "It's weird, too, that he had a girl with him and she took off. You think it was Amber?"

I shook my head. "She doesn't have the guts to walk out on him, let alone walking out on him in the middle of the woods."

"Did he mess around on her?"

"Obviously. Don't ask me how, but he could always find a girl. He cheated on Amber from the day they started going out. But she stayed with him. That's why it couldn't have been her tonight."

"Did he have any regulars that he had sex with?"

"Megan, Katie."

Nancy's body stiffened. "Megan Naki and Katie Youngblood?"

"Yeah."

"Weren't they her best friends?"

"Amber's not real good when it comes to picking friends or boyfriends."

Nancy snorted. "Obviously." She paused. "Maybe it was one of them, and they didn't want anyone to know—"

"Everyone knew. 'Cept Amber."

We were silent for a minute and watched the two cops pack up. The paramedics pulled out their body bag. Sorrow rose in me. As much as I hated Serge, there was something horrible about seeing somebody's life end in a generic plastic body bag.

"You said his parents came to watch practice."

"Mm-hmm."

"Was that usual?"

I frowned. "Mrs. Popov went from what I heard, but I don't know how often—I don't really go to practices. And the reverend...never, except tonight."

"Oh...why were you there tonight?"

Heat saturated my cheeks.

Her "Ah" said everything. "Is that why you were driving around? Practice didn't end the way you'd hoped?"

"I thought we were talking about your side of the investigation."

"His tank was empty," she said.

I blinked, then realized she'd steered the conversation back to Serge.

"He couldn't have driven anywhere. Maybe that's where the unknown girl went, to get some gas."

I considered the theory. "It would make sense. Serge drinks himself into a stupor while the date does the hard work."

A few minutes later, one of the paramedics came to tell Nancy they had Serge's body stored.

I repressed a shudder. An entire life, "stored."

She thanked him as she pushed herself off the truck. "Now comes the worst part. Telling the parents." She looked at me, turned and waved Dad past the crime scene tape.

The officer holding him back let go and he rushed to me. His open coat flapped with the energy of his movements and his face was cemented into determined lines.

"Let's get you home," said Nancy and held up a warning hand as Dad closed in. "I had to talk to her alone. You couldn't be here. You're here, now, so don't bitch at me."

He pressed his lips together.

I squeezed her fingers. "Thanks."

I climbed out of the trunk, and into Dad's minivan. He stood by the driver's door, talking to Nancy. Then he got in and we headed home. The ambulance was in front of us. My car was behind me, driven by one of the other cops. It was a weird, depressing kind of processional.

"She should tell Amber too," I said.

"I'm not sure that's appropriate," said Dad. "They notify next of kin."

"Nancy should bend procedure."

He glanced at me and turned back to the road. "Why?"

"His parents couldn't stand her. If they say anything to her, it'll only be to blame her." I fiddled with the heat gauge. "I think that's really the only reason he dated her—not because he liked her but because it pissed off his dad." I stopped. Anger at Serge was an arrow that pierced my stomach with its sharp toxicity. He was dead, I reminded myself.

Dad dug in his jacket pocket and pulled out his cell. "Tell her."

I phoned Nancy and gave her my story.

"Do you think the Popovs would phone her tonight? Did they hate her that much?"

I shook my head. "No, but they'd do it first thing in the morning."

Dad headed down Rydl Street. The shops were dark and the only light came from Rory's gas station.

"Tell you what," said Nancy. "I'll tell them tonight. Tomorrow, I'll head over to Amber's."

I nodded.

"She can't see you," Dad said with a chuckle. "You're on the phone."

Oh. Duh. "That sounds good." I hung up.

"You have a soft spot for Amber, don't you?" asked Dad.

"She's fragile—one of the people that will twist themselves inside out just to be liked. He was horrible to her."

"He's gone now, and he can't hurt her anymore."

I sure hoped so.

Dad pulled into the driveway. I headed inside and dumped my stuff on my bed. The animals knew what had happened—they always knew when it was a bad case of the dead. Ebony curled around my feet and Buddha butted my hand with his head. I sat on the floor. The cat crawled on my lap as the dog flopped down beside me.

I buried my face in Buddha's neck and inhaled the scent of cinnamon buns that he gave off and pretended Serge's death didn't hit me on a deep, disturbing level. Kitchenware rattled and I heard the sound of a plate being pulled from the dishwasher. Ebony jumped off my lap and Buddha shoved me in the shoulder.

"Okay, okay." I stood. "I can take the hint." I headed downstairs.

"The tea's on the table." Dad opened the oven door and pulled out thick white toast and butter. Then he turned. "Just what you need, right?" He gave me a lopsided grin. "Just about the only thing I don't burn."

I nodded, tears filling my eyes as I ran for his embrace.

"Was it fog?" he asked.

"Yeah." I buried into his flannel shirt and inhaled the woodsy scent of his cologne. "It was purple."

He hissed. "Did you see anything else?"

"Fire," I sniffled against his shoulder.

"Anything else?"

"He's not around." I pulled away. "But I heard The Voice on the radio again."

"I'm so sorry. I don't know why—I'm so sorry."

I didn't know, either. No one on his side of the family saw the dead or heard the voices. Maybe it was on my mother's side, but she'd abandoned me long before I'd had the ability to ask. The only thing I really knew was that she was East Indian.

"Come on," he said, as he pushed me toward the table. "Eat."

Whenever I dealt with anyone who died a violent death, the only thing my body would ingest for the next few hours would be white bread and tea. Dad brought the items to the table and I ate in quiet. He didn't ask for information because he knew there was nothing I could tell him.

I wasn't called to every death. And not every death or dead person I'd seen had been offed in criminal circumstances. The voice on the radio, though, only showed up when things went really wrong. I choked down another piece of toast and swallowed my drink. Then I pulled myself up.

"I'll be here if you need me," said Dad. "Don't worry about the time or if I fall asleep. You wake me, okay?"

I nodded and trudged up the stairs to my room. My fingers curled around the knob. As the door swung open, I stepped inside.

Serge was sitting on my bed.

CHAPTER SEVEN

"What happened?" He blinked quickly. His bloodshot gaze catalogued the room and lingered on the panties I'd left on the floor. He frowned, staring at the red lace as though unwilling to believe I wore sexy undies. Pulling his eyes to me he slurred, "How'd you get me here?"

Serge shook his head. His blond hair swung left then right. He crawled off the bed and stood. Well, tried to. He swayed and fell back on the mattress. "What did you give me?" He licked his lips. "Geez. Is that tequila? I hate that crap. Tastes funny, too. How did you get me to drink tequila?" He rubbed his chest, pulled the red jersey material from his body. "I feel itchy."

Nice. I get a ghost with eczema.

"And sick."

Wow, this night was just getting better all the time.

"You knock me out, kidnap me, and now you're ignoring me?"

Great. Of all the luck. I not only get the ghost from hell but the one who can't remember his death.

The vein in his neck pulsed a quick, angry rhythm. A red flush swept across his face. "Answer me, you freak! What are you doing?" He glanced around. "Is this your bedroom? Why am I here—you think I'd be your sex slave?" He snorted. "Forget it."

Yeah, right. The nightmare images of me and him intertwined were going to haunt me for years.

Serge groaned and put his fingers to his temple. "Seriously, how did you get me to swallow tequila?"

I didn't answer him. He didn't know he was dead and that put me in the power position. Serge hadn't figured out all the crazy stunts ghosts could pull—that needed time and effort. If I ignored him, maybe he'd get bored and disappear. I went to the desk and booted up my computer.

"Fine. Ignore me—not that it'll help. I'm going to sue you—bring criminal charges. Freakin' Deadhead." He rolled out of the bed, strode for the door and touched the handle. Electric blue lightning flashed from the metal and blasted him across the room.

Holy! I'd *never* seen anything like that before. I caught myself staring at him and whipped my gaze back to the laptop.

He groaned, struggled to get to his feet and failed. "What was that?"

Good question. An acrid, burning odour filled the room, though I knew I was the only living person who could smell it. Something was keeping Serge trapped in my bedroom. Something that obviously hated both of us.

"I hate you. What is with the trap? You think you're going to keep me prisoner?" His limbs shaking, he pulled himself to his knees, then stood.

But he didn't come near me and that said that on a very basic level, he knew he was dead. I kept ignoring him and headed for the bathroom to change.

When I came out he was sitting on the bed, his legs doing a weird, fast twitchy thing. "You're going to pay for emotional and physical damage—your stupid electrical trap did something screwy to my muscles."

In the kitchen, pots clattered. Serge's head tilted to the side. "Is that your dad?" A calculating grin spread across his face. He fumbled for his shirt and pulled it off.

Oh, for cryin' out loud.

His fingers clumsy, he fought with his jeans and finally ripped them off to reveal grey polka-dot boxers.

Huh. Never figured he actually wore underwear.

"What will the old man say when he hears his little girl screwing her brains out with me?"

He'd probably say, "Who knew you could have sex with a ghost? Gee, Maggie, at least we know you'll never get pregnant."

Serge hopped on the bed but whatever had zapped him remained in his system. He fell. His head bounced against the wooden post. Cursing, he struggled to his feet and started jumping on the mattress.

He slammed the headboard against the wall and started screaming, "Just like that! Ride it! Ride it hard!"

Wow. Those were his sweet nothing lines he used during sex? Why did Amber stay with this guy?

After a few minutes, he was out of breath and hope. No one was coming up the stairs. Poor schmuck, I actually felt a little sorry for him. He was only solid and real to me.

"Fine." He hopped off the bed and yanked his clothes back on, wincing when his fly got caught. "Look, Maggie, whatever. I'm—let's just forget about what happened tonight. Let me go."

I heard the trace of fear in his voice. He wasn't the only one that was worried.

"Shut off whatever bizarre electric trap you have rigged to the door, and let me go."

I should have said something. Should have acknowledged him, but I suddenly realized, he was *trapped* in my bedroom. Serge of the Constant Insult and Bullying was prisoner to an invisible force. He was contained in the room of the one person he hated most in the whole world, and it struck me as funny. Hilarious. Karma was a bitch, but she had a dark sense of humour and I was laughing at the punchline. Let the bastard rot in my room. What did I care, there were three or four other rooms I could use. I went to the door.

"Maggie! C'mon, fun's fun but this is stupid."

My fingers made contact with the handle but it didn't do anything to me. I opened the door and stepped out. Then I went back in.

"I knew you couldn't do it," he said, relief flooding his words. He stood and shoved his feet into his sneakers.

Oh, I was doing it, all right. I grabbed the blanket by the door and left.

Dad followed me into the living room, a dishtowel in hand. He frowned. "Sleeping down here?"

"Figure it'll be more peaceful."

He didn't question me, except to ask, "You sure everything's okay?"

I thought of Serge trapped in my room and grinned. "Peachy-keen."

"Okay." He turned and went back to the kitchen.

That's when I noticed Serge standing behind him, looking as confused as I felt.

"What was that?" He looked down at his hands. His gaze went back up the stairs. "What the—"

And then it hit me. Serge wasn't bonded to the room.

He was bonded to *me*.

Wherever I went, he'd go.

Man. Karma really was a bitch.

CHAPTER EIGHT

A bad night turned into a worse morning, but around 3:00 AM Serge had screamed himself hoarse and fallen asleep on the couch. His constant snoring and occasional farting kept me awake for another three hours. It felt like just as I'd fallen asleep, there was someone at the door, ringing the bell.

I stumbled off the couch and shuffled to the door. Dad came up behind me, saying, "Nine o'clock? Early for visitors."

"Nine? Can't be—I barely fell asleep—"

But he was opening the door and letting Nancy inside.

She ran a worried gaze over me. "You look horrible."

"I feel horrible."

From his position on the couch, Serge roused himself. "Hey! Sheriff! They're holding me prisoner! They've kidnapped me and"— he stopped, blinking at the fact no one was looking at him—"they're ignoring me. No food, no water. Help me!"

No one turned.

"What is this? Some twisted—" He stomped to the adults and waved his hand in front of Nancy's face.

"You didn't sleep?"

"Not really."

"I can make you some oatmeal—"

"I'd rather have some coffee and come with you."

She frowned. "Come where?"

"When you talk to Amber."

Sympathy softened her face. "Oh, sweetie. You can't."

"She'll need someone."

"She's got her—" Nancy glanced at Dad and sighed. "You still can't come. It's a police matter."

"But—"

"I didn't let your dad in when I talked to you last night, honey. I'm not bending the rules, now."

"But we have a bond."

"Oh boy. I'm going to need coffee for this."

"Enough! Someone pay attention!" It was enough for Serge. He pushed Nancy's shoulder. His hand went through her. He jerked back like he'd been electrocuted.

Nancy turned and went to the coffeemaker.

"Hold up," said my dad. "I'll pour."

Serge followed them.

I followed Serge.

He reached out and tried to touch Nancy again. Once more, his hand went right through her. "No way." Disbelief mixed with mounting terror.

"I could use some tea," I said, as a way to negotiate myself past Serge but still stay in the room. From the corner of my eye I saw him look at me. Then he turned and faced the wall. He took a deep breath and went straight for it.

And, of course, he bounced off like a rubber ball.

I started laughing.

He whipped around to me, but I said, "You know how some mornings you're so tired, everything seems funny?" I held up a mug that had "I'm with Stupid" written on it. "Somehow, this just seems hilarious."

Serge looked at me and rubbed his nose.

Moron. If you think you're dead, but you're not exactly sure if you're corporeal, why would you run into a wall? Shouldn't you touch it first, gently, and see what happens? That was Serge's second plan because he pressed a finger to the wall. It didn't give. Frowning, he went to Nancy and tried to grab her boob.

I rolled my eyes. Even dead, some things never change with this guy.

His hand went through her. He stared at his hand, then at the wall, a confused expression on his face.

For this I had sympathy. Next, he'd be wondering why he didn't fall through the floor or float in the air. Sure enough, he turned his stare to his feet. I made my tea and headed toward the stairs. One day he'd figure out that he was being a ghost according to Hollywood standards.

"How are you feeling?" Nancy asked as she took the cup from Dad. "Really feeling?"

I shrugged. "Okay. How did Serge's parents take the news?" I twisted, adjusting myself so I could watch her and Serge.

"Mikhail didn't say anything, but Lydia—"

To my left, Serge flickered like a television that momentarily lost its signal.

"—seemed devastated. Started crying and praying—" Nancy's expression darkened. "She shut up, though, when Mikhail started talking."

"What did he say?"

She pressed her lips together.

"That bad?"

"I know they had problems, but their kid's dead. Probably murdered. How does he not give a f—" She glanced at me "—how can they be so callous? He said that it was just a matter of time and they'd been waiting." The muscles in her face tightened. "He said, 'at least it was sooner rather than later.'"

Serge lost his features, his body went black and turned him into a shadow. A second later, he looked like himself again.

If my dad had reacted like his, I'd have turned into shadow too. "Are you serious? His son dies and that's all he says?"

"No, he said more." Her voice turned hard. "He wanted to know when we'd release the car."

Not the body. The car. No wonder Serge was a nutcase. I didn't say anything and neither did he. He flickered once more. A second later, he disappeared.

"Be back." I went to the bedroom and found him by the dresser.

"Maggie—"

If I didn't pick up on the terror in his voice, I saw it in his face. His skin was white, his eyes were wide.

"What the—can you hear me?"

Nope, baby, I'm blind, deaf, and dumb to you. Maybe Karma wasn't punishing me, maybe this was my final punchline. I was the only one who could hear him, and as long as I ignored him, he was stuck in an earthly purgatory.

I grabbed my clothes and headed to the bathroom. I didn't expect him to follow, but when I walked inside, he was sitting on the low-flush toilet.

"What?" He looked down at his body. "How can I do that?"

What, indeed, and wasn't this a fine pickle? If I acknowledged him and told him to get out, my final revenge was over. But if I kept pretending I didn't see him, I'd have to act like it too. Smart move, Maggie. So much for my shower. Reminding myself that loads of people go to topless beaches, I gritted my teeth and took off my sleeping shirt and tossed it on the beige countertop.

"Whoa—nice tits. Small, but perky."

I swallowed my sigh and ignored him.

He checked me out hard enough for me to considering hiring him instead of using a doctor to get a mammogram.

I yanked on my bra.

"You know," he said dubiously. "You're too small to really need that."

Oh, *screw off*. I pulled on jeans and a thick ivory sweater and jogged downstairs.

Nancy was gone.

"I'm going to Amber's."

Dad looked up from his tablet. "I don't know if that's a good idea."

"Nancy's gone there right now, right?"

He nodded.

"So, I'll give it twenty minutes and head over. I'm Amber's—well, I'm the closest thing she's got to a friend. And when she gets the news, she'll need all the help she can get."

Dad looked at me for a long moment.

"It'll be fine."

"She's got a Taser and a gun. Behave accordingly."

CHAPTER NINE

I gave him a quick kiss and headed out. The rain poured down from a dark sky, heavy and hard enough to make the eaves spill over. I raced for the car and dived inside. I wiped water from my face. Serge appeared in the backseat. Buckled up. Man, this guy had fewer brains than a skeleton. What did he think the belt was going to protect him from? I ignored him, started the car. The streets were quiet and I looped the town. After half an hour, I figured Nancy was done and I headed to Amber's house.

When we pulled into her driveway, the glower on Serge's face lightened. "Finally."

I went up the porch steps and rang the bell. Amber's mom opened the door. The smell of stale cigarettes and fabric softener wafted past. Like her daughter she was curvy and had red hair. She frowned.

"What's going on?" she asked.

I shivered and pulled my jacket closer. The overhang protected me from the rain's bite, but the wind still nibbled.

"Hello May. I need to talk to Amber."

Her brown eyes narrowed. She took a step back, pulled the collar on her velour robe. "Is she in trouble?"

"No, no." I was quick to soothe. "Nothing like that. Just some stuff I wanted to talk to her about in person."

May watched me for a moment. She stepped back and opened the door wide. "Come on in. She's sleeping, but I'll get her. Go in the living room. Or kitchen—there's coffee in the pot."

"She's sleeping? Wasn't Nancy here?"

May shot me an incredulous look. "What would she be doing here?" Her soft features tightened. "What's going on?"

Before I could answer, the doorbell rang.

Oh, crap. I followed May to the door.

Nancy stood on the porch. "Mornin' May, I—" Her gaze flicked to me.

I gulped. If she'd been my mom, I'd have been grounded, for sure. But she wasn't my mom. She was a cop. And that meant—"I'm unarmed."

She snorted. "Hardly." She stepped inside. "Get out."

"I thought you'd be done by now!"

"What did I tell you?"

"Yeah, and Amber's going to need someone—"

May cussed, loud and sharp. "What's going on?" She crossed her arms in front of her chest. "No one's getting near my kid until I get some answers."

Nancy smiled. "Be happy to give you all the answers you need, May. Soon as Maggie's gone."

May laid a restraining hand on my arm. "The kid's staying." She tossed a dirty look in Nancy's direction. "I don't trust pigs."

The cop didn't react to the slur.

"I want witnesses." May turned. "Don't touch anything. You don't have warrants and I have a right to remain silent."

"I wish you would," muttered Nancy. After she watched May walk down the hall, she turned to me. "Seriously uncool, kiddo."

"I wasn't trying to be a jerk. I really thought you'd be done and Amber would need a friend and—"

Nancy held up her hand. "Stay out of my way. I'm going to talk to Amber in the kitchen. You stay in the living room. Clear?"

I nodded.

She sighed. "I'll never admit to saying this, but it's probably good you're here." She snorted. "Right to stay silent? Only in America."

I went down the two steps into the carpeted area and took a seat on a worn, dark blue couch. Nancy took a position by the window. I looked around for Serge, but I didn't see him.

May returned with Amber.

I stood. "I'll wait in the kitchen."

"No. I told you. Stay."

"Nancy wants to talk to Amber alone—"

"She talks with witnesses," May sneered, "or she doesn't talk at all."

Amber blinked, sleepy, and asked, "What's going on?"

I moved towards her, stepped through a cloud of cold air, and realized Serge was here. Invisible but present.

Nancy made eye contact with me and nodded to the kitchen.

"Where do you think you're going, bean pole?" May asked.

I sighed. Why are adults such idiots? Stay. Go. Go. Stay. "Uh, I'm just giving everyone space. I'll be right here." I took a spot at the edge of the living room. Smiling, I gave May a thumb's up. And avoided the death stare coming from Nancy.

She nodded. "Amber, I'm here about Serge."

"Huh?" Then the reality of a cop standing in her living room seemed to wake her up in a way caffeine never could. She whipped around to look at her mom, then her gaze went to Nancy. Protectively, Amber wrapped her arms around her bubble-pink flannel pyjamas. "What about him?"

Serge materialized beside me.

"He died last night," I blurted.

"Oh!" She jerked back.

"I'm so sorry—" I wanted to do something to comfort her, but didn't know what to do. I stepped back. "I'm so sorry. There was—" I caught Nancy's glare. "Nancy will tell you." I edged to the kitchen.

Serge remained in the living room.

Trust him to be the difficult dead. I moved out of Nancy's line of sight, took a spot behind the kitchen wall, and started eavesdropping.

"What happened?"

I crouched and peered around the edge of the wall.

May came up behind her daughter and put her arms around her shoulder.

"He was found at the lumber mill." She took a breath. "I'm sorry Amber, he's gone. First glance, looks like it was alcohol poisoning."

The blood fled from May's face. Then she made a contemptuous sound. "Figures. That boy had no brains."

Serge's nostrils flared and I felt a hit of anger. May should talk. When it came to alcohol, there wasn't a brand or kind she didn't like.

She seemed to catch herself. "Oh, I'm sorry, baby, I didn't mean—" She brushed her daughter's hair with her fingers. "It's a horrible shame."

"Thanks for telling me," said Amber.

I didn't know much about how people reacted when given tragic news, but something was off about Amber. It was like I'd told her that the lawnmower was broken or we'd had to do an extra chapter for English class. The reality of her boyfriend's death didn't seem to sink in. I glanced at Nancy. She, too, was watching the teen, but she was doing it with cop eyes and that didn't bode well.

"You know, May," Nancy stood, "I think I will take that coffee."

I scrambled to my feet and got my butt in the chair just as they came into the kitchen. My plan was to stay there but then I heard Serge's voice. Nancy was focused on May, asking her about Amber. I snuck back to the living room.

"It's okay," crooned Serge. He reached out but couldn't make himself solid to touch her. "I'm here, I'll always be here."

"Amber?" I asked. "Do you want to sit?"

She nodded and shuffled to the couch. I sat beside her. "Um, I'm really sorry."

She didn't say anything, just stared ahead with an unfocused gaze.

"You guys were together for a long time," I said, trying to get any kind of emotional response from her.

"Yeah. Long."

Tentatively, I touched her hand. When she didn't move, I took her fingers. "You must have really loved him."

That broke her shock. Her eyes filled with tears and spilled down her face.

Serge crouched in front of her. "She did love me," he said. "Deep down, we were soul mates."

Amber started sobbing.

I patted her on the back and felt completely inadequate. "I'm so sorry," I said. "I know it's hard to hear, but I didn't want Reverend Popov telling you."

She clutched me tighter and heaved a breath. "No." It came out as a moan. "You don't understand."

I rubbed her back. "What don't I understand?"

Beneath my fingers, her body tightened. She pulled away, yanked her sleeve over her fingers and used the material to rub her face.

"Amber?"

Contempt curled Serge's lip. "Geez, give her a minute. The only person who ever understood her just died."

She sighed.

The wind pelted rain against the window.

Serge rubbed her knees. "You're crying for the lost future, right, babe? 'Cause we never made up?"

"I'm crying because he's gone," Amber said.

I frowned at the way she spoke the words.

So did Serge.

She glanced at me, a dull flush crept up her cheeks. "He's gone. I'm finally rid of him."

"What?" I jerked back in surprise.

Serge did the same.

Amber started to cry again. "The past few weeks, I've been thinking about how to break up with him. Now he's dead and I'm so happy, and I feel horrible about it."

Serge bolted upright. He stumbled backwards, toward the window. "Happy? She's *happy* I'm dead?" The air turned heavy, charged with electricity.

The hair on my arms rose, my teeth vibrated. A low humming filled my ears, followed by a sharp, crackling sound punching the air. The glass in the living room window cracked.

Amber recoiled.

So did Serge.

"It's the wind," I told her. "It's really bad outside—it probably tossed a pebble."

She nodded and I hoped none of them would notice that the crack was on the inside.

"Tell me about being happy."

"It's horrible, isn't it?" She curled her feet under her body. "I should be sad or something, but I couldn't stand him."

"But—you were together since junior high. You never seemed—well, I mean, sometimes you seemed embarrassed, but never out of love."

She huddled into herself. "I did love him." She looked at me. "But he was horrible. You know he was."

"Yeah," I said, "but I never dated him or kept dating him after I'd stopped loving him."

She shook her head. "You don't know Serge." She laughed, the sound dark and heavy. "Not true, you did know him. He could be cruel and heartless."

"But I supported you!" He kicked the rocking chair, but only ended up losing his balance and falling on his butt.

"Back in the summer of grade ten—" She blanched. "I let him videotape us—y'know—"

Serge froze. He pressed his lips together until the edges turned white. His limbs rigid, his body tight, he stood.

"Yeah, I know."

"I was afraid if I broke up with him, he'd post it on the Internet." She looked at me, grabbed my hand. "You saw what he did with you and the car. Do you know what would have happened to me if he'd posted it?"

Yeah, she'd be town slut and the running punchline for years.

"My mom works as the church secretary, I'm there all the time—" Amber's eyes went wide with horror. "Can you imagine what Mrs. Popov and the women's circle would have done to her—to me?"

I didn't even want to think about it.

"Work's hard to find right now." She gestured to the worn furniture and scuffed wood floors. "We're barely making it. If she lost her job—"

"I would *never* have done that to her. Never," Serge said through clenched teeth.

Amber shook her head. "He cheated on me all the time—"

"You knew?"

She shot me a cutting glare. "I may not be smart, Maggie, but I'm not stupid."

"Okay, um"—God, this was awkward—"uh, it looks like he was with someone the night he died—"

She snorted.

"So…you don't know who it would have been?"

She shook her head. "He liked to do anything in panties."

"I didn't—" Serge stopped, a look of misery on his face. "I wasn't that bad."

And then I realized he'd never told her that he loved her. Had probably never shown her, either. In a weird way, I was getting what I wanted: the ultimate revenge on Serge. He was finding out no one gave a rat's ass about him. But instead of feeling gleeful, I felt bad for him, and guilty that I'd ever wished this on him.

"He was mean to everybody—I barely had any friends." Her face contorted with anger and pain. "And the ones I did have, he just screwed when he thought I wasn't looking."

"But surely," I said, not quite believing I was actually defending him, "there must have been some good times."

She sighed and rubbed her eyes. "Maybe. In the beginning. But lately, all we did was fight. He was really angry—"

"Wasn't that just his natural state?" I caught myself. "Sorry—"

"No, it's fine. He *was* always angry, but lately, it was worse. Something was setting him off—"

I waited to see if Serge would say anything, but he remained hunched by the chair, and said nothing.

"Do you know what made him so mad?"

She shook her head. "Every time I asked, it just caused a fight." The words rushed out her mouth as tears fell down her cheeks. "Everything caused a fight."

One of the outcomes when you deal with the dead is learning to spot a liar, and the acid churning in my gut said Amber was lying.

Serge got to his feet and stormed to the window, but remained silent.

"He always made me feel like I couldn't do anything right," she sniffed.

More tears fell. Instead of making me feel sympathetic, I got the gross vibe that she was trying to manipulate me.

"What about you?" He whirled to face her. "What about your pissy attitudes and screwed up crap? If I took you to a movie, you wanted to go for pizza. If we went for pizza, you wanted to go for a drive. You wanted more time together, less time together!" He jerked his hands through his hair. "At least your friends didn't bitch at me or complain!" Serge was crying. Twin tracks of dirty red tears—blood and betrayal—left gritty trails on his skin.

I turned from him, the sight of his raw pain too much to bear.

"Why don't you tell the Deadhead about all the ways you screwed up this relationship!"

The air started to crackle and made the hair on my skin rise.

"Amber, he didn't have a shirt on. Do you know who he would have been with?"

She snorted. "Who wasn't he with?"

"And what about your mom!" He paced to where the television stood. "Why don't you tell Deadhead about all the times she made you cry and I was there for you! I was the *only* one who was there for you!" Rage mottled his face.

My teeth vibrated, a high-pitched ringing sounded in my ears. *Crap.* "Amber, seriously, who do you think he was with last night?"

"Why don't you talk about that night—all the times I took it from *him* because of you! No! Of course not! Poor, innocent Amber. It's all big, bad Serge's fault. Right? Mine! Not you, not your whore of a mother!"

The window exploded. Shards of glass, rain, and wind blew across the chairs and floor.

Amber screamed and pressed herself against the couch.

I twisted one way, then the other, looking for the ghost, but all I saw was pelting rain and dark skies.

May and Nancy ran into the room. The cop shot me a look.

Oh, crap. I was in *so much* trouble.

CHAPTER TEN

"What happened?"

"The wind." The lie rushed from my mouth.

Nancy turned to Amber's mom. "Do you have any wood? We need to board this up."

She nodded and left. I took a steadying breath and stood.

"You and I," said Nancy to me in a tone I'd never heard before, "will discuss this later."

While May was gone, we pulled the chairs away from the gaping hole in the wall. She returned with wood, hammers, and nails. May and Nancy knocked out the broken panes and fixed the window, Amber and I swept the broken glass into the trash.

"I think that's the best we can do," said May. Her forehead puckered. "Not sure where we'll find the money to fix this"—she pasted a smile on her face—"but at least no one was hurt."

No one living, I thought. I glanced around the room, but Serge was gone.

Nancy glanced at me and I didn't need the push. I didn't want to be here anymore. Between Amber's behaviour and my newfound sympathy for Serge, I'd lost my inner grounding.

"I should go," I said.

Nancy nodded.

Amber reached for me and I gave her an awkward hug

"Thanks for being such a good friend," she said.

The acid bubbling in my stomach began to churn. For sure, she was lying. The fact she was trying to force a bond between us said as much.

I took my coat from May, ran into the rain and to the car. Serge wasn't in the backseat. And for the first time in my life I found myself wondering where he was and hoping he was okay.

CHAPTER ELEVEN

Nancy stepped into the house.

"Dad's not home, but I let him know you'd be coming over."

"Worried about witnesses?"

"You looked pretty pissed."

"I'm not pretty pissed." She dropped her coat and headed up the stairs. "I'm gorgeously furious."

I winced.

At the top of the steps, she turned, looked back at me. "You and your dad have a unique relationship and I love you kid, you know that. But this is a police investigation, this is a murder, and you *cannot* pull a stupid stunt like you did."

"It wasn't a stunt!" I rushed up the steps. "You were with May—"

"And you should have kept that cute derrière of yours in the chair, Maggie! What were you thinking?"

"That she'd lost her boyfriend and maybe she needed someone who would feel badly for her and not treat her like a suspect or a means to an end."

"She is a means to an end!" Nancy put her hand on my shoulder. "You're a smart kid, Maggie, but there are things you don't understand."

I turned away from her. "I could say the same thing back to you."

"I'm not busting your balls to be a jerk. I'm doing it to protect you."

I nodded.

She sighed. "You want something to eat?"

If she was willing to feed me then she probably wasn't as mad as I thought. "Yeah."

Nancy moved into the kitchen. "So. Tell me. What don't I understand?"

"Huh?"

"You talked to Amber. What did she have to say?"

"So, you're going to give me grief for talking to her but you want the information?"

She took a long look at the bread and butter on the table. "I don't have to feed you. I could go back to the station. Leave you to toast and tea."

"No, I'm starving—I'll trade information for food."

"Thought so. What did she have to say?" Nancy busied herself at the fridge and I sat at the table.

"Not much. They were having problems and she's happy he's dead, not sad."

"Did she say anything about being with him last night?" She flipped the knob of the oven.

"No, and she says she doesn't know who he'd been with, but she's lying."

Nancy frowned. "Why? What's the point?"

"I'm wondering the same thing...unless—" I stopped. "You don't think she was in on it?"

"Does she have a motive?"

"A dirty video he took of them."

She tilted her head to the right then the left, as though shifting the words. "I'll look into it. Kids have killed for less. Only..."

"Only, she's not the type. Let's face it," I said, "Amber's nice but she's not smart enough to have killed Serge like that. If she'd done it, she'd have left evidence everywhere." I glanced at Nancy. "Unless you got some crime scene results—?"

The cop laughed. "This isn't prime-time TV. I don't get fingerprints back in an hour. It'll take a few weeks, but even so, my gut says she didn't do it."

"Did May say anything?"

"Not really. Guess Serge was having trouble at home—"

"Yeah," I said dismissively. "But we already know that."

The sides of her lips quirked.

I blushed. "Sorry. What did she say about the fighting?"

"Just that it had been worse the past few months. A couple of times, Serge came to the church office and it looked like it would come to blows."

"Not that I'd cheer for violence in a house of God, but if anyone deserved to get decked, it was the reverend."

Nancy's brow wrinkled. "No, he was fighting with the mother."

"Mrs. Popov?" I thought about the night at the pool. "Are you sure? He seemed protective of her, not mad."

"I'm just telling you what May said."

"Did she hear what the fights were about?"

Nancy frowned, but I wasn't sure if it was at my question or the deli meat in her hand. "She said she didn't…"

My ears pricked. "But?"

"It's a police matter."

"C'mon, you know you want to tell me."

She laughed.

"Anyway, that's not news—Serge fighting with his parents." I thought back to all the times I'd seen them together. "Mrs. Popov was always telling him he needed to respect his father. I'll talk to Amber again."

Nancy glared at me.

"Okay, sorry, but if she talks to me, I'm not going to tell her to shut up." As much as I loved Nancy, I had a ghost to get rid of, and Amber was my way to do it.

Nancy made me a sandwich and salad. After we'd eaten, she left me to the dishes and went back to work.

I pulled out my phone and called Dad. "Hey," I said when he answered. "You don't have to worry. I'm okay. It's been a few hours, I can eat again."

"I know." He sounded affronted. "I'm not worried."

I glanced at the table, at the bread. "Liar."

"No—"

"Dad, I could find dead bodies and hear The Voice every day for the rest of my life, and still not get through all the bread you left."

"Thought you might be hungry," he said gruffly.

"Just tired," I said.

"Are you sure you're okay?"

"Yeah. Sure."

"I'll be home in a few hours."

"We'll talk then." I ended the call. I brewed myself a pot of black tea. Then I took the last bits of lunch to my room. My empty room.

Two days later, I came into my room and found Serge hunched on the window seat, staring out at the pouring rain. He didn't turn or acknowledge me.

Before, I'd ignored him out of spite. Now I did it out of respect. I crawled on the bed. The animals moved out of the way. Ebony jumped on the window seat. She studied Serge, head-butted his knee, and rubbed her face against his leg. He turned. Watched her. Then, he reached out and stroked her temple. She purred, circled three times, and curled into a ball.

The hum of the furnace was the only sound in the room. I flipped on the television. At this point, I regretted not speaking to Serge sooner. If I had, then I could have said something comforting now. Who was I kidding? If I had tried to say anything before, we just would have fought, and this moment would be even more awkward. Crap. I should have been happy for his pain. God knows he'd been the cause of too many tears in my life. So, why did I pity him? Wish that even one person were sorry for his passing?

I clicked through a bunch of channels. The oldie station caught his interest. It was showing one of the police dramas from the '80s. I wasn't a huge fan of the pastel-wearing cop duo, but I figured Serge needed something pleasant so I left the station on. I drank some tea and decided it was a good time to catch a shower. Twenty minutes later, dressed in jogging pants and a sweater, I came back in the room.

Serge was on my bed, the animals sleeping beside him. Absentmindedly, he rubbed Buddha's head. The sound of the front door opening caught my attention.

Maybe it was the result of living together for seventeen years, maybe it was the psychic skills, but there was nothing good about the way dad closed the door. Buddha hopped off the bed and we both headed downstairs.

I found Dad hanging his coat up in the closet. "Hey. What happened?"

He glanced at me.

I saw the anger in his face and took an instinctive step back. "You look ready to take a baseball bat to someone's head. What happened?"

"Nothing."

I followed him into the kitchen. "Dad?"

As he turned towards the coffeemaker, his profile came into view. His lips were pressed together in a tight, thin line, and his jaw was clenched.

"It's not Nancy, is it?" I swallowed my ballooning panic. Was I going to get in trouble all over again?

"No. I don't want to talk about it."

"Okay. Fair enough."

Dad brewed a pot of coffee. The scent of medium-roast beans filled the air. He poured himself a drink and I helped myself to another mug of tea. I didn't want to go back upstairs, so I went into the family room and sat down. Dad came in a couple of minutes later. I handed him the papers from the coffee table.

"Thanks," he grunted and sat down in the old leather recliner.

That thing was an eyesore, all ripped material covered with duct tape. If Nancy ever moved in, it would be the first thing to go. I knew it. I also knew it was dad's favourite piece of furniture and he was more likely to give me up than the chair.

"What are you doing in here?" he asked.

I started. "You want me to leave?"

He looked at me from over the top of the newspaper. "No, I'm just surprised. You're usually in your room."

"Oh." I glanced around, pointed up, and dropped my voice to a whisper. "I have a visitor."

His papers fell to the floor in a crinkled rustle. "Dead Falls's most recent contribution to the ghostly set?"

I nodded.

He moved to the spot beside me. "When did he get here?"

"He's been here on and off the past few days."

Dad frowned. "Why didn't you say anything?"

The heat of shame burned my cheeks. "I was being an ass."

I moved closer to my dad and, wrapping my arm around him, inhaled the scent of soap and cologne. I leaned my cheek against his flannel shirt. "I thought it would be this great revenge. Leave him to silence—"

"Oh, Maggie." In his voice was disappointment and understanding.

"But I feel like crap," I said. "Amber was actually relieved he's dead. Serge was there for the whole thing. It was horrible. He was so angry and hurt. I thought it would make me feel good—" I lifted my face. "But instead, I feel like a jerk, and worse, I actually feel bad for him. He's just sitting upstairs watching TV and hogging my bed."

Dad gave a small chuckle. "There's a sentence I never thought I'd hear: 'Dad, Serge is in my bed and hogging the space.'"

I snorted. "Yeah, not really a sentence I thought I'd be saying."

The smile left his face. "That poor kid."

"Bet you never thought you'd say that."

Dad shook his head. "I may never have said it, but I thought it often enough." He sighed. "Even when he was being a jerk-off to you. It was my second thought, right after 'I'm going to kill that little prick.'"

I laughed. "Thanks."

He sighed and squeezed my fingers. "It gets worse, you know."

"What does?"

"I just came from a consultation with the Popovs." His face contorted with distaste. "It's like they're burying a stranger—some derelict off the street." He took a breath. "They don't want flowers—they don't even want a service."

"No—!"

"It's like they want him gone, not just physically, but psychically, as well."

My brain spun with possible reasons for their decision. "Maybe they're afraid no one will come?"

"Come on, Maggie. In this town? People would come just out of respect. They'll come out of morbid curiosity."

"Yeah, I know."

"There's no reason for this."

"Who led the charge?"

He grimaced. "They both did. He suggested it; she backed up him."

"Wow."

Dad took my hand. "Even if you were the worst kid in existence, if you died, I'd want to give you a proper burial."

I squeezed his fingers. "Thanks."

"How can parents do that?" Dad took a sip of coffee. "Didn't they love him? Aren't they a *little* upset he's dead?"

I was starting to wonder the same thing.

CHAPTER TWELVE

The next morning, I headed to the Popovs. Ten minutes of driving and I climbed out of the car. The rain had tapered off, leaving the smell of moulding leaves and a damp chill that seeped through my bomber jacket. I stood looking at the bungalow on the tree-lined street. The living room curtain flicked open for a second. Good. They were home. Hoping that Serge only needed a memorial to send him to the Great Beyond, I headed up the walkway. There was no bell, so I knocked on the metal door. No answer. I knocked harder. Still nothing. I did it again and started calling, "Mrs. Popov? Reverend? Are you there?"

Of course they were there, and if they didn't want the entire neighbourhood hearing our conversation, they would open the door.

"I wanted to talk to you about Serge," I called loudly. Making eye contact with a few of the people on the street, I continued, "I know you're very upset, but it's about the funeral preparations. There's been a mix-up. He's been tagged for cremation—"

That got 'em. They were all about traditional burials. The door opened a crack and Lydia Popov peered at me.

"Mrs. Popov. I wanted to talk to you about—"

"I'll fix the cremation," she said, and went to shut me out.

"No—" I put my foot in the jamb and winced as the edge of the door slammed into my foot. "It's not that."

Giving me a look like she wouldn't mind making me an amputee, she opened the door. "What is it?" She shivered at the wind and wound her hands in her apron.

I moved so I stood in the doorway. Let her try to slam it on me now. "My dad said you didn't want a service or anything."

"That's right."

"But why?"

"Because he didn't deserve it." Her voice had a sudden vehemence, an anger and hatred. "I tried so hard and he repaid me by being ungrateful. He was a bad kid—" Desperation corrupted her words. "You know what the good book says. I did my best and he ruined everything!"

"He was your son and—!"

The door swung wide and I found myself staring up at the gaunt face of the reverend.

"Miss Johnson. Your father's still raising you well, I see."

"Better than some fathers," I said.

He didn't blink. "Why are you disturbing us during this time of mourning?"

"Who's mourning?" I asked. "Dad says you're not doing anything for Serge—"

"That's our decision," he said.

"But—he was your *son*. Shouldn't you do something to remember him?"

"We have, but putting him on display for people to gawk at him is not how we'll proceed. This is private. You don't know us and you have no right to be here."

"Folks will want to say goodbye—"

His thin, delicate eyebrows rose. "Like who? You?"

He leaned toward me and it took all my effort not to recoil.

"Will you shed tears for the boy, Maggie?"

"No—maybe." The reeking scent of rotting wood coming off him made me take a step back. "But your son had friends—"

"And look where it got him. Go home, Miss Johnson, and leave us to mourn in peace." He clamped his bony hand on my shoulder, pushed me onto the cement steps, and slammed the door.

"What about the memorial at the game tonight?" I wasn't sure if the team was planning anything but, knowing Craig, I figured it was a good hunch. "You going to ignore that too? No funeral? No remembrance for him? What's your congregation going to say when they find out what you're doing?" I yelled as loudly as could, hoped the entire block would hear me. "Think they'll still want you as their reverend when they find out your mercy and forgiveness couldn't extend to your own kid?"

Nothing.

I walked back to the car, avoiding the puddles of water on the sidewalk. The wind whipped my hair around my face. I climbed inside and found Serge sitting in the back. Did he want to visit the house? Or see his parents? I didn't know and I still couldn't bring myself to say anything to him.

He climbed across the console into the passenger seat. I let him get comfortable, then I started the car. Air pumped out of the vents and warmed my skin. I wondered if he could feel the heat.

"All I ever dreamed of was leaving this crummy town, getting out of that stupid house," he said. "Now, I'm dead and stuck here forever." He gazed up at the shingled roof of what used to be his home. "But at least, I'm outta there. One out of two isn't that bad."

I opened my mouth to acknowledge him, but the front door slammed open. Reverend Popov raced towards me. The hem of his burgundy cardigan flapped against his body and made him look like an overfed vulture swooping in for an after-dinner snack. He came around to my window and pounded on the pane. I rolled it down.

"Get off my property."

What could I say? *Just a sec, Reverend. The spirit of your son is waxing philosophical and I don't want to interrupt.* "I was just letting the car warm up."

His face contorted. "You weren't on our doorstep long enough for the car to get cold."

"Fine, I'm taking a minute."

"You've had it," he said. "Get off my driveway or I phone the cops."

"What's your problem?" Even for the reverend, this was over the top.

He shoved his finger in my face. "I don't know what your little game is, but I won't have you making a mockery of my family."

I slapped his hand away. "You're doing a good enough job of that all by yourself!" Before he could say anything more, I rolled up the window.

"Good one," said Serge. "He's such an ass."

"No kidding," I muttered, and shoved the gears into drive.

Oh-uh.

Serge whipped around and stared at me. "What the—can you hear me?"

I pulled away from the curb and drove towards home. I sighed. "Yeah, I can."

He smacked the dashboard. "Can you see me, too?"

"Yep."

"No kidding!"

"Yeah, I've just got the luck of the Irish, don't I?"

"So...how long have you been able to see me?" His words picked up speed as his excitement grew. "Did it happen when you stood up to my dad? You found your courage and your voice and stood your ground and suddenly—"

I glanced at him. "This isn't some movie, Serge. This moment isn't a turning point for the plot."

"Oh." His shoulders deflated. "So? When were you able to first see me?"

Crap.

"Well?"

"It's a little complicated—"

His body went still. "You've been able to see me the whole time, haven't you?"

I hesitated. "Yeah, yeah, I have."

His face turned purple. "You bitch!" He went to punch the dashboard, but his fist swished through the material. "You scum-sucking, pathetic, little—"

"See? That's *exactly* why I didn't say anything. Who wants your rage?"

"Bull!" This time he managed to hit the dashboard. "You ignored me because you knew it would hurt." His fist bounced off the side of the door. "You did it to get back at me."

"Fine, I did! Can you blame me? You're an asshole!"

"That doesn't excuse—"

"You're freakin' right it does. You deserved everything you got!"

His face went white and memory flashed through me.

"I didn't mean that." I took my foot off the accelerator. "Look, at first it was a way to get back at you. I admit it, okay? But after that thing with Amber, I felt bad—"

He shoved his finger in my face. Geez. Must be a genetic thing for the men in his family.

"You say anything to anyone, and I'll get you."

I batted his hand away. "Did death take what little brains you had? How can I tell anyone anything? You're dead, remember?"

He dropped his hand. "I knew there was something wrong about you," he muttered. "Seeing dead people. Figures." He glanced at me. "Deadhead."

"Your lucky break," I told him. "If it wasn't for me, no one would know you're still here." I frowned. "Why are you here, anyway? Shouldn't you be in hell?"

"Ha ha. Funny." He shifted. "I don't know why I'm here. I didn't even know I was dead until I saw Nancy and your dad."

I pulled into the school parking lot. It was deserted, which meant no one would question why I seemed to be talking to myself. "Do you remember anything?"

His eyebrows pulled together.

"Gimme a break. Either you come clean or we spend a lifetime together. Is that what you want? To spend your eternity with me?"

"Water polo practice—" His face went grey. "Mom and him being there."

"What about after that?"

His frown deepened. "It's just blank." He shook his head. "No, I don't remember—what happened? What do you know?"

"You were found in your car, in the parking lot of the old mill."

Serge shook his head. "No—are you sure?"

I nodded.

"What would I have been doing at the old mill?"

"Uh, well, you were found with your shirt off."

He snorted. "I definitely don't do that at the old mill."

"Are you sure?"

He shot me a look.

I raised my hand. "Okay, point taken."

He stared out the window. Shoving his hands in his letterman's jacket, he asked, "Is it possible to die without knowing it?"

I shrugged. "Yeah, but usually, you remember soon enough."

He fiddled with the radio knobs.

"Are you sure you don't remember what you were doing after you left the pool?"

"Why can't I adjust the stations?"

"'Cause you're dead."

"But I blew out the window in Amber's house."

"Are you really asking or just avoiding the subject?"

"Me, not wanting to talk about my death. Go figure."

I sighed. "Why are you haunting me?"

"Shouldn't you know the answer to that one, Deadhead?"

"So far, all I can think of is that I made Karma mad at me."

His eyebrows pulled together. "Who's she? Some new kid?"

"Apparently, the myth of death bringing the ultimate wisdom really isn't true. At least, not in your case."

"Screw you."

I smiled. "I'd like to see you try it."

And the reality of him being stuck with me as his only source of companionship must have hit, because he slouched down and cursed.

"Let's try again. What did you do after practice? Showered, dressed—"

"Went for a burger."

"Okay. Then what?"

Nothing.

"Did you go to meet somebody?"

His face tightened. "It's stupid, you know? You have all these plans, all these ways you're going to make the people you hate pay for all the ways they screwed you over. But then, suddenly, you're dead and nothing matters anymore."

"What do you mean?"

But he only shook his head and went silent.

CHAPTER THIRTEEN

The polo game was going to start in forty minutes and already the parking lot was full. I wedged my car in between a minivan and truck. After unhooking my cell from its charger, I headed to find my friends. McNally's pool was closed for renovations, but the Cottondale Rec Center had agreed to host the game. For this I was grateful. They had the best poutine in town.

I stepped through the glass and metal doors and, weaving around the crowd, walked to the concession stand. Nell was already there and waved me over to her spot.

"You'll never believe who's here tonight," she said.

I eyed her retro neon pink shirt, stirrups, and legwarmers and said, "The 80s?"

She rolled her eyes. "Don't try to be funny. It makes me feel bad—like watching a puppy trying to tango."

I frowned. "When did you ever see a—"

"Focus, Johnson. The Popovs are here tonight." She gave me an approving smile. "I guess your acting like a lunatic earlier today worked."

"If you're going to call me names, I'm going to stop texting you about my adventures."

"No you won't. You can't help yourself." She pointed to herself. "Flame." She pointed to me. "Moth."

I rolled my eyes. "I think your brain is sputtering."

"Me. High watt bulb."

"Dimwit."

"You wanna bask in your victory or are you going to start something I'll finish."

I grinned. "I do deserve some basking. Mrs. Popov came to a couple of games—according to Craig—but His Righteousness—"

"I know. You must have really freaked him out with the congregation thing. I think the church pays for their house, too. If he got ousted, there goes their home."

We moved up as the customers in front took their popcorn and hot chocolate and left.

"What do you want?" Nell asked.

From the corner of my eye, I spotted Mrs. Popov sitting by the windows that overlooked the pool. "Uh, a coffee and fries."

"Coffee? With fries?"

"It's not for me." I nodded to the row of plastic yellow chairs.

Nell's gaze followed. "Oh." She turned to the junior-high kid behind the register. "Gimme large fries, two Cokes, a mega-burger, hot-dog, large popcorn—" She turned to me. "What do you want to eat?"

The kid laughed.

"She's not joking," I said. "She's made medical history with her invisible tape worm."

He frowned, not sure if I was serious.

"I'm still having the coffee. Add in a burger, change the fries to poutine, and a large Coke." I fished into my jacket.

"I got this," said Nell. She turned to the cashier. "Listen, can you grab us the coffee right away?"

He nodded. "What size?"

"Medium," I said.

He returned a minute later. "Cream and sugar are over to the side."

"I'll be back," I told Nell. Threading my way past the green-jerseyed McNally supporters, I headed to the bank of napkins and condiments. I grabbed a couple of sugar packets. Maybe she preferred the artificial sweeteners? I stuffed a couple of them in my pockets.

The smell of rotting wood prickled my nose. I glanced up. "Mr. Popov."

He ignored me and took two napkins.

It ticked me off to have to play nice, but I needed to send Serge to the Great Beyond. "I was hoping we could talk—" Holding up the coffee, I said, "I'm sorry. I only saw your wife. I bought her a coffee, but if you'd like one as well—"

"I don't drink coffee."

There were no s-words in his sentence, but I got the distinct impression of a snake hissing.

He pushed two straws into his jacket pocket. "Stay away from me, Miss Johnson."

I held up the coffee. "What about your wife?"

The corner of his lip curled.

"What about the coffee? Can you at least take it to her? I don't know if she likes cream or sugar—"

"And I do?" He snarled the question then strode away.

"That went well."

I turned and took my pop from Nell. "Yeah, he's a real prince." I glanced over my shoulder. Mrs. Popov sat alone, her fingers entangled with each other. I scanned the crowd, but the reverend was nowhere in sight. Handing my drink back to Nell, I said: "I'll meet you at the pool."

I strode to where the older woman sat and held the coffee to her. "Here."

She turned and frowned at the cup in my hand. "What is that?"

"Coffee...I thought you might be cold."

"Serge used to make me coffee." Her lips pressed into a straight, narrow line. "He was always doing naughty things like that."

Feeling like a total idiot standing there with my hand stretched out, I set the cup on the white plastic tabletop. "He was just trying to be nice—"

"By making coffee." She shook her head. Oily wisps of hair fell across her lined forehead. "Caffeine isn't good for the body. He knew Mikhail disapproved." Her fingers clawed at her green cardigan. Pulling the wool around her, she said, "He's out of pain now. There's peace, finally." Her eyes lost focus. "All I wanted is for him to be at peace."

The scent of burnt sugar and mouldering excrement made me gag. "You're not talking about your son, are you?" I wanted to hit her.

She pushed her chair back. The metal legs of the chairs shrieked against the floor; the sound echoed off the high ceilings. "I should go. He'll be waiting."

"What about your son—doesn't he deserve anything from you?"

Our gazes met but if eyes were the windows to the soul, then Mrs. Popov had the curtains closed and the lights off.

I stepped back. She pushed past me. I grabbed the coffee and dumped it in a nearby wastebasket. My phone chirped. It was Nell, texting to ask what was taking so long and to just "*woo-woo*" Mrs. Popov.

I stuck my cell back in my pocket and turned to go. My gaze caught Amber emerging from a narrow hallway, a drink in her hand.

"Hey! Amber!" I sped to her.

She swung my way, her expression startled.

"Whoa." I skidded to a stop. "Are you okay?" Her face was puffy. Tear left wet trails on her red cheeks.

She shoved her drink at me.

Too stunned to refuse, I took the cup. Melting ice cubes rattled in the almost empty container.

"What—?"

"I hate orange juice."

"So why did you order—?"

She pulled at her blue and white striped scarf.

The action drew my attention to her neck and the small red bruises on her skin. "Amber—"

"It's fine. I'm fine." The words came in a breathless rush.

The smell of mould on wood caught my nose. Mr. Popov came out of the same hallway. He glared at both of us then disappeared into the crowd.

"Did he hurt you? Did he say anything—" I reached for her shoulder.

Amber wrenched herself free. "No! It's fine. Just stay out of it, Maggie." She pulled her goose down jacket close to her chest and hurried away.

"Great," I muttered. "Glad to help." I dumped her drink and went to find my friends.

Until I walked into the rec centre , my dealings with Serge had preoccupied my thoughts. But seeing Craig, wet and hot, warming up by the pool's side, brought my heartache back. It flooded me, sharp and ice-cold. Everyone was pairing off, finding boyfriends and girlfriends.

All I had was a maladjusted ghost who'd hated me in life and despised me in death. He'd stayed home instead of coming to the game, and his will was strong enough to keep us apart. Too bad it wasn't strong enough to fully break the bond between us and send him across the bridge that separated the living from the dead. I scanned the bleachers. Amber wasn't around. I spotted Nell and the gang and headed over. The whispers of kids followed me, but I ignored them.

"Finally," said Tammy as I sat down and grabbed my food from Nell. "We can get totally caught up on everything. Your texts didn't really say much."

"Can't blame me for not wanting to put details in writing."

"But it's true, though, you're the one who found Serge?"

I nodded

"Geez, Tammy." Bruce rolled his eyes. "You think infomercials are true but don't trust the Dead Falls grapevine." He pivoted in my direction. "I heard he was by the old mill."

"Gross." Tammy's nose scrunched in distaste and made her freckles crinkle. She turned to me. "That must have been disgusting. Finding him, I mean."

I glanced at Nell. "Uh, yeah."

The girl to my left was almost in my lap, she was leaning into the conversation so hard. I elbowed her to get some space and said, "Maybe we should talk about this later."

Nell cut her eyes at the girl. "You got it. A *private* discussion."

The girl sniffed and turned away.

Coach Thiessen left his players and, standing by the referee, said, "As many of you know, the Warriors lost one of its most valued players in an accident last week—"

"Accident?" whispered Tammy. "I thought Serge died of alcohol poisoning."

"Do you think he meant to do that on purpose?" asked Bruce.
She blushed.

"—and so we invite his parents to come up as we dedicate the game in his honour." He looked to the left.

I straightened, craned my neck to get a better view. Sure enough, Lydia and Mikhail Popov were sitting in the front row. Neither of them moved.

The coach shifted from one foot to the other. "Mr. and Mrs. Popov?"

Slowly, Serge's dad stood.

I did as well.

Nell yanked me down. "What are you going to do?"

I leaned in. "Maybe Serge needs a send-off to...y'know...*go.*"

"And you think confronting his parents in public will make them agree to a memorial."

"Shame is a highly unused negotiation tactic." Rising, I made my way poolside. I got to the floor at the same time Mr. Popov reached the coach.

He took the microphone. "Thank you," he said stiffly. Handing the mic back, he turned.

"Reverend Popov."

He froze at my voice. Only his eyes tracked my position.

"Sir, I want to ask—on behalf of the town—for you to reconsider your decision about Serge's funeral."

"We already discussed this." He pressed the words through closed lips. "You must remember the exchange, Miss Johnson. It was when you trespassed onto my property."

"Sir, please. I understand your feelings—" I moved towards them and grabbed the mic from Coach Thiessen.

He blinked, stunned, and reached for it, but I was already moving away. "I know there were issues between your son and many of the townspeople. I was his favourite target, but sir, even if it was a crappy relationship, it was a relationship. I have a right to say my goodbyes—to say the things to him in death that I couldn't in life. I have a right to have closure."

Serge appeared in my peripheral vision.

Crap. My talking about him must have called him to me.

The skin on Mr. Popov's face went leather tight and red. "*Your rights? How dare you?*" He spit the words.

"He was a stupid kid." My words bounced off the tile. "But he was a kid, and he doesn't deserve this kind of annihilation. He'll never get a chance to be the person he could have been. Please give us the chance to find closure—"

Craig stood, gave me a thumbs-up.

"Miss Johnson," Mr. Popov hissed. "Sit down before you embarrass yourself further—"

"Funerals are expensive." Mrs. Popov stood.

Her husband's head snapped in her direction, the hate on his face naked and raw.

She stumbled back and dropped in her seat.

"If money's an issue," said Coach Thiessen. "We can hold a fundraiser—"

"We are not poor!"

"Then why won't you do it?" I asked quietly. The question echoed into silence.

"Your selfishness is only exceeded by your stupidity, Miss Johnson. His death, like his life, is of no concern to anyone but his mother and me. Leave my family alone." Mr. Popov turned on his heel and with slow, deliberate steps, stalked to the exit.

After a brief pause, his wife scurried after him.

I watched them leave. Their path took them straight to Serge. They couldn't see him, but it didn't matter. In death as in life, they walked through him.

He stretched his arms out to his mother and tried to grab her as she moved past.

Everything in me crumpled at the pain and torment etched on his face.

The coach put his hand on my shoulder. He took the mic and, giving me a small smile, said, "Why don't you go and find your friends?"

I nodded and went back to my seat.

The ref blew his whistle and the game started. I saw Amber get up and leave.

Nell grabbed my arm. "You did good."

I tried to get Serge out of my head and away from my thoughts. His hurt haunted my heart and swept through the chambers of my mind, a hot, blistering wind that seared everything it touched.

I forced myself to watch the game—mostly because everyone was watching me, but my eyes seemed to hone in on Craig. And every time, it left me feeling cold and alone, bereft of hope and happiness, and terribly lonely. Who was the girl he'd been with and why couldn't it have been me?

By the time the match was over, I felt like I'd been the one in the pool, getting tossed around and held under.

"Man, what a game!" Bruce draped his arm around my shoulder. "Craig saved it in the last minute, eh?"

I didn't even realize we'd won. "Yeah, he sure did."

Bruce pulled me close. "Don't let the Popovs screw up your night. You tried your best, Mags, and that's better than Serge ever deserved from you."

I nodded. "Yeah, I guess."

Nell's eyes narrowed at my tone. "Hey, let's go to the Tin Shack to celebrate."

"Wanna take my minivan?" asked Tammy. "It'll fit all of us."

"No," said Nell. "Maggie and I will catch up."

"No telling the dirty details of finding Serge without us," said Bruce.

"Promise," I said.

They moved off and Nell pulled me to the side. "Spill."

I shrugged. "There's not much to say. I felt the pull—"

"Not that. The zombie act."

"I'm fine."

"And I'm flat-chested. Start talking. What was really going on when the Popovs walked out?"

I sighed. Pulling her away from the crowd, finding a quiet spot where no one could hear us, I started from the beginning and told her about Mrs. Popov smelling like rotten apples.

Nell's nose scrunched. "I don't get it—rotten apples?"

"You ever hear the saying 'as wholesome as apple pie?'"

Her eyebrows pulled together. "Maybe..."

"Moms smell like apples—it's nurturing, loving. Rotten apples is motherhood gone wrong." I pressed my fingers to my eyes. "I feel really conflicted, Nell. Whatever she was to him, it wasn't a good mom. Earlier, when I was talking to her, she smelled like poop and burned sugar. Her obsession for her husband, her unquestioning devotion, and loyalty—it's at the expense of her son." My throat clogged with tears. "You should have seen him tonight, reaching to her. It was horrible. I can't stand Serge, but I'm tormented by what was done to him."

"Wire monkeys," she said.

"How much sugar did you have tonight?"

"No—in psych class, they were talking about this horrible experiment with monkeys." Her head tilted to the side. "Or was it chimpanzees?" She waved away the question. "Doesn't matter. What matters is that they took the babies from their real mothers and put them in a cage with two fake monkeys."

"Holy crap."

"I know, eh? Anyway, one fake mommy was wrapped in terrycloth. The other one had milk, but it was a wire monkey. What they found was the babies would cling to the terrycloth mom, even though she couldn't do anything for them. They'd only go to the other one when they were hungry."

"We are a real screwed-up species, aren't we?"

"Forget the animal rights aspect for a minute and focus. What I'm trying to say is that Serge had a terrycloth mom. She didn't do anything for him, but—"

"—she was the only mom he had."

"Exactly."

"I was much happier when I just hated him."

"Tell me about it." She nodded to the boys' locker room. "What else is going on? Usually, when you're watching Craig, you look like you're experiencing the rapture. Tonight you looked like you were trying to drop a deuce but were too constipated."

"Nice imagery."

She grinned. "I try."

I told her about Craig and Widow's Peak.

Nell shook her head. "No way. Craig doesn't have a girlfriend."

"Maybe. But he seems to have a friend with benefits."

She frowned. "It doesn't make sense. If he was rubbing skin with anyone in the school, I'd know."

I scoffed. "Yeah, why?"

She gave me a hard look. "I know about you, don't I?"

"Well—"

"Believe me, I know everything."

I thought about my ghostly roommate. "Do you know who Serge saw the night he died?"

She made a face. "Okay, *almost* everything."

"I feel comforted already."

"Don't be petulant," she said as she threaded her arm through mine.

Her soft hair brushed my face and tickled my chin.

"I may not know about Serge, but I know Craig. You must have gotten the cars mixed-up."

"With the level of my obsession with him? Not likely."

She chewed her bottom lip. "I guess, but still…"

"You know what? I really don't want to talk about this." I shook my head. "I'd rather talk about the dead guy."

Nell gave me a sympathetic half-hug. "Okay, no more talk about love. Let's go discuss death."

"Do you think it's strange that the place townsfolk go to have sex is called Widow's Peak—I mean, it's a death name. That's weird, right?"

Nell grunted. "This whole town's weird."

We left the arena and headed to my car. A few minutes later, I pulled into a parking spot and saw Tammy and Bruce outside the Tin Shack. Craig was with them.

"Holy crap," I muttered as we headed over. "I just can't catch a break."

Nell squeezed my fingers.

"Hey, Maggie," he said. His breath clouded the air.

"Hey." I shoved my hands in my pockets and wished I'd brought my gloves. "Good game."

He grinned and stupid me, I went weak in the knees. "We toasted them."

"Winning by two goals isn't toasting," said Bruce.

Craig's grin widened and the too-familiar blade of love and rejection sliced my heart.

"Any win is toasting." He bumped my shoulder. "Right?"

"Yeah, right."

We went inside and the smell of grease, fries, and meat mixed with the dry heat of the room.

"We should grab a table," said Bruce.

Nell shook her head. "Let's eat in Tammy's ride. It's more private."

I looked around and realized she was right. The small restaurant was full of kids, and most of their attention seemed to be on me. "Good idea."

I ordered my food and headed to Tammy's minivan. The chairs were worn and the hinges squeaked, but it was big enough to give us room to spread out. I sat on the left of the last row, Craig took the right, and we set the food in between us.

Tammy started the car and flipped on the interior lights.

"So, what happened?" Bruce asked around a mouthful of fries.

"Uh." I took a sip of the shake and gave myself a minute to think. "I was driving around and saw the car."

Bruce frowned. "That's it?"

I shrugged. "I thought it was weird for his car to be there—plus, we'd had words at the pool. I wanted to have it out with him."

Craig stiffened. "What did he do?"

I reminded my hopeless heart that his protective tone had more to do with being a genuinely good guy than with nursing a crush, and said, "Nothing. He was just on edge about his parents."

Serge appeared on the chair next to Nell. "What happened to the TV? They were just going to shoot the drug dealer." He glanced around the van. His gaze stopped on me. "I felt you calling—a tug."

Tammy turned on the vehicle and adjusted the heat gauge. "Getting cold."

"Kinda sudden." Nell's gaze caught me. Her eyes narrowed.

I nodded and glanced to the seat beside her where Serge sat.

She gathered her food closer, and he shifted into a more comfortable position.

"Are you going to be calling on me a lot?" he asked. "Because we'll have to figure out a schedule." He leered at me. "Like when you're in the shower."

"Not likely," I muttered.

"What?" asked Craig.

"Unlikely," I said. "I thought it was unlikely that we would solve anything, I thought I'd face him anyway. He'd just been a jerk about me talking to his parents."

At the mention of his folks, Serge went grey. He regained colour and said, "I told you not to talk about it."

I didn't answer him.

"You said they didn't say anything to you." Craig took a bite of his burger.

Serge watched me. "Maggie—c'mon—" He swallowed and his Adam's apple bobbed. "—c'mon, *please*."

"They didn't."

His breath left in a rush.

"Serge was just freaking out about nothing."

"I don't freak out over nothing!"

"Amber said he'd been weird lately."

Bruce snorted. "He was always weird."

"The guy wears thong underwear," muttered Serge, "and I'm the weird one."

Craig looked up from his burger. "Tammy, what did you mean about Serge acting weird?"

She shrugged. "All I know is that Amber used to be gaga over him, but since the start of school, things had been going downhill."

"It's true," said Nell. "One time she came to cheerleading practice and she had a bruise on her upper arm."

Red light sparked from Serge's body. "That wasn't me."

"Did she say Serge did it?" I asked.

"She denied it," said Nell.

"I believed her," added Tammy. "The marks were too small for his hand."

We looked at her.

"How did you notice that?"

She moved, uncomfortable and embarrassed. "Amber used to brag about Serge's—"

Bruce grunted.

"She said you could tell by how big his hands were."

Both guys spread their hands and looked at them.

"I can't imagine Serge letting someone else manhandle his girl-friend," I said.

"I didn't," he told me, his voice hard.

"Who did it?" I asked.

"She never said," answered Tammy. "But whoever it was, she was scared out of her mind."

Nell nodded.

"That explains why Amber would have drunk herself to death, but Serge is the one who's dead," said Craig. "It doesn't make sense. He drank too much and too often to do something stupid like overdose by accident."

"Do anything long enough and you get careless," said Nell.

"Maybe there was something else going on," I said, looking at Serge, "something that was eating at him and he couldn't go on."

He leaned over the chair back. "I didn't drink myself to death."

"He wouldn't drink himself to death," said Craig.

"See?" Serge smiled.

"He would have been more likely to beat up whoever was giving him problems."

"Is it true his pants were off and his wiener was hanging out?"

Tammy hit Bruce. "Nice."

He rubbed his shoulder. "It's an honest question."

"It's a stupid question."

"Now that"—Bruce reached over and plucked a few fries from Tammy's container—"doesn't make sense. Serge was a pig when it came to girls, but even he wouldn't take a chick to the old mill."

"Why?" I took a bite of my cooling burger and wiped ketchup off my face. "Isn't any spot useful?"

Serge rolled his eyes. "You're such a virgin."

"When the wind comes in from the northeast the place stinks," said Craig. "No one's that horny."

And that just reminded me again about his romp on Widow's Peak. "Oh."

"Amber wouldn't have done it there. No girl would."

"But some girl was with him," said Nell.

"Or some boy," said Bruce.

The lighting in the van waned and buzzed.

I shot Serge a look.

His eyes widened. "Is that me? Can I do that?" He stared at his hand, pointed at the steering wheel and tried to zap it.

Nothing happened.

"Maybe I need incentive," he muttered. His eyes went to Nell's breasts and he grinned. Spreading his hands like an evangelical pastor about to perform a miracle, he squeezed his eyes shut and tried again.

I sighed and ignored him.

"He was a flaming heterosexual," said Craig. "As long as it was female, he'd do it."

"You guys hung out—"

Craig's face twisted with disagreement.

"Kind of," I clarified, "You kind of hung out."

"That was just because of the team," he said, "we weren't friends."

"But Serge wasn't private or anything. You must have known the girls he was screwing."

Craig made a face. "Who didn't he try to have sex with?"

"I've got a normal sex drive," said Serge, "is that such a bad thing?"

"The guy was like a rutting pig."

Serge tried to zap him, but couldn't get the electricity to work.

"So," I asked, "who was he with the night he died?"

"No one," said Serge. "I saw Amber after practice"—his face went to shadow—"that was it."

"Girls that would have gone with him to that place?" Bruce went silent. "Minerva, maybe."

"Minerva? That mousy girl from bio?" Craig shook his head. "No way."

"She's the only one desperate enough for a boyfriend to have gone with him," said Bruce.

"Please," said Nell. "Minerva doesn't want a boyfriend."

"How do you know?" Bruce shot at her. "She barely talks to boys."

"Because she's too busy chatting up the girls."

"Huh?"

"She's gay."

Serge looked at me. "She talked to you, a lot. Anything you want to confess to me, Deadhead? Promise, I'll take it to my grave."

He laughed at his joke, but the sound was empty and held the hollow ring of desperation covered by bravado.

I rolled my eyes. I put my arms on the back of the chair in front of me. Looking at Serge, I said, "Who could it have been? Amber?"

No response.

"Kim?"

Still nothing.

"Beverly?"

No reaction.

"I think he was screwing some old lady," said Bruce.

Whoa, that got a reaction. Serge's body sparked like fireworks.

I turned to Bruce. "Really? Somebody's old lady? Or some old lady?"

"Some old lady," he said.

"How do you know?" asked Craig. He crumpled the wrappers and stuffed them into the bag.

"Followed him."

"You followed him? Why?"

"Because he was a ball hog and he needed to learn how to share. I saw him sneaking out of the locker room one time after practice. I thought maybe he was scoring drugs. That could have gotten him kicked off the team."

"I didn't do drugs," said Serge.

I gave him a look.

"Alcohol doesn't count. That's a drink."

I rolled my eyes.

"Anyway, I saw him with somebody's mom. They snuck into her car and drove off."

"Whose mom?" asked Nell.

He shrugged. "She had on a hat and sunglasses."

"Of course she did," muttered Craig.

"She did!"

Nell frowned. "How do you know it was someone's mom?"

Bruce's forehead wrinkled. "I dunno. The way she drove, maybe?" He blinked. "Or maybe the car was familiar…"

We waited in the silence.

He shook his head and his hair flicked over his eyes. "I can't remember. But it was someone old. I know it."

"You think she's the reason he drank himself to death?" I asked. "Maybe she went back to her husband."

Craig took my empty wrappers. "Forget it. Serge would never kill himself over a girl."

I glanced over. Serge's arms were folded in front of him, his shoulders tight and stiff, his mouth set in a straight, hard line.

The bag in Craig's hand crinkled. "Serge would never kill himself. Period."

Serge lifted his gaze.

I saw the bleakness in his eyes and it left me wondering if Craig was wrong…if we'd all been wrong.

CHAPTER FOURTEEN

"Hey, Maggie, can I catch a ride home with you?"

I stepped out of Tammy's minivan and turned to Craig. "Uh, yeah, sure."

Nell overheard the exchange and said, in true rat-from-a-sinking-ship form, "Cool. I need to talk over some cheerleading stuff with Tammy, so I'll catch you later." She yanked me close. "Now's your chance to ask about the Widow's Peak."

Oh, yeah, I could *so* see that coming up in casual conversation. She trotted off before I could do anything—like glue her to me. Sighing, I led Craig to my car. We climbed in and I started the engine.

"I just have to let it warm up for a bit," I said. "What happened to your car?"

He made a face. "I think the springs are shot. Maybe the shocks."

"Must have gone over some wicked bumps," I said, and immediately thought of the night on the hill. Man, she must have given him some ride.

"They were going for a while now." He looked at me. "Tammy would have given me a ride—"

Yeah, me too, one day. Maybe not enough to wreck your car, but it would have been memorable, anyway.

"—but I wanted to talk to you. About Serge. ."

"Oh."

He shifted his body, turned so he faced me. "How are you doing?"

"Um—"

"I imagine it was a bit of a shock—"

I nodded.

"You're probably feeling really weird."

Yeah, I was feeling plenty weird.

"Did you want to talk?"

"About..."

"Serge."

The last thing I wanted to do was talk. At the sound of his name, Serge appeared in the back seat.

"What is this?" he asked. "A loser make-out session?"

"Maggie." Craig reached out, touched my hand. "Did you want to talk? You seemed out of it tonight—"

"Talk? *Talk?*" Serge shook his head. "No wonder this guy hardly dates."

"I really don't feel like talking about Serge," I said.

Craig pulled back and I missed the warmth of his hand. "I get it. It's the creepiness of finding the body of the guy you hated."

I nodded. "That was definitely a night I could have done without."

"He was a total jerk to you."

"I wouldn't say 'total,'" Serge muttered from the back seat.

"He was mean and cruel to you—"

Serge pushed his face between Craig and me. "What about her? She gave as good as she got."

"But it still would have been crappy to be the one who found him." Craig made a face. "Especially if what they're saying is true, and he was naked and covered in vomit."

"Not covered, not naked," corrected Serge. He shook his head. "I still don't know how I ended up like that."

I put the car into gear and backed out of the spot.

"Sorry," said Craig, "You said you didn't want to talk."

"What a wuss," said Serge. "Who asks about feelings, then apologizes?"

"No, it's not that—"

In the rear-view mirror, I saw Serge frown and lean towards me. "You got a weird glow going, Deadhead. Kind of fuzzy and—oh!" He fell against the back seat and started howling. "You got the hots for Captain Polo?" Serge laughed again. "Stop wasting your time. The guy's gay."

I squeezed the steering wheel.

"The memory's probably too fresh," said Craig. "Serge may be dead, but I bet it doesn't feel like he's out of your life."

"You don't know the half of it," I muttered. The light turned red and I pulled to a stop beside Tammy's minivan.

Nell caught my eye and gave me a thumbs-up.

I gave her the finger.

She laughed and turned away.

"Probably doesn't help that we were asking all those questions." Craig pulled at the seatbelt and adjusted his position. "It's just weird. He was supposed to meet up for pizza after the game. I couldn't go—"

"Because of your sister." The light turned green. Tammy went right and I drove straight.

He nodded. "Serge usually books when it's his turn to pay, but it was Bruce's. And every time Bruce has to pay, Serge is there, eating everything he can shove in his mouth." He nodded at the retreating lights of the minivan. "You know about Amber and Bruce, right?"

I frowned. "No. What?"

"They sort of dated over the summer."

"How is that possible—Amber and Serge—"

"They were on some kind of break. All I know is that pizza night, Serge would eat enough to leave Bruce totally broke. At least, he tried."

I glanced at Serge though the rear-view mirror. "The dysfunction of this guy still amazes me."

"Like you should talk," he muttered, slouching down. "You see the dead and you're hot for this loser. I may need therapy, but I'll have to get in line behind you."

I looked away and focused on the red taillights of the car in front of me. "Maybe something called him away."

"His parents?" Craig glanced out the window. "It's not like them to show up to the practices or games. His mom would come to the games. Sometimes." Craig made a face. "And I always got the feeling she was doing it behind the old man's back."

Serge snorted. Fog crept along the edges of the windshield. I put the defroster on and cracked one of the windows

"You don't think Mr. Popov approved of sports?"

"I know he didn't," said Craig. "He tried to get Serge pulled from the team earlier this year."

I glanced at him. "Are you serious?"

Craig nodded. He put his long fingers to his lips and tapped his mouth.

I wrenched my gaze away. "How did he manage to keep playing?" The question came out as a croak.

In the back seat, a slow, satisfied smile spread across Serge's face.

Craig shrugged. "I don't know. One week we were told he wasn't coming back. The next practice he was gone, but the third week, he was back in the pool again."

"That's weird." I thought for a bit. "Do you think it has anything to do with him and the older woman?"

Craig made a disgusted sound. "Don't believe Bruce. There was no older woman."

I glanced at Serge. "Are you sure?"

"I'm positive."

"How do you know?" I braked and turned the car left.

Craig grimaced. "Serge doesn't like wrinkles. Didn't you ever hear him telling Amber she'd be old by twenty-one?"

"I did my best not to listen to him."

"They were having all kinds of problems. Big ones, even for them."

"Like what?"

Craig shifted.

"Like what?" I repeated.

He shrugged. "Neither of them ever confided in me."

He spoke with sincerity...so why did I feel like he was lying through his perfectly straight teeth? I pulled into the cul-de-sac and braked to a stop in front of his house.

Craig sighed. "I saw Amber at the drugstore one night." He paused. "By the family planning aisle. She didn't seem happy to see me."

I kept my focus on the road. But I wondered why she would've been ticked at Craig seeing her. Everyone knew she and Serge were sleeping together.

"Sorry." Craig frowned. "We weren't supposed to talk about Serge."

"It's okay. I think he's going to be a big topic of conversation for the next while."

He reached over, touched my hand. "Do you want to come in? I know it's late, but—"

Man, I had waited for so long for that invite. But knowing he'd been with someone else just soured the fantasy.

"Maybe he isn't gay," said Serge. "Go on. I can't wait to see what happens"—he leaned towards me and gave me an eyebrow wiggle— "especially if tits are involved. Even your little mosquito bites. It's been awhile since I've seen flesh. I'll even settle for you."

"Thanks," I said, "but I'm feeling stressed. I just want to forget about everything."

Craig flinched a little, like I'd hurt his feelings, but it was so fast, I thought maybe I'd just misinterpreted everything.

"Okay," he said. "No problem. See you later?"

"Yeah, I said. "Later."

He got out and went in the house. Serge climbed into the passenger seat.

"There's something weird about him," he said. "I wouldn't trust him."

"Then he must be okay." I pulled away from the curb.

"Why do you gotta be like that? I say something and you're just a hosebeast."

"Better to bite first than be bitten."

"Aw—" He scowled. "Is it my fault you can't take a joke?"

"Jokes have punchlines—"

"I was wrong," he muttered. "I thought I'd died and been left here in limbo." He glared at me. "Obviously, I've died and gone to hell if I'm giving you dating advice."

I snorted. "When did you ever date? From what I hear, you're more like a hit and run driver."

"See? Hosebeast."

I sighed. I was tired and exhausted and heartbroken. "What did you do?"

He looked at me.

"To get your dad to let you back on the team?"

He grinned. "We had a heart to heart."

"Now who's being a hosebeast?"

He exhaled, impatient. "Look, I just pointed out that if I was on the team, I couldn't be at home. He liked that."

I glanced at him. "You guys really had a sucky relationship, didn't you?"

"With detective skills like that, you should go into policing. Think of how much the crime rate would drop."

"Don't be a jerk." I slowed as the light in front of me turned yellow. "I only meant that most kids complain about their parents and vice-versa, but they love each other."

His face tightened at the word "love."

"You really hated him and he couldn't stand you."

"In a nutshell."

I stepped on the accelerator. "Why?"

He shrugged. "Why not?"

"Because it's not natural for parent and kids to actually hate each other."

"Maybe not in your perfect little world, but not everybody's dad is their best friend."

"Maybe, but he must have done something to you."

His face hardened, a rough slab of flesh and bone. "He didn't do anything to me."

"That night, at the pool," I said, "I saw the way you were standing in front of your mom—"

"Lay off it, Deadhead."

"I'm just saying—"

"And I'm just telling you to shut up!" His voice rose, anger made it raw. Serge's body sparked, flashed white.

The light blinded me and I lost sight of the road. I hit the brake, but turned the wheel at the same time. A big rig's horn blared in my ears. I blinked, trying to see past the flash.

The horn sounded again.

That's when I realized the light blinding me wasn't Serge.

It was the semi's headlights, bearing down on me.

CHAPTER FIFTEEN

I swerved back into my lane. The rig barrelled by. Its wheels hurled gravel at the windshield and the air shook like thunder. "You could've killed me!" I yelled at Serge.

"Shut up! It's not like I did it on purpose! I can't control the— whatever this is."

Shaking, I pulled the car to the shoulder. I put my head on the wheel, and unclenched my grip. "I can't do this anymore. We have to get you to cross over."

He didn't say anything.

"Craig said Amber was in the drug store, buying condoms. But that aisle also sells pregnancy kits. Did you knock her up?"

"None of your business."

I turned to face him. "Yeah, it is. Until we get you to leave this plane, we're stuck with each other. You want to spend a lifetime with me?"

He said nothing.

"I didn't think so."

The muscle in his cheek pulsed and his jaw worked back and forth, like he was getting ready to spit. "Do you know what's out there," he asked, "on the other side?"

"No, I don't."

"Then you don't know what happens when I go?"

"Is that why you're holding on?" I asked the question soft and easy.

He shook his head. "No, something's keeping me here. I feel it."

"But you don't know what it is?"

"No."

"What were you and Amber fighting about?"

"Not her being pregnant."

"You're not going to tell me?"

He looked out the windshield, to the cars coming our way, and squinted against the lights. "It doesn't matter. It was boyfriend-girl-friend stuff, and that's over with."

"Maybe not. Maybe that's why you're still stuck here."

He half laughed, half moaned. "I doubt it. We were thinking of breaking up, okay? If that was what was holding me, I'd be haunting her, not you."

Point taken. I sighed. "We have to figure out what's tethering you."

"It's usually about unresolved issues, right?"

I glanced at him.

"Why people don't move on. It's because we have unresolved issues."

"You think we have unresolved issues?"

"Not you and me, Deadhead. Me and my mom."

Oh, right. Of course. Wait. "Shouldn't it be you and your dad?"

He made a face. "No. He hates me. I hate him. There's nothing to resolve."

Okay. "So, what needs resolving?"

"Mom and I argued all the time." He shifted, pulling at his blue sweater as though it was too tight. "I wanted her to leave him."

"So. You need to what—realize the decisions in her life are hers and let her go?"

He shot me a death glare. "You really are a Deadhead. I need to get her to leave him."

"How are you planning on doing that? You're dead."

He stared at me and cocked his head. A slow smile crawled along his mouth and lifted the right side of his lips.

"No, no way."

"What the—who else is going to help me?"

"What am I supposed to say? Hi Mrs. Popov, I know your son is dead, and I know your religion tells you after death people either go to heaven or hell, but here's a kicky little story. Serge is here. Right beside me, and he wants you to leave your husband."

"I'll give you information only she and I know."

"Listen to me." I took off my seatbelt and rotated to better see him. "I know you're here. You know you're here. But you're dead, and I'm not. And if I go and start telling people I see your ghost, I'm going to be living all alone. *All* alone because they'll think I'm too crazy to be allowed to adopt cats."

"You won't be alone," he said. "If I don't move on, I'll be with you forever."

"You're new at the art of making things better by conversation aren't you?"

"You have to tell her." His voice rose. "There's no one else who can do this."

I buckled back in. I checked the road and pulled into traffic and manoeuvred the car back on the road. "No. There's got to be a better way."

"There's no other way."

"She's a grown woman. Don't you think it's her right to decide who she wants to spend her life with?"

"No."

"Nice."

He fiddled with the air vents. "Look, she's bought into the whole righteous women of God submit to their husband and never get divorced."

"Does he abuse her?" I asked softly.

"Hit her?" Serge made a face. "No, he never does anything physical. All his weapons are mental and emotional."

I didn't bother to point out abuse didn't have to be physical. "Why was he at your practice?"

His face went blank. "I don't know."

"You were fighting."

"We were always fighting."

"Yeah, but does it have anything to do with how you died?"

He didn't say anything.

"Listen, if you want me to help, you can't stonewall me."

"I don't know," he said, his voice quiet. "There's a bunch of stuff I can't remember." He looked away from the window and met my gaze. "Is that normal? To die and forget huge chunks of your life?"

"I don't know." I turned left. "Most dead people don't really linger. I mean, they stick around for a last message, but the ones who actually haunt the town, they've been doing it so long, I don't think they remember anything about their lives."

"When you're alive, they call it repression."

My eyebrows rose. I glanced at him.

"I'm not as stupid as you think."

"I'm getting that."

"So, is it the same with the dead?"

"I don't know. You're the dead one. Do you think you're repressing or do you think you're still transitioning from one plane to the other?"

He shrugged, frustrated. "I don't know. The only reason I can think of for lingering is my mom, but if there's no way to get her to leave him, why am I here?"

It was a good question and I wished I had the answer.

When we got home, Serge went upstairs and disappeared into the bedroom. I went into the kitchen and called the police station.

"Sheriff Machio."

"Hey, it's me."

"Hey kid." The pleasure in her voice dimmed as she said, "You're not in any trouble are you? Everything's okay?"

"Everything's fine."

"Promise?"

"Promise."

"Are you calling to come clean about your fixation with Serge?"

Eek. Silence stretched as I vainly tried to think of an explanation.

"I didn't think so."

I heard the humour in her voice and relaxed. "I was wondering… do you have a file on Serge's parents?"

"A file?" The line hummed with curiosity and suspicion. "What kind of file?"

"I think"—I dropped my voice in case Serge heard—"his parents were beating him."

"Oh."

The hair on my skin prickled at her tone. "Why do you say it like that?"

"I can't talk about it."

"What?" I tapped my fingers against the crackled finish of our ancient mustard-yellow telephone. "We're like sisters—how can you *not* tell me."

"Oh, boy."

I could almost see her rolling her eyes.

"When did that happen? Us being like sisters?"

"Ever since—"

"Ever since you wanted to use me for information."

"I love your cannoli," I said softly. "And I dream about your lasagne."

She chuckled. "Nice try, sweet face, but it won't work." She took a breath. "I trust you and you know I love you, but these are department regulations."

"I won't tell."

"If they fire me, I won't have any money to make you pasta."

She had me there. "Okay," I sighed. "It was worth a try."

"Why do you care, anyway? I thought you'd be dancing on that creep's grave."

"Yeah, me too." I fiddled with the twisted phone cord. My fingers picked at the tangled mass, uncurling and uncramping the line, but as soon as I let go, it tangled in on itself again. "I guess...I guess I just feel bad for him. What sucky kind of life did you lead when your parents are anxious to erase you from existence?"

Nancy's sigh was heavy with compassion and weighed down by pity.

"I know." She paused. The silence went on. Then she said, "Sorry, kiddo, I can't help you on this."

"Yeah," I said, a smile spreading across my face as I realized who could help me. "Too bad."

"Gotta go. Be good."

I hung up and dialled Nell. "We need to see your aunt."

She hesitated. "Which one?"

"Don't be a moron. Debbie-Anne—your only aunt."

"I'm the moron? You want to go into the den of the drunk woman and I'm the moron?"

"Functioning alcoholic."

"Lunatic."

"You gonna help? We could go tomorrow."

"Why?"

"Serge."

The line went dead. Nothing like mentioning the drama with a dead guy to get Nell's attention and co-operation.

Nell phoned at 6 AM the next morning.

"Seriously?" My voice came out groggy. "You think your aunt's even awake?"

"We'll wake her up."

"You think alcoholics enjoy that kind of thing?"

Silence.

"Oh my—are you thinking of an answer? It's no! No, because she'll take a bottle to our heads. We'll go this afternoon." I hung up the phone.

Six hours later, the doorbell rang. "It's 12:01," said Nell. "Technically, it's afternoon. Let's go."

I jogged up the stairs and found Serge on the bed, pressed in between Ebony and Buddha. The theme music for *Miami Vice* pounded through the television speakers.

He looked up. "Why can I work the television?"

"It's electrical."

He didn't blink. "I said I'm not dumb. I never said I was smart."

"Energy is electricity. You can work the TV because it's electrical and so are you."

"Why can't people see me?"

"They don't want to."

The skin on his face tightened.

"Not you personally, though I wouldn't mind never seeing you again. In general, we think death is the end. So no one sees you because no one expects to see you."

"And why don't I sink through the floor?"

I moved to the closet and tossed on a red hoodie. "I'd love to continue this discussion, but Nell's coming to get me."

He shut off the TV and wriggled off the bed. The bed sheets scrunched together.

"What are you doing?" I asked as he pulled on his sneakers.

"You said we're going out with Nell."

"No, *I'm* going out with Nell. You're watching television."

His white and black sneaker dropped to the floor with a *thunk*. "Are you kidding? You're going to leave me?"

Darn straight. "Yeah, unless you want to come and talk to her aunt about her hysterectomy."

"Holy crap." His face scrunched together. He kicked off his left sneaker. "No thanks."

I shrugged. "I figured."

He flipped back on the TV.

I turned to leave.

"Hey...Maggie."

"Yeah?" I looked at him from over my right shoulder.

"Why don't I get hungry? If energy is energy, doesn't it need to be replenished?"

"You don't have a body."

He blinked fast. "Oh. Yeah. Right."

"I'll be back soon," I said. "We'll figure it all out."

His shoulders went up and down. "Yeah. Whatever."

I stepped out. Looking back, I saw him rubbing Buddha's head, his gaze unfocused, his expression lost.

Nell and I headed to Debbie-Anne's trailer. We pulled up the driveway, and Nell cut the engine.

"Why are we doing this?"

"Because," I said, "I figure S—his parents beat him."

She glanced from the dark sky to me, the question in her eyes.

"I think when I call his name it acts as a homing beacon and brings him to me."

"And you don't want him to know what you're doing."

I thought about the bright light and the semi, and shuddered as the memory pressed its cold lips against the back of my neck. "No, I really don't."

"So...why crazy Aunt Debbie-Anne?"

"Because Nancy will be fired if she gives out confidential information. Whereas—"

"Debbie-Anne already lost her job and she's a drunk, so it doesn't really matter what she says." Nell sighed and nodded.

"You can stay in the car, if you want."

Shadows cast by the trees and lamplight rippled across the upholstery and dashboard. "No, it's fine." She glanced my way and gave me a humourless smile. "Family's family."

I squeezed her hand.

"Lunatic," she muttered. She yanked the key out of the ignition and hauled herself out of the car.

I followed her up the crumbling steps of the porch to the doublewide.

Nell took a deep breath, curled her fingers into a fist, and knocked on the door.

Nothing.

She tried again, louder.

From inside, we heard the muffled sounds of Debbie-Anne careening down the hallway, thumping as she banged into the walls. A moment later, the door opened and she was staring at me.

She blinked red-rimmed, bloodshot eyes and said, "Eh? Maggie? Whaddya want?"

"To talk." I smiled and pushed past her.

Nell followed. The strands of her hair swayed as she shook her head.

"'Bout what?"

"The Popovs."

Debbie-Anne's lip curled back. "Poor bastard. Best thing that coulda happened to him was death."

Nell flinched.

"I'm not saying it was good the way he died," Debbie-Anne rasped, her voice ravaged from years of alcohol and cigarettes. "But that kid didn't stand a chance."

My heart contracted and in a blink, Serge was in front of me.

Oh, man.

His head rotated in a slow semi-circle. "What am I doing here?"

Debbie-Anne shuffled down the hallway, her ragged pink slippers sanded the dirt-crusted linoleum floor.

Nell pulled me close. "Let's get this done. The house smells like laundry left in the washer for too long."

I nodded.

She let go and went to her aunt.

I waited until both women were farther down. "Go home," I whispered.

"What am I doing here?"

"Annoying me."

"Be serious."

"Obviously, I accidentally called you."

"Why?"

Because pity is instinctive. "Who cares? Just go."

He shrugged. "Fine—"

Debbie-Anne turned and yelled, "Whaddya want to know about the Popovs?"

Red blotches obliterated the freckles from Serge's face.

Oh, boy.

"This is what you're doing here?" The words came quiet, venomous.

I ignored him and went into the cramped living room. "You were a nurse at the hospital—did he ever come in as a kid?"

She snorted and reached for a beer bottle, its amber glass slick with condensation. "When *didn't* he come in?" She took a long pull of her drink and eyed me through the limp strands of hair that covered her eyes. "No kid's that accident prone."

In my peripheral vision, small, bright flashes of light began to spark from Serge's body. Thin and wispy, the purple, green, and pink tendrils shot skyward and burnt out, mid-flight. I moved away, putting the ripped green and brown striped couch between me and him, and asked, "What kind of injuries?"

Her fingers played with the opening of the bottle. Then Debbie-Anne grasped it by the neck and swung the beer in a lazy circle. "The usual injuries: broken arm, broken leg—" She glanced at her lap. Her gaze swung up and impaled me. "Fingermarks on his right arm."

A fuzzy, red aura outlined Serge. His body began to hum, buzz. Trying to look casual, I edged into the corner.

Nell frowned and cocked her head.

I glanced at the hallway, then at Nell, and finally at the window she stood beside.

Her frown deepened. She turned, eyed the window, then focused on the hallway. The lines on her forehead faded and she moved away from the glass.

"He used to be a sweet kid." Debbie-Anne sucked in her lower lip. Her eyelids fluttered.

The smoky wisps of colour sparking off Serge's body grew solid and took on the consistency of yarn. Their speed slowed, their trajectory smoothed until he looked like a sun, surrounded by the ever-changing colours of its rays.

"Bubbly, bright." Her watery eyes grew unfocused, her fingers stilled. "Then it all changed. He became sullen. Angry." Her mouth tightened into a hard line. "Who could blame him?"

The rays of colours retreated and melted into Serge's red aura.

"I did what I could—reported my concerns, tried to talk to the police." Her lips curled back into a sneer. "But that was years ago—Dead Falls was so small we didn't even have a town cop, just an RCMP guy who'd drive through." Light returned to her eyes, barren and dim as a rocky moor. "You do what you can and when that fails"—her gaze lingered on the bottle in her hand—"you do what's necessary. He didn't come in after he turned ten. I tell myself that's cause the bastard stopped using him as a punching bag."

The band of light that outlined Serge's body began to turn in a clockwise rotation. The humming increased, a million angry wasps looking for a body to sting.

My teeth began to vibrate. The hair on my skin rose. Oxygen rushed out of my lungs, leaving my muscles tight. "We should go, thanks."

"But I haven't even told you about—"

I glanced at Serge.

He wasn't there—mentally. His eyes had retreated leaving black holes. The empty sockets glistened like oil. His fingers, tightened into fists, hung straight and rigid at his side.

I reached over, grabbed Nell's hand. "That's okay. We can talk later." I took a breath and made my way to the front door.

Nell kept pace, but I pushed her behind me. "Just in case, keep a few feet back," I said quietly.

"Maggie, *oh my God.*"

I frowned and looked back, wondering why Nell's voice seemed so far away.

Light from Serge spread in a flashlight's beam, wrapping her in a pale-white circle and casting a grey shadow that convulsed on the nicotine-stained walls. Her head twitched from side to side, her breath came out in rapid, shallow panting. Her hand lifted, slow, smooth, and she pointed...*at me.*

Spreading my arms wide, I checked my body. My clothing rippled along my torso. The shirt twisted, turned, the cotton puffed as though a snake slithered underneath.

Nell's gaze lifted from my clothing and raised itself to my face.

I ran my hands along my skin, feeling the heat radiating off my flesh. My hair felt as coarse as straw. I glanced at the wall and saw the shadow I cast. Strands of hair stuck out, slowly rippling in an invisible breeze.

"Go back," I told Nell, dropping my hands. "Get Debbie-Anne and get out through the other door."

She didn't move.

"Nell!"

She gasped and stumbled back.

Air blasted me from behind. Hot and rotting, it seared my back.

"*Maggie.*"

"Stop watching and go!"

Her throat bobbed up, down. She swallowed, pivoted on her right heel and ran down the hall.

Looking down, I saw the blisters on my skin. My blood felt hot, like it was turning solid in my veins. My skin pulled and tightened as the flesh bubbled. I turned back to Serge. Taking a step and hissing at the exquisite pain, I said, "I'm sorry."

He said nothing. He saw nothing. His aura continued to spin and rotate like a neon sign advertising "eat here!" or "nude girls! live!" In this case, the sign flashing above Serge would have warned, "Abandon hope." He closed his eyes.

"Serge." I moved closer, ignoring the furnace heat, pretending the blisters on my skin didn't hurt. "We need to know. You can't cross over if the truth doesn't come out."

At the mention of "truth" his head cocked to the right, then twisted left as though he was stretching his muscles in preparation for... *something*.

"Serge—don't you want to leave? Don't you want to be gone from here? Don't you want to be...free?"

His eyelids snapped open.

Though his eyes were gone and nothing but darkness remained in the sockets, the sensation that he stared at me, stared *through* me was as certain as the ground beneath my feet.

His aura stopped rotating.

Air pulled away from me, rushed toward Serge. For a moment, the world stopped. Reality and action hung in silent suspension.

The smell of fire—charred tinder and ashes—singed my nose. I pivoted, turned my back on the ghost, and ran.

CHAPTER SIXTEEN

The air roared, loud as a lion's bellow and just as terrifying. I raced for the open patio door, sensing rather than seeing the shock wave of red energy rolling toward me. My feet slipped on a stray magazine, my sneaker slid on the glossy snapshot of the model, twisted on her digitally heightened smile, and sent me pirouetting toward the ripped armchair.

My hip slammed into the armrest, bone rammed wood and steel. I spun in a crooked arc and fell to the ground. My knee smashed into the floor. Shockwaves of pain made my teeth rattle. Struggling to my feet, I raced for the door; the breath of destruction belched its hot air down my neck.

I stumbled through the patio exit and banged my shoulder on the frame. Nell and Debbie-Anne stood close to a propane barbeque. Too close.

I grabbed them and shoved them down the path. "Serge won't listen."

The explosion rocked the trailer and lit the sky with orange-red flames. It pushed us forward and down. Shattered glass rained down, the tinkling sound mixed with the boom of the propane tank rupturing. The furnace rocketed into the dark sky then hurtled earthward. Black smoke plumed into the air and the heat from the fire roasted my skin.

Nell, stomach on the grass, raised her head and rolled onto her butt. "Jesus." The word came out as a prayer, not a curse.

"Yeah." I turned to Debbie-Anne. "You okay?"

She also lay face down on the ground.

Nell shook her. "Debbie-Anne?"

She didn't move.

"Tell me again. What happened?" Nancy stood by the driver's side door of her Sheriff's SUV. Yellow police tape separated us from the curious gawkers. Even the cold bite of the falling night didn't deter the inquisitive. They huddled together in clumps, curlers in their hair, thick robes wrapped around their stout bodies, and whispered their theories.

"Maggie?"

I turned from the crowd and my gaze glanced off Debbie-Anne, seated on a gurney with a grey blanket wrapped around her frail shoulders. "Is she going to be okay?"

Nancy nodded.

"Are you sure? She was out for a long time."

She nodded again. "The amount of alcohol in her system—when she was knocked to the ground, it hit her harder than you." She grimaced. "No pun intended." Putting her hand on my shoulder, she said, "Come on."

I tightened the scratchy blanket around my shoulders and followed her to where Nell and Debbie-Anne were.

"It's amazing none of you were seriously injured."

I glanced at my hand, at all the places where Serge had burned me, and all the places where the psychic wounds had knit together. My skin still ached and I couldn't get the bacon-smell of fried flesh out of my nose. "Yeah. A real miracle."

We moved to the ambulance.

"I tried phoning your dad—"

My memory went to the calendar on the fridge. "I think he has a consult with the Chanthy family. He turns his cell off." I shrugged off my blanket. "Anyway, it's better that I tell him. I'll go see him at work."

Nancy frowned. "I have a few questions left for you. Are you sure you don't want me to get a deputy to get your dad?"

I shook my head.

Her mouth pulled down.

What could I say? *Don't worry, Nancy. Dad and I have been through worse. This isn't my first exploding building.*

I turned to the paramedic. "Is Debbie-Anne okay?"

"She's fine," said the paramedic. He smiled as Nell came around the corner. "They both are." He glanced at the smoldering, wet wreckage of the house. "Do you know what happened?"

"Furnace, most likely," said Nancy. She smoothed a strand of hair from Debbie-Anne's forehead. "Can you remember anything?"

She didn't answer the sheriff. Instead, she looked at me and said, "Serge did it, didn't he? He's angry."

The paramedic and Nancy exchanged worried glances.

"Maybe I should check you for head trauma again," he said.

He reached for her, but she batted away his purple-gloved hand. "I'm not traumatized, you moron. I know what I heard."

Her eyes locked on mine with the accuracy of an F-150 fighter jet. "He's angry and looking for revenge, isn't he? He's pissed because no one helped him."

Nancy nodded at the paramedic. "You better take her to the hospital. Just keep her overnight."

He gently pushed Debbie-Anne down on the gurney and began to strap her in.

She fought, but her strength had been wasted by alcohol and despair. "I know what I heard—tell them, Maggie! Tell them what you said!"

Nancy turned to me. Her eyes searched my face. Her fingers played with the holster of her gun. "What did you say?" she asked. "What did you see?"

"Tell them the truth!" Debbie-Anne's bony fingers reached out and clamped onto my arm.

I shook my head and directed my comment to the woman in the gurney. "No one's looking for revenge."

Nancy's hand fell to the side.

Debbie-Anne's face hardened. "Even you." The words came out with a venomous whisper. "Even you betray him." She took a breath. "And me." Her head dropped to the pillow and she turned away from me.

I swallowed and looked away, too ashamed to maintain eye contact. I hadn't lied, but that wasn't the entire truth and we both knew it. I'd done my best to protect her and myself. Better to let the town dismiss her statements as the rantings of a drunk woman than to have them add "the woman who believes in ghosts and fairies" to her tag of "alcoholic."

Nell didn't say anything. She only edged away from me.

The paramedic called his partner over, and they wheeled Debbie-Anne into the back of the ambulance. The police on duty moved the tape and cleaved the crowd. With a path before them, the ambulance drove away, the lights flashing but silent.

Nancy turned to me. "If you hadn't been here she could have been killed in the fire."

I swallowed. Acid burned my stomach.

Nancy cupped my face. "I see that look. Don't you go giving yourself a hard time about what she said. She's a sick, sad lady, but she has you to thank for her life." She watched me for a moment. "Maggie, you weren't...investigating, were you?"

"Is it okay if Nell and I go?"

"Because we talked about this."

"I think I should get Nell home."

"Sweet cakes," she said gently.

I avoided her gaze.

"Go ahead. I know where to find you."

"Thanks." I glanced at Nell.

She didn't look at me. She didn't say anything.

But when I moved, she followed.

I ducked under the yellow tape. The crowd, bathed in mawkish light, reached out, clawing, grasping. Voices twittered insipid lines of condolence and sympathy. Insincere masks of concern covered their faces. I ignored them all and made my way to Nell's car. Judging by the look on her face, it would be the last time I'd ever get a ride from her.

The air remained heavy with ash and soot, acrid in the stench of burnt rubber and plastic. I stopped at the passenger side of the car. Gravel crunched as I turned and made eye contact.

Tried to. She wouldn't look at me. Her head remained down, her gaze focused as though she'd lost a contact lens and was determined to find it.

The car chirped.

I sighed and reached toward the cold steel door handle.

Nell's hand appeared out of my peripheral. Fast and smooth, she shoved her palm against the window and slammed the door shut.

I sighed again, not ready for another battle, but thankful she couldn't burn my skin, only sear my reputation...on second thought, I think I'd rather have taken on Serge again. Turning, I eyed her.

The features of her face scrunched together, making her look less pixie-fairy and more gargoyle troubled by indigestion. Her mouth worked side to side, up and down, but no sound came out. She kept shaking her head.

I noticed her hand tremble. Finally, when I could stand it no longer and was about to say all she couldn't—this friendship is over; you're a freak—the lines of her face stiffened further.

She looked up, her eyes wide, frightened, and unseeing. Again, she tried to speak and failed. And since words couldn't give her what she needed, she chose action: she flung herself into my arms.

I rocked into the car. For a little girl, she had momentum, and she drove me back into the side mirror.

Then she began to sob. Hard. Hot streams of salty tears soaked my shirt and left my neck wet. Pre-Nell, I'd been dumped by a lot of friends, though never in such a pitiable manner. Stumped for what to do, I did the cliché: I patted her on the back and murmured, "There, there. It's all right."

She looked up. Streams of tears joined a river of snot and ran in rivulets off her cheeks and chin. "No, it's not." She tightened her grip.

Her fingers dug into my skin—my freshly seared flesh. I winced and hissed, but she didn't notice.

The tears renewed themselves. "All this time." She raised her head. "I love you, Maggie, but all this time, I've judged you. I thought you were such a wuss—with your gift, Serge, and Craig."

Oh, boy. This night was just getting better.

"I could never figure out why you were such a pussy. If it had been me, the whole town would have known I saw dead people—"

I glanced around to see if anyone could hear her, but the night was empty, save the ashes that floated on the ghost waves of air and wind.

"—and I would have paid for my university by holding séances. And Serge. What fun! What an adventure. But now…" Her face crumpled as though invisible hands had reached out and shoved the muscle and skin together. "Maggie. He could have killed you."

"Well"—I opted for a joke since she seemed a breath away from being buckled down next to Debbie-Anne—"that's nothing new. In life he could have done the same."

Angry lightning flashed across her face. "It's not funny. It was *horrible*. Seeing you—seeing what his energy did…" She yanked me back into her arms. "You are the bravest person I know."

Her hug held warmth. The tight steel bands of rejection—the unflinching certainty that she was going to bail on our friendship— rusted and broke under the tears of her love.

I hugged her back, ignoring the pain lancing through me, because, save Dad, she was all I had to protect my heart and soul.

"I will never, *never* question your courage again."

I laughed. *Yeah. Right.*

"Maggie?"

I frowned and turned, bringing Nell with me. "Craig?"

He emerged from the shadows. The lone lamplight in the parking lot shed its sickly fluorescence but the majority of him remained in darkness, a black figure wrapped in the cloth of night.

Why did I find this so sexy? "Hey. What are you doing here?"

"It's all over town, about the fire. I didn't care—but someone said"— he glanced at Nell, who clung to me with the ferocity of a Siamese twin— "you guys were here. Maggie. First Serge, now this. Are you okay?"

My heart boomed loud enough for astronauts to hear, and Nell must have heard because she gave a mighty sniff, dissected herself from me, and not so subtly shoved me in his direction.

Craig caught me on the first stumble.

He wrapped me in a strong embrace but before I could feel too smug, he reached out and caught Nell with his other arm.

"Are you guys okay?"

It was my hair he pressed his face against, my cheek that warmed under his breath, my nose that gloried in the spicy-sweetness of his cologne, and I told myself it mattered, that it was an omen. Then I remembered the hill and clung tighter to him because this could be my only chance to ever have the memory of his body next to mine.

His grip tightened and his lips brushed the top of my head...maybe. Or maybe that was just my fantasy taking hold.

"Let me drive you home," he said. "Nell, we'll get your car later."

She pushed away and said, "Okay."

He let her go, but he held close to me.

My foolish heart tried to make sense of this.

Taking my hand, he led us to the back of the parking lot, where a grey sedan sat.

"My parents' car," he said as the lights flashed and the vehicle chirped.

"Your car's still in the shop?" *Duh, Maggie.*

The interior light lit his grimace. "Yeah, it's like some weird car virus. We're just taking turns putting the vehicles in the shop."

Nell shoved me to the passenger side and climbed in the back. "Do you want to listen to the radio?"

I flinched. I'd never told her about the static.

"I'd rather know what's going on with you." He looked my way.

I shrugged.

The engine revved and he slowly backed the car out of the spot. "That's not an answer."

"I don't know what you want me to say."

"Drop me home, first," said Nell. "I'm too upset to see any fighting tonight."

"No one's going to fight." Craig turned on the signal light and pulled on to the road. "I just want the truth."

Yeah, right, and give up my opportunity for more Craig hugs? I don't think so.

He glanced my way. "You're trying to figure out who killed Serge, aren't you?"

Close enough. "Yeah."

"And you think one of his parents might have played a part."

"Uh. Yeah."

Craig shook his head. "Maggie, that family is seriously screwed. *Seriously.* You can't go around them, and can't be digging into their history."

"Who said—"

"Give me a break."

He spoke softly, easily, but I heard the "don't BS me" tone.

"You're at Debbie-Anne's house. She's the biggest gossip in town *and* she used to be a nurse."

My head tilted sideways. "How do you know that?"

"I may be new to Dead Falls, but word spreads. You were trying to find out about what—previous abuse charges, right?"

I shifted, uncomfortable.

"They're bad news," he said. "Stay away from that family."

The car turned silent.

"If we're going to go all awkward," Nell's voice sounded from the back seat. "Can we turn on some music?"

Craig cranked the dial, but all that came out was static.

My body broke out in chills.

He turned it off. "The radio doesn't work sometimes." He glanced at Nell's reflection in the rear-view mirror. "I could always sing."

"I've heard about your singing," said Nell. "I'd rather not have bleeding eardrums. The night's been tough enough."

He grinned. "How about an ice-cream cone, instead?"

"The Tin Shack's closed."

"My house."

Geez. My heart just stopped.

"You and Maggie can—"

I heard the smug tone in her voice—the one that always precipitated a trademark Nell pep talk-lecture.

"—but I'd rather go home. My parents will be freaking out."

"Mine too." My tongue tripped over the words.

"I doubt it," said Smug Nell. "Nancy's there to talk to your dad and—"

I glanced at Craig. "I should still talk to him. Let him know what's going on."

"I can do it," said Nell as the car pulled up to the curb of her house. "I'm practically like a daughter, anyhow."

Craig cut the engine and looked at me, his face shrouded in shadow. "It's fine if you don't want to—"

Don't want to? *Don't want to?* I'd have crawled over desert and shattered glass, lived through a million Serges if it meant time alone with Craig. But, watching him eat ice-cream—seeing that delectable tongue doing things to creamed dairy that I wanted him to do to me—and knowing his sexy mouth had been on someone else's lips. I couldn't stand it.

Nell's seatbelt slid into its holder with a canvas rasp. She popped open the door and said, "Thanks, Craig." Then she climbed out of the seat.

I followed, tossing a "Be right back" at the object of my obsession and scurried after Nell.

"Stop following me, and get back in there."

"Haven't I suffered enough?"

"Maggie. You need to figure this out and clear it up."

I translated the words. "Be brave."

"Something like that."

She traipsed up the flagstone steps, and I resisted the urge to toss her into the shrubbery. "I thought we decided you weren't going to question my courage."

"I'm not. There's no question about your lack of it when it comes to Craig."

"I don't care if there are witnesses. I'll drag you into the back and drown you in the pool."

"It's been drained for winter. Besides, we're not talking about courage." The bell-shaped lamp on the porch lit her face. "We're talking about bravery."

"Semantics."

"Kazuntight."

"Do you ever get whiplash from the sudden turns in logic?"

She grinned. "It's why I'm a cheerleader. It keeps my muscles limber." Her smile faded.

"All joking aside, Maggie, you deal with enough craziness and dysfunction." Her eyes locked onto mine. "There's a lot of crap in your life. Don't add extra fertilizer if you don't have to."

"What if he doesn't want me?" Turning toward the car and assuming he was watching, I held my hand up in a "one more minute" gesture. I dropped my voice and said, "He's seeing some girl right now, fine…if I don't ask him about it—if I don't tell him how I feel, I can tell myself that *one day* he'll see me and love me. But if I ask—" The ache of unrequited love sent its barren sigh through my body and left my lungs spent of air. "What if he says, 'no, Maggie. I could never see you in that way.' What if he never wants me as a girlfriend. Ever." I looked down at my fire-smudged sneakers, then back at Nell.

"Why hold on to a dream? If he doesn't want you, move on."

"The dream keeps me warm." The cold air hitting my skin was nothing compared to the Siberian freeze coming off my heart. "You, Dad, Bruce, Tammy, and Craig are really all I have. You and Dad the only ones who really seem to *see* me. Everyone else—I'm just a satellite orbiting their planet. With you and Craig, I can at least say I have a couple friends. If he was gone, all I'd have is you. I'm already pathetic. I don't need to be tragic."

Nell folded her arms across her chest and did a little jig to warm up. "You're not giving him enough credit. Just because he may not like you doesn't mean he'd stop being your friend."

"I see the dead. I don't read minds, and I can't afford the risk."

She grinned.

"What?"

"You're hyper-anxious about this guy but totally in love and obsessed, and you think seeing dead people is what makes you freaky."

I rolled my eyes. "Jerk"

"Yeah, but you're my friend, so what does that make you?"

She had me there.

Nell moved to the swing by the railing. "If you won't go home with him, stay with me. You haven't said anything, which means Serge hasn't appeared—"

"He won't, not for a little while. That kind of energy takes a lot out of a ghost. He won't be around 'till morning. Maybe longer."

"Still, you shouldn't be alone and I know your dad probably won't be back until late. Go with Craig or stay with me, but don't be alone."

I nodded, the pull of my heart too strong for me to consider staying with Nell. "I'll see you tomorrow."

"Maggie?"

"Yeah?"

"This"—she made a face—"is going to get worse before it gets better. A fantasy may keep you warm, but if you do it at the cost of reality, it'll leave you out in the cold." Her lips split into a wide grin. "Did you see what I did there? Pairing hot and cold—"

"Yeah, and it left me all wet."

"Green. Left you green with jealousy."

"I'm going. Tonight's events have obviously upset what little mental stability you had." I turned to leave.

"I'll talk to your dad."

I looked back. "He won't be too worried. This isn't the first time I've had a building blow up. It's not even the fifth." Even in the darkness, I saw her face go white.

"Be careful."

I nodded again, pulled her into a hug that threatened to break her ribs, then sprinted to Craig's car.

"Everything okay?" he asked as I ducked inside.

"Mm." I buckled myself in and pointed the heating vents toward me. Dry, warm air pushed my hair off my face and thawed my fingers.

He put the car in gear and slowly pulled away from the curb.

We drove in silence for a bit, which was good for me. Close proximity to Craig made my brain melt.

His hand slid from the wheel and circled the gearshift.

I found this erotic. The light cast by the street lamps sent rippling shadows of dark and light on his skin, and I found this *immensely* erotic. And the fact that I was obsessing about a gearshift could only spell disaster.

But I *couldn't* pull my gaze away from it. His fingers were long and lean and tapered, and the gentle way they played with the gearshift just about sent me out of my skin. Plus, every time I looked at his hand, my peripheral vision came into contact with his long legs.

His long legs covered by those sweet jeans.

And I knew what was under the denim.

He looked at me, his eyes suddenly on mine.

My guilty conscience sent my head jerking back and I smacked it on the window. "Son of a—" I rubbed my head, no longer worried about erotic fantasies.

"I'm glad we have some time together," he said.

"Me, too." *Kind of.*

"I wanted to talk to you—"

My heart did an involuntary contraction, hard and painful. "Yeah?" I squeaked the question. "About what?"

"Us."

My insides twisted and twisted again, until fear left me wrung of hope. "Yeah?"

He turned his focus back to the road "Are we okay?"

We were fine. *I* was going to have a coronary. "Yeah, why?"

"Because you're acting weird."

My brain zeroed in on my obsession with his hands. Had I been so obvious? "When?"

"Since the water polo practice."

My mind limped back in time, hobbled by the certainty that The Conversation—the one where he dumped me as a potential girlfriend and was so creeped out by my devotion he stopped being my friend—was two breaths away from starting. "The practice?"

"I asked you to look out for any weakness in my play—"

His quiet voice held a curiously hurt tone, like he'd let me in to something private and personal, and I'd scorned him.

"—and everything was fine. Then there was the game, and after that—" His dark eyes turned my way. "You got weird."

Widow's Peak, I wanted to say. It's the fault of Widow's Peak.

"What happened?"

I couldn't talk, couldn't get breath past the hold anxiety had on my lungs. Five years from now, it wouldn't matter if he liked me or not. Five years from now, I'd be out of university and will have dated. Hopefully, I'll have had sex, too. So, why did it feel like my life would begin or end with this moment? Why couldn't my brain just be relaxed? Nell had love affairs go wrong all the time and she never lost a breath.

I, meanwhile, was about to go into a full-fledged panic attack.

"Maggie?"

"I—I—"

He took his foot off the accelerator. "I thought we were friends."

Deep in the recesses of my frantic brain, I found a mental valium. Taking a breath that stumbled and hitched over my tight lungs, I said, "Yeah, I thought so, too."

He slowed even more, stared at me. After a second, he must have remembered that he was supposed to have his focus on the road, because he stepped on the accelerator. "You lost me."

"I asked if you wanted to go for pizza that night."

"Yeah." Annoyance, faint as early morning dawn. "But I couldn't— I had to babysit my sister."

I swallowed, grabbed my falling courage and said, "I was out driving that night. I saw your car."

He looked over, his eyebrows pulled together.

"On Widow's Peak."

He started. "Widow's Peak?" Craig rocked back in his seat. "*The hill?*" His head spun in my direction, and his hands followed the action. The car swerved to the side of the road. Craig stomped on the brakes, and the sedan screeched to a stop on the shoulder. For a moment, there was no sound save the rumbling of the idling engine. Craig hunched over the steering wheel, a statue etched in stone.

He muttered something but all I got were the words "hill" "life" and "twisted." Craig took a long, deep breath and said, "Excuse me." His fingers slid to the metal catch of the seatbelt and he released the restraint. Then he got out of the car and closed the door.

I sat, unsure. Hunching down, I peered out the back window.

He leaned with his back against the car.

In the pallid light, I saw his left fingers drumming against his right arm. I sat back, stared at the red lights of the dashboard. Then I twisted round and looked at him.

Tattered shreds of breath, transparent and white, spiralled down.

I figured I'd survived a raging ghost and an exploding house, I was pretty sure I could live through the confusing antics of a teenage boy. I climbed out and followed the line of the car to the trunk. "Craig?"

He twisted his head. "Widow's Peak." He half said, half laughed the words.

There was no humour in the laugh, only the forced air of someone trying not to be angry.

Craig turned, rested his arm on the roof of the car. "The hill."

"You lost me."

"My parents. My—" Words seemed to fail him because he leaned forward and muttered, "My parents."

Logic said this was a weird thing to go all twisted over, but I spend my days talking to the dead. I probably wasn't the best judge of "weird." Instead of saying anything, I put my hand on his shoulder.

His gaze lifted from the ground to me. The night air turned his skin silver and his cheek shone like burnished marble. Craig turned his focus back to the ground, and the sharp lines of his profile—the straight nose, the hard sweep of his jaw—were swallowed by the darkness. He sighed low and tired.

"I'm sorry—I—"

"Don't be." His voice was more than low. It was quiet and empty, as though the world had left him alone to fight the demons that hid in lonely valleys. He chuckled, his breath streamed in a wind tunnel that funnelled toward the wheel. "My parents were the ones having sex in my car." He straightened. "It wasn't me you saw that night. It was them."

Okay, so it would be gross to have your parents having sex in your car, but I didn't understand his reaction. "Um—"

"No wonder you were acting weird."

"I just didn't—"

"I was really babysitting my sister," he said.

"I believe you."

"I'm not seeing anyone."

I tried not to grin like a moron, tried to keep my mind focused on the subject at hand, but I couldn't help the happy lift in my voice when I said, "Oh."

He dropped his hands from the car and, crunching the gravel under his feet, stepped toward me.

I moved to him—seemed the friendly thing to do. The air was shifting around us, but I didn't need ESP or a Hollywood orchestra playing violins to know—hope—where this was headed.

He took another step.

I was too transfixed in the heady elasticity of the moment, in the sweet caramel energy between us, to do anything but stand still. So close, he was *so close*.

"Maggie?"

He was a breath away from me. Literally. I had to go cross-eyed to stay focused on his face, and his nose was almost touching mine. "Yeah?"

And then he was kissing me. His lips were cold but his breath was warm and his tongue hot. It swayed into my mouth, supple and easy, doing a slow samba and hypnotizing me into its rhythm.

The air crackled and a jolt of electricity ran through me. It was high voltage and hit like a thousand-watt light shoved into a forty-watt outlet. Sparks and coloured fire, but, strangely, no pain. My body pulsed as the wave of energy rode me like a Hawaiian surf and left my muscles buzzing.

Craig broke away to look at my face.

As soon as contact was interrupted, my body snapped back to normal.

"Whoa. You always kiss like that?"

I blushed and decided on a partial truth. "Uh, you're the first guy I've ever kissed."

His breath warmed my skin. "No kidding?"

"No kidding."

He laughed, gentle and easy, and every part of me melted into the sound. Craig cupped my face, his fingers curled around my neck, and his thumb caressed my cheek. Smiling he said, "Let see if it was just a one-time thing."

It was either hormones or love, but I was all for another go.

His smiled widened into a grin. "I promise to take it slow."

Electricity zapped my body again. "Okay." It came out as a breathy sigh.

He tilted his head, leaned close, and pressed his lips to mine.

I closed my eyes.

He smiled against my mouth and kissed me again.

I softly moaned.

His tongue traced the outline of my lips. Then he slid it into my mouth.

I welcomed him, silently telling myself to play it cool, but all of me wanting to devour him bit by bit. I loved the feel of his tongue on mine. Our breaths tangled and he pulled me close.

He turned and leaned against the side of the car...I think. I was too busy glorying in the thick waves of his hair, inhaling the sweet scent of him, and memorizing the feel of his long legs against mine to really pay attention to anything.

After what seemed like a too-fast kiss, he pulled away.

"C'mon," he said. "Let's go somewhere comfortable."

I must have started or flinched because he laughed.

"I don't mean that kind of comfortable. We haven't even been on a date, yet, and I'm not that kind of guy."

Relief made my breath whoosh. "I guess I'll have to buy you a lobster dinner, first?"

He put his hand in the small of my back and guided me to the passenger seat. "Don't they come from the same family as cockroaches?"

"Gross."

"Yeah, you're not getting anything out of me if you feed me mutant insects." He kissed my cheek. "Let's get you home."

CHAPTER SEVENTEEN

When I walked through the front door of the house, I heard the shrill ring of the phone. "I gotta get that," I told Craig, kicking off my shoes but not bothering with my coat. "Just toss your stuff in the closet and meet me in the kitchen."

"No worries."

I rushed up the steps. Using my socks like ice skates, I slid into the kitchen, twisted around the corner, and grabbed the phone. "Hello?"

"Maggie! Can't you answer your phone?"

"Dad?"

"Yeah. Dad. The guy who pays the bills and freaks out when his daughter's almost blown to smithereens."

"Whoa. Chill. Why didn't you call my cell if you couldn't reach me at home—didn't Nell phone you?"

"Maggie." He drew out my name with the exaggerated singsong tone he used when he was trying not to go ballistic. "Nell *did* phone me. She was thorough, detailed, but you can understand how, as a parent—*your dad*—I'd want the update from *you*."

Yeah. I glanced over as Craig strode down the hallway. Now was probably not the time to admit teenage hormones had gotten the better of me.

"I tried phoning your cell but the battery's dead."

I blinked, surprised. "Are you sure?"

He didn't say anything.

I could almost hear the "yeah, dumb-dumb, I'm sure" humming down the line. Digging into my pocket, I pulled out my cell. Yup. Dead.

"What was the agreement about the phone?"

"Dad, I *swear* I charge it every night—you know that. It's always beside yours on the counter. You know it was plugged in."

In his sigh, anger retreated to neutral territory and the horn sounded the end of the battle. "Maybe the battery's going. We should check up on that."

I nodded, then said, "Yeah. Sure" when I realized he couldn't see my head movement.

"Nell said a friend of yours was bringing you home?"

The sudden memory of Craig's kiss kicked me in the solar plexus. "Mm," I grunted because I didn't have the breath to speak.

"Who is it?"

"Uh. Craig."

Silence.

In my mind's eye, I saw our armies freeze, our respective generals twitching at the scent of another battle in the air.

"Why're you saying his name like that?"

"Like what?"

"Maggie." The soldier blew his horn.

"Uh—"

"You like this guy, don't you?"

My eyes slid to Craig.

He frowned, blinked. In a split second, he caught the gist of the conversation because he suddenly became interested in the nubs of fabric on his black socks.

"You *do* like him."

I winced and turned away from Craig. "Yeah."

Dad sighed, long and heavy. "Of all the—"

My back straightened, ready to brawl it out.

"Does he like you, too? Capital 'L' like?"

"Yeah."

Another sigh. "The mother in me is thrilled you've finally found someone. The father in me wants to shove a shotgun in his crotch and threaten him with severe harm if he does anything to hurt or take advantage of you."

"Let's stay in your feminine side."

"I feel very conflicted about all this."

I glanced behind me. "I'll hide the shell casings."

Craig's head jerked back, and he stared at me, wide-eyed.

Dad sighed again.

"Careful. You're starting to sound like one of those indecent phone perverts."

"Does he know? About...you?"

The light feeling in my heart, buoyed at the moment Craig kissed me and floating since our lips touched, plummeted to the ground. "No."

"Be careful."

"I will."

"On all levels."

Blood rushed to my cheeks and the tips of my ears. I turned my head away from Craig and whispered, "We're not there, yet."

"This makes me feel less conflicted."

"Good."

"I'd still hide the shotgun shells if I were you."

I didn't push, just waited to see if the bugler would put down his horn or sound the beginning of an unnecessary battle.

"Where's Serge?"

I kept my voice low. "With everything that happened, I don't think he'll be around for a couple of days. He exploded pretty badly."

"He's the reason behind the fire?"

I sighed. "Yeah." I could almost see him rubbing his forehead. "I should go—Craig's here...and stuff."

"Yeah, right. *Stuff.*"

I waited.

"Maggie, I trust you."

"I know."

"On all levels."

"I know."

"Fix the phone tomorrow."

"Okay."

"And Maggie?"

"Yes?"

"I love you."

I smiled. "Me, too." I hung up.

Craig stood and ran the palms of his hands on his thighs.

Man, I loved those thighs.

"Everything okay?" He nodded toward the phone.

"Yeah. Everything's great."

He grinned.

I melted. "Uh, do you want something to drink?"

"Maggie."

The hoarse, guttural voice that groaned my name would have made the hair on the back of my neck prickle, and the sight of Serge, burned and flambéed, would have made me shriek had I not experienced the funhouse of horrors when I was five and Dad took me to a pioneer settlement in North Dakota.

Still, Serge's appearance wasn't likely to make any Top Ten Sexiest Bachelors lists, here or in the otherworld where—I assumed from the imaginative manner death can take—the standard was far lower.

"Maggie."

I ignored him, partly because I didn't want to explain to Craig why I was talking to air, partly because I was pissed at Serge. I figured since he'd tried to blow me up, I deserved to be a little peeved.

Craig moved to me. "It's Serge, isn't it?"

Now *that* made the hair on the back of my neck prickle. Prickle, tickle, and stand straight.

"What?"

He stepped closer and reached his arm out.

I moved, dazed, into his embrace. "What?"

"Serge. You're thinking about him, aren't you?"

Sudden relief that my gift stayed buried it the moist darkness of secret earth jousted with the piercing disappointment that I was still alone with this talent and in this life. "Um—" I pressed my forehead against his shoulder. "Yeah."

"Me, too. Sometimes, it feels like he's still around." Craig pulled away.

"Yeah," I said and kept a straight face as I continued, "me, too."

"*Maggie*. Please. *What did I do?*"

I stepped back from Craig. "Can you excuse me for a second? I want to check on the cat and dog."

"You have pets?" He moved to follow me. "Can I see them?"

I looked over my shoulder and grinned. "They're in my bedroom. That would cost you at least three chicken dinners."

He smiled and stopped.

I walked down the hallway, subtly brushed close enough to Serge to trail my fingers on a spot of his jeans where no blood had stained the fabric. "Come," I whispered.

He turned and followed, his steps squelching on the floor and leaving dark, red marks in their trail.

I went up the stairs, and when I was certain Craig could neither see nor hear, I faced Serge.

Then wished I hadn't.

Soggy chunks of skin hung off his bone like flesh curtains, exposing the yellow fat and bright red muscles of his face. His eyelids had seared shut, his mouth drooped to the side. Serge's clothing had fused to his body, and the parts of exposed flesh that weren't covered in bright blisters, glistened with clear fluid.

The sight didn't faze me. It was the smell. Charred skin, decaying rot, crisped cotton, and bacon. It was the bacon that made me want to vomit. The salty scent swarmed around me.

"Maggie?"

I took a shallow breath. "Pretty big freak out."

He whimpered.

I sighed. "Look. I'm sorry if the questions I ask make you—"

"Did I hurt anyone?"

I blinked. "What?"

"Did I hurt anyone?" Hysteria made the words pitch upwards. "Tell me I didn't—" He shoved his head into his hands. Bits of flesh slid to the floor. "Tell me I didn't—"

"No," I said softly. "Everyone's fine."

He didn't say anything, just kept his head buried in the raw meat of his palms.

I stepped forward, quietly called his name.

He remained silent except for the soft snuffling.

I shuffled in place, unsure of what to do. In my life, I'd dealt with many incarnations of him: Angry Serge, Belligerent Serge, Asshole Serge. I didn't have a clue what to with a Broken-Hearted Serge.

"I've never hurt anyone—"

That rocked me back. "Never—you made my life hell. Called me names—almost beat me up—"

"*Almost*," he mumbled. "I never hit you."

And that stopped me cold. "Does it hurt?" I nodded toward his body.

He shook his head. Then he looked up. "How come? How come it doesn't hurt? I've been able to feel everything—the heat from your car, the sheets on the bed. Why can't I feel this?"

I didn't answer. Usually, when the dead go off their nut, they return to this existence in the form they want. That Serge came back burned, his insides left exposed to air and elements, said a lot.

He wasn't ready to hear it.

I wasn't ready to say it.

"Am I fading? Going to...going away?"

"No," I said softly. "Not yet."

He pondered this. Then: "Do you think it hurts?"

I strained to hear the words. "What?"

"The other side."

Compassion was like a bellows in my chest, expanding my lungs, inflating my heart, and creating a space inside me that I'd never thought would exist: a soft spot for Serge. "No, I don't think so."

"I'm sorry...about blowing up the house."

"I know," I said quietly.

"I'm sorry—" He took a breath.

What I could see of his face seemed to contort in pain.

"—I'm sorry about everything."

Sharp needles of tears pricked my eyes. "It's fine." The words rushed out, fast and tumbling. They poured like antibiotics pushed into the body, and thrummed through my veins, speeding the healing of a wound I hadn't realized existed. "Do you want to come down-stairs? Hang out?"

He shook his head. "I'll just go back to the bedroom. Maybe lie down."

I made a mental note to wash my sheets. Just because the living couldn't see the marks of the dead didn't mean I wanted to sleep in them. "Are you sure?"

He nodded, keeping his gaze downward.

"I'd rather you stay with me." Wow. Talk about sentences I never thought I'd utter.

"No," he said, thick and muffled. He lifted his head and a chunk of flesh slid off his cheek and *sploshed* on the floor. "Sorry."

"Don't worry. No one can see it. I'll clean it later." And yet another sentence I never thought I'd say to Serge: *no problem, buddy. I'll wipe up your desiccated flesh. You sit. Relax.*

"Maggie?" Craig's voice rose up the stairs.

I jerked my thumb in his direction. "I should go—if he comes upstairs and sees me talking to the wall—"

Serge nodded. "Go." He turned away. His steps squelched on the wood. Bits of black soot and specks of ashes floated in his wake.

I turned and went down the steps to Craig.

He knelt by the stove, stroking Ebony. Looking up, he smiled. "She must have gotten by you when you went upstairs."

"Must've. You wanna a pop or anything?"

"Sure."

I grabbed two cans of Coke from the fridge and we headed down into the living room. My ears strained for the sounds of *Miami Vice* coming down from the second floor, but if Serge was in bed, he wasn't watching TV.

Craig moved to the edge of the couch, gracefully fell into it and stretched his legs on the cushions. He patted the spot beside him. "Come here."

The way he said it made me shiver, like he was going to protect and possess me all at once. My feet took me to him.

He pulled me between his legs and wrapped his arms around my waist.

I leaned into him. The heat of his chest seeped into my back, loosened the muscles at the same time it made my stomach tighten.

Craig kissed my temple. "How are you doing?"

"Okay."

"Sure? Pretty intense few days."

Serge flashed into my mind, and in the silence between heartbeats, he appeared.

He blinked, his head moving slowly and taking in the room as though he'd never seen it. Serge spread his arms. "Maggie. I don't want to be here."

I could have answered him telepathically. But I wouldn't. That kind of connection required a high level of intimacy. I wasn't sure yet what Serge was to me, but I knew who he had been. Though the waters of forgiveness quietly rolled and dutifully eroded the walls of hate and hurt that had been built between us, I wasn't ready to drop my defenses and let him in.

He frowned. "Why can't I leave? Why do I feel bound to this room?" He lifted his gaze and lidless eyes stared into mine. "Why do I feel bound *to you?*"

Craig threaded his fingers through my hair. "How are you feeling? Truthfully?"

"Out of my element."

His voice dropped. "What about Serge? You found his body and you seem...I dunno, determined to find out his past. What's going on?"

The sound of his voice soothed me. It rumbled and resonated through my chest.

"I don't know."

He chuckled, soft and low. "Yeah." The word rippled in the air. "You do."

Serge watched me, his body tight.

I sighed and hoped he was too weak to inflict further damage. Dad would freak if a lingering ghost blew up the house. And he'd doubly freak if it was Serge. "I feel conflicted."

The tension ebbed from Serge, slowly peeled back like a lazy ocean wave.

He remained alert, wary, but his posture no longer reminded me of a tsunami looking for a hapless island village.

"Conflicted." Craig shifted. His hips pulsed into mine as he moved us further down the couch.

"He was terrible to me..." The memory, the *weight* of all the years was mortar, heavy and wet. It spackled the crumbling wall, cementing my bitterness and blocked out the river of mercy that tumbled by. "I never did anything—"

Serge bowed his head, shook it side to side. Red tears fell from his cheek and splattered the floor.

"He'd slam me into the locker, push me off my chair." My voice cracked. "And all I could think of is *I don't deserve this*—"

"You deserved it."

Serge's voice crawled on a snake's belly and hissed in my ears.

He folded his arms across his chest. His foot pounded the floor. "You deserved it. You and"—his face contorted, meaty, chunks of muscle and fat twisted in hate—"your *dad*. You all deserved it. From the moment, I saw you and him"—his voice broke, shattered like smashed glass— "saw you at the school, *laughing together*. I hated you." He looked up.

His gaze shoved me back.

"I still hate you." Confusion replaced contempt, and, weeping again, he returned his gaze to the floor. He stumbled sideways and collapsed into the chair.

"You didn't deserve it," said Craig.

"I know." I kept my gaze on Serge. My insides quaked. In my home, in the safest place I knew, he'd managed to metaphorically slam me into the wall. I hated him. And I pitied him. And I *despised* him for making me pity him. "I didn't deserve it."

"What about me?" asked Serge.

I didn't just restrain my temper. I locked it in iron shackles. Keeping my gaze on Craig, I thought of love and light and not of all the ways I wanted Serge to burn in hell.

"People have choices in life," said Craig. "He made his."

"Easy for him to say." Another slab of flesh fell to the floor. "What's the worst thing that's ever happened to Captain Polo?"

Craig shifted, moving further down the couch and taking me with him. "But then I wonder if he *really* had a choice."

"You're excusing his behaviour," I said. "You're saying it's okay that he was a bastard to me because his dad beat him."

Behind me, Serge took a sharp breath that hissed in the air.

"I think he was trying to survive and that's what came out. People do weird things to make sense of their world."

"You're *excusing* him."

"No, I'm trying to understand."

I didn't say anything.

He smiled. His fingers touched my mouth, traced the outline.

The hard, tight line of my lips softened.

"Understanding is power. Power is freedom."

"That's bull." Serge rolled his eyes. "He's playing deep and sensitive to get in your pants."

"His dad despised him," said Craig.

"That's what he said."

Serge froze.

So did I. The words had fallen from my mouth before reason and logic could erect a dam, and now I was going to drown under my stupidity. While he was alive, Serge had never talked to me. Bullied. Intimidated. Cajoled, maybe, but talk? Never. My brain churned, trying to create a possible scenario under which I could have gleaned this information.

If Craig noticed the screw-up, he chose to ignore it because he nodded and said, "Can you imagine?"

"I'm sure his dad loved him—deep down."

Serge grunted.

"Why do you think that?" asked Craig. "You've seen the way his parents have behaved since his death."

"People mourn differently."

"And all the things we've seen—his dad refusing to allow the school to do a memorial, the fight your dad is having with them to actually give him a funeral are—?"

"Misdirected grief. They can't undo what they did, can't go back or admit they're—" I raised my head and looked at Craig. "You don't agree?"

His mouth pulled sideways. "Sometimes, people's actions line up with their hearts."

"His dad really hated him." I glanced over to see Serge nodding.

"I don't think his dad hated him," said Craig. "I think his dad *despised* him."

The wounds on Serge's body gushed blood. Bright and red, it spilled from the white chair to the floor in a thick, crimson waterfall.

"Have you ever thought why it was you Serge picked?"

"I don't know," I lied.

Serge didn't contradict me. He remained silent, the only sound the quiet rush of red. It pooled around the couch, a scarlet riptide he would drown in.

"He still had a choice," I said. "And he chose to torment me."

"You're talking like he was in an everyday situation, but he wasn't. People cut off their limbs to save themselves. Resort to cannibalism. Kill other people."

"You're talking about catastrophic, physical situations."

"And a parent beating out the crap out of you on a daily basis isn't a catastrophic, physical situation?"

Blood covered the floor, thick and luminescent.

"Beating you and justifying it with religion and God." Craig sat up. "You've heard Popov. Serge lived in hell."

The remaining foundation of un-forgiveness splintered. "It still doesn't…"

"When you're an adult and someone violates you in the name of God, you know they're full of crap. But when you're a kid, what do you really know?"

Craig's unrelenting gaze held me tight.

"And your mother won't protect you. The church won't step in. Teachers get mad. Kids don't understand." Craig took a breath and the hard light in his eyes dimmed. "I'm not justifying it, not excusing him. But I am saying if you're going to get over this, you have to take more than yourself into account. If you hang on to what he did, then you'll never be free of him he'll haunt your life, forever."

The words, simply said, made without judgment or condemnation did more than splinter my justification to hang on to bitterness. They blew a hole in the wall.

"Do you think there was a moment when he was ever truly happy?"

Blood flowed past my feet, turned the ground red.

Serge said nothing.

"Maggie?" Craig jostled me.

"I—" I couldn't speak the truth, not with Serge sitting within hearing distance, not while the copper smell of his life rushed past me. "I'm thinking." I peeked at Serge. "When was the last time he remembered true happiness?" I turned and willed him to lift his gaze.

He did.

"The last time? When was the last time—joy without spikes or taunts?"

Serge blinked.

An invisible bridge formed between us, humming like a million wheels on asphalt and vibrating as though electricity ran along its perimeter.

He blinked twice.

Blood receded, slow motion, flowed backwards and retreated into his body. Fallen flesh shimmered then evaporated. Skin knit itself, slotted into the missing chunks of his body like puzzle pieces, which then sealed themselves, leaving no indication of wounds. The charred remnants of his clothes, now woven, covered his body in bright, freshly knit threads.

"When was he happy?"

Craig's voice sounded low, calming, hypnotic.

"I don't know," I whispered.

Serge shimmed, glowed. He began to grow younger, younger, and younger still. Seventeen, fifteen, twelve.

"It's been years, I bet," I said, "since he knew happiness."

And still Serge grew younger. Until his clothes were more like blankets. Until his cheeks grew chubby with childhood fat. Until he was too young to use words.

I blinked, rapid and fast, to keep myself from crying.

When he reached the stage of a newborn infant, his face wizened by wrinkles, his fingers not even as big as my pinkie nail, he stopped and looked at me.

The tears fell, large in his small face, silent from the eyes that said everything.

His cells broke apart and he was gone.

CHAPTER EIGHTEEN

T hree mornings later I came downstairs and found Dad in the kitchen. He was making my lunch—and giving me Brussels sprouts. I sighed. That meant the cold silence between us was about to ignite into a fight. I dragged a stool over to the coffeemaker, sat down, and filled a cup. Gesturing to the sprouts, I said, "You still can't be that mad at me about Craig and Serge."

He eyed me from over the top of his metal frames and heaped another handful of sprouts into the container. "I've never treated you like a child, Maggie. Your gift precluded that." He sliced into the ham. "And your brains. You've never been a stupid kid."

An instinctive flash of wounded pride lit up my insides. I took a long drink of coffee and ignored the urge to justify my position and give fuel to the still-burning fight between us.

"But this is stupid."

The cup hit the counter with a *bang*. Hot coffee sloshed over its rim, scalded my skin, and stained the roughened fibres of my cotton bathrobe. "It's not stupid." I spoke slow and enunciated every word.

His gaze moved from the ham sandwich he was making to the spilled beverage. "The iron hold you have on your emotions proves that?"

My breath escaped in a hot hiss. I pushed the stool back and went to the sink. Grabbing the sponge, I leaned over and wiped the mess. "You're purposely baiting me and you know it."

Dad didn't say anything.

I rounded on him. Cinching the belt about my waist, I said, "At least admit to trying to push my buttons."

He sighed and reached for the lettuce. "I admit it. I'm ashamed but I admit it. I just"—he slapped the vegetable onto the ham—"we don't fight and I don't like it."

"I'm not that fond of it, either." I shuffled back to my stool and grabbed my mug.

Dad scrubbed his forehead with the back of his hand. "A house explodes, you're dating, and Serge has disappeared into nothingness."

"He's back," I said. "I left him sleeping on the bed."

"Let him rest." He dropped the knife and spun toward the coffee-maker. His steps were jerky, as though he was walking on pins and needles. "You have to drop this, Maggie, *now*."

Ugh. This was the same fight we had when he came home last night. "Not this again. You—"

"I mean it, Magdalene." He gave me a full-on dad stare. "Drop it."

"No! I won't—I *can't*—"

"I've gone along with a lot of things when it comes to your gift," he said. "I've trekked through bogs and swamps searching for lost bodies, I've stayed up late and gotten up early. I've put up with walking into the kitchen and seeing my plates flying through the air, and I didn't bat an eye with that whole sausage thing—"

"You said you'd never bring it up again—"

"It's not like this is even the first time you've been in an explod-ing building—" He bent his head and ran his hand through his hair. "What kind of father am I?"

"A good one—"

He kept his gaze pointed at the floor. "I can even deal with a dis-appearing boyfriend—"

"Craig's not invisible," I said, exasperated. "But after Serge blipped out of existence I was a total mess. I'm *sorry* I didn't ask my boy-friend to stay late and watch me sobbing, just so you could meet him but—"

"It has to stop."

The way he spoke made me freeze. There was finality in the way the words flowed, like wet cement turning hard and cold.

"I can't stop—he's tethered to me."

"Untether him."

"What do you think I'm trying to do?"

He wrenched the coffeepot off its element. "Can't you"—Dad swung his hand in a circular motion. A wave of black liquid arced out of its glass container—"break the bond or something?"

"There's only one way: I'm trying to guide him to the other side."

"Tell him to find someone else."

"In Dead Falls? Who's he going to go to?"

"Aren't you the one who's always telling me about the flexibility of the universe? Time and distance don't matter—tell him to find someone else."

"I can't," I said quietly. "And we can't keep arguing about this."

He pointed the pot like a gun. "We're not arguing. He's a murdered kid. Let him be—go—go find a hobby!" He scowled at the coffee and shoved it back on the warmer. Then he stalked back to the sandwich.

My eyebrows went down. "I help murdered people all the time."

He lifted the knife. A dollop of mayo dropped to the counter. "Long dead people, honey. People who were killed thousands of miles away and in different countries. But the guy who killed Serge is still around and he's not going to let you meddle in his plans."

I grimaced. "I'm not meddling in *his* plans. I'm trying to get a ghost off my bed and into the afterlife."

"The guy who murdered Serge doesn't know you're asking questions and digging into this kid's past just so you can transition him to the other side. As far as he's concerned, you're some wannabe detective who's getting in his way."

My breath burned its way down my throat and hit the acid churning in my stomach.

"I'm putting my foot down, Maggie. Tell Serge to find someone else."

"Where?"

He frowned.

"Where are you putting your foot down? Over there?" I jerked my chin toward the floor. "Because that has Serge's dried blood on it. Or are you going to put your foot down in my bedroom? The sheets on the floor are stained with him." I stood. "When the night comes, the ghosts find me, not you, and I'm the one who deals with the fallout of their lives and their deaths. There's blood everywhere—*his blood*—and

I see it. I'm the one who saw his burned body, who saw his skin dropping like dough. I'm the one who"—my voice cracked—"saw this kid
regressing into a baby, desperately trying to find a *moment* where he
was happy and not finding anything. That's me, Dad, not you. And
until you're the one cleaning charred flesh off the landing, don't talk
to me about *putting your foot down.*"

The skin on his face tightened.

"This is my life. This is what I live," I said bitterly. "Don't I count?"

"Not if you're dead."

"He's right."

I spun around and saw Serge standing by the table.

He pulled the sleeves of his grey sweater down his arms and
rubbed his hands against his jean-clad thighs. "Tell me how to unbind
myself from you and I will," he said. "Your dad's right. Whoever did
this to me isn't going to let you ask questions." He paused. "I should
have thought of that."

Dad followed my gaze. "Is he here?"

I nodded. "By the table."

He set down the knife and walked around the counter. "How are
you doing?"

Serge jerked back. He blinked and shook his head. "I'm doing all
right..." A frown creased his forehead. He looked at me, confusion
clouding his eyes. "I feel weird—"

"Like how?"

"Dunno. I'm fine, but I'm weird."

"You said it, not me."

"What did he say?" asked Dad.

"He says he's doing okay."

"Does he know why he's bonded to you?" Dad folded his arms
across his chest and leaned against the counter.

"No," I said.

"Tell him I said he's right." Serge walked to me. "Ask him if he
knows how to break our tie."

"He doesn't."

"What?" asked Dad. "What did he ask?"

My eyes squeezed shut. "This is going to be the world's longest conversation, and I'm not in the mood to play otherworldly translator."

"I want to talk to him," said Dad. "Ask him if he understands the dangers he's putting you in."

"I do." Serge walked over to me. He didn't smell like bacon anymore.

"And I don't want to do this...not to you."

"What's he saying?" Dad straightened.

"Bloody—fine. Everyone come with me." I led them to my bedroom, to my laptop. "Turn it on," I said to Serge.

His eyebrows formed a line. "How?"

"You're energy. This works on electricity. Just try."

"I don't know—"

"You're doing it with the television. Just turn it on."

"Yeah, but—"

"Serge!"

"Okay!" He closed his eyes, raised his hand like he was in school and wanted the teacher to call on him.

I waited.

Nothing.

He raised his hand higher and started to wiggle his fingers.

"What are you doing?"

"Trying to turn it on," he whispered. "Shut up, I'm trying to concentrate."

"You look like a holy roller trying to summon Jesus."

His eyes snapped open, and his hand flopped to his side. "Nice."

I rolled my eyes. "It's not about whatever that was you were trying to do. Just imagine the computer being on."

"Imagine." He said it like I'd suffered oxygen deprivation.

"Yeah. Thought is energy. Energy is electricity—just trust me. Imagine."

He stared at me.

Dad rolled the office chair from under the desk and sat down. "What's going on?"

"I'm just supposed to close my eyes—"

"You don't have to close your eyes—"

"Why's he closing his eyes?" Dad leaned forward.

I looked heavenward. This was a bad Abbott and Costello routine. A Three Stooges skit without the blunt weapons. "Serge."

"Fine." He closed his eyes.

I sighed.

"It's not working," he said. He pried open one eyelid. "Is it?"

"Turn on the television," I told him.

His head swivelled in its direction and a second later, it blipped on.

"Just like that," I said. "Turn on the computer."

He swung toward the laptop.

It flared on.

"Whoa. I didn't know it could transfer." Serge strode to the desk, stood beside Dad.

"Open Word," I said.

Serge did. "If I could have done this in life, I would have been a better student."

I hopped up on the desk. "Go ahead," I told my dad. "Have your conversation."

"Can I surf the internet, too?"

"No!" I grabbed Serge's shoulder. The wool of his sweater tickled my skin. "No porno on my computer."

"Spoilsport."

"Serge—" Dad adjusted his spectacles and faced the computer. "How are you doing, really?"

"What do I do?" asked Serge.

"Imagine the words on the screen."

I'm okay.

"Really?"

No.

Dad's shoulders dropped, and a soft light went into his eyes. "How do you feel?"

I couldn't speak for Serge, but I felt weird. Dad had asked the question in the same tone he'd ask me. I wasn't sure how I felt about my father caring about the guy who bullied me. Then again, I wasn't sure how *I* felt about the guy who bullied me. There was pity and sympathy...and in a twisted way, I think there was some respect. Which made me feel *super* weird. All I know was that if I had been him that night, unable to remember a single moment of happiness and living a life devoid of compassion and mercy, I probably would have off'd myself by the time I was thirteen.

Free and chained. Serge opened his eyes and stared at me. *I'm sorry, Maggie. I didn't hate you.*

Invisible fingers gripped my stomach. "I know—I mean, I get that, now."

His eyes glistened. Tears left twin tracks down his cheeks. *I'm really sorry.*

"I know."

I screwed it all up. He choked on a sob and more tears fell, and dropped to his sweater. *I wish I could do it again—I'd do better this time.*

Dad took my hand. "No one knows what really happens when you cross over, Serge. You may get another chance."

Not with you. Not with her. I could—He buried his face in his hands.

Instinct made me move to him, put my arms on his shoulders.

He gripped me on either side of my waist, hard, and threw himself into my arms.

So weird—*so weird*—to hold onto this guy, this guy who'd made my life such a living hell, to hug him and whisper comfort...and to *really* feel the need to make it all okay for him. I heard my dad hiss, like he'd taken a body blow. "You okay?" I turned to look at him.

His glasses were off and he swiped the tears from his eyes.

"Dad?"

He shook his head but didn't say anything.

Serge pulled away. *Sorry.*

"It's okay." I stumbled back, putting space and air between us.

Dad blew out a breath and put his glasses on. "What did that feel like?"

I frowned. "What? Are you talking to me or him?"

"Both of you."

I cocked my head.

Serge wiped his eyes and looking at me, shrugged.

"Maggie—" Dad spoke slowly, seeming to choose every word with hyper care. "Just now, when you touched...did you feel anything?"

I shook my head. "No—just...just that I wanted to make it right."

"Serge?"

No. The words stood out, black etchings against the white background of the computer screen. He frowned. *Relief, maybe, but that's it.*

Dad looked at both of us. "You changed."

I blinked. "What?"

What?

"There was—Maggie, you glowed."

"I *what*?"

"Glowed," he said, "You glowed. There was an aura around you—pale green, then purple, then white. It was bright, luminous and—" He took a breath. "I saw Serge. Transparent." He frowned. "Foggy but transparent and he glowed white, too."

What does that mean?

My lungs burned from holding my breath, but I couldn't release the air. "I have no idea."

Dad stood, rubbed the whiskers on his face, and walked toward the bed. He turned and looked back. "I've never seen that happen with any spirit you've helped."

I sank into the chair.

What?

"I don't know." I looked at Serge. "But this goes beyond a tether or bond."

Whatever Serge was to me, it was more than a simple transition.

But you don't know?

"No."

Crap.

I finally took a breath. "You said it."

took a few days off school. Ignored all the texts from everyone but Craig and Nell. Somehow, math and biology didn't seem half important as finding out why I glowed when touching Serge.

Serge and I sat on my bed. Our legs dangled over the side. The scent of clean sheets filled the air with the aroma of wildflowers and baby powder. Ebony and Buddha lay in a criss-cross pattern on the duvet. Whatever was going on, it didn't freak out the animals, and I took that as a good sign.

"You're sure this has never happened to you?"

"Positive."

He ran his hand through his hair. "What do you think it means?"

I stared at him. "Seriously? Having never experienced this before, you think I suddenly have all kinds of theories in the five minutes I've realized that I glow around you?"

"It's been a few days."

"It's called exaggeration. I don't have the answer. I don't have any answers."

He rubbed at his chest. "Don't snap. You have more experience with the dead than I do."

"Not like this."

"What do you really know about the other side?"

"Not much. I've never been."

"Yeah, but—"

I sighed. "Look, all I know is death. Technically, all I know is what holds souls back from crossing over. That's my area of expertise. And it's pretty easy, once you get over some of the gross ways people have died. You talk to them about their life, the things that made them sad. They let it go, and poof, soul transitioned. You"—I eyed him—"are a whole new world of WTF for me."

He pushed back, rested on the lavender pillows, and crossing his legs yoga-style, asked, "Why did I come back burned? The night of the explosion? I'm dead. Why would I have burned?"

I hesitated.

"Maggie, c'mon."

My gaze moved around the room in a zigzag pattern. I wanted to look everywhere but him. Taking a breath, I said, "You may not like—this may make your current state worse..." I winced. "Maybe. Or maybe it'll—"

"Holy crap. You're killing me and I'm already dead. Just say it."

"Spirits tend to come back as they were in life." The words rushed out.

He gave a "have you lost your mind" look. "What?"

"When a spirit freaks out, goes all poltergeist, then comes back—they come back as they were in life."

"I've never been burned in life."

I didn't say anything, just watched him.

After a moment, comprehension lit his eyes. "My whole life was one burn after another."

"I think the words you're looking for are 'living hell.'" Reaching out, I touched his kneecap. "I'm sorry," I said softly. "I didn't think... I didn't know how bad it was for you."

He shrugged, but the muscles at the side of his jaw ticked a rapid rhythm.

"I thought"—I shifted sideways—"it seemed like you and Amber—"

He snorted.

"Weren't you ever—" I stopped because there was no point in asking if he was ever happy with her or if he'd felt loved by her.

"She—we weren't anything." He took a rasping breath. "You're saying the reason I didn't feel anything the night I blew up the house was because I'd stopped feeling, a long time ago."

I nodded. "Basically."

Pain contorted his face. "I screwed it up, didn't I? One day after another."

I kept silent—what could I possibly say?

A tear slid down his cheek. "I gave him all the power. I destroyed myself and everything that was good around me, thinking I was torturing him, but it did nothing." His Adam's apple bobbed up and down. "So I'm still here because…" He shook his head. "Why am I still here?"

"Something happened in your life and it's chained you to this existence," I said, then immediately felt lame. Of course he knew that.

He looked at me from glassy eyes. "Do you believe in reincarnation? Do you think I'll get another chance if I cross over?"

I shrugged. "I don't know. Maybe. I don't know what happens after you transition. No one's ever come back to tell me."

"I might go to hell," he said quietly. "For everything I did to you and everyone else—"

My heart lurched. "You don't know that."

He snorted.

I made eye contact. "Fine. Maybe, but I doubt it. Haven't you ever read the bible? Doesn't it say something about forgiveness and redemption?"

"I tried to stay away from the reverend's favourite book," he said dryly.

"Come on. In Holy Popov's House of Prayer and Pain? No way you didn't read it. You must know how holy a person has to be to get into heaven."

"If you're a regular person, heaven's hard to get into. If you were a guy in the bible, then I think you got a reserved spot, no matter what. Lot committed incest and made it into heaven. David murdered a man and got in, Solomon had a sex addiction, and Elijah had serious anger problems."

Wowsa. "Trust me, if those guys got in, you'll be fine. Besides, I don't think that's what's holding you here."

"Me either." He looked away, pulled Ebony into his arms. She purred and gave him her belly. "Have you ever seen hell?"

I shook my head. "No, but I don't think you're headed there."

"How do you know?"

I made a face. "Dunno—I just…the sense I get is hell always claims its souls. If you were doomed, you'd be there by now."

"Some comfort." He scratched the cat under her chin.

She purred harder and snuggled into him.

"What now?"

"I don't know. Dad's afraid if I keep trying to figure out what's holding you, whoever killed you is going to come after me."

"The great and mighty reverend."

"What?"

"He killed me."

I stared at him. "You remember that?"

He shook his head.

"Then how can you be sure?"

He shot me a look. "It had to be him—it was always just a matter of time." He trailed his fingers along Ebony's tail. "I bet if I proved it, I could cross over."

"You think vengeance is holding you back?"

"Justice," he said. "It could only be that."

I shifted closer to him. "How do we prove it?"

He gave a humourless laugh. "What a life. What an afterlife. You don't know about hell, for sure, do you?"

I rolled my eyes and hid behind annoyance so he wouldn't know my uncertainty. "You're not going to hell."

"I am."

The thought of him burning in eternity made my stomach hurt. "We don't have to solve this—you could stay here—"

"And haunt you forever?" He gave me a small smile. "Don't you think I've shadowed your life for long enough?"

"But—"

"I deserve it." The words came, full of quiet conviction. "I never faced up to anything in my life. And I hurt a lot of people. All the time. I can't run from that. I won't. It's cowardly and I spent my life being a coward—I'm not going to be that in my afterlife, no matter what."

I didn't know what to say, except, "How do we prove your dad murdered you?"

"I have a flash drive," he said. "I keep it hidden in my locker. Get it and take it to the sheriff. If I have to pay"—his face hardened—"so does he."

CHAPTER TWENTY

I headed downstairs and found Dad at the desktop in the family room. "Hey."

He turned his head, but kept his eyes on the screen. "Come here. I've been looking up those aura colours."

"Yeah?" Pulling my hand out of my kangaroo hoodie, I walked to him. "What do they mean?"

He squinted. "I'm not sure. I think the colours are on a scale. Green can be anything from healing to jealousy." He rolled the chair back and gestured for me to look at the screen. "White is the melding of all energies."

I scanned the definitions, went back to the search engine's list, and scanned a few more websites. "This is so not helpful. I've never been jealous of Serge, but it was me glowing green, not him."

Dad grunted and took a sip of coffee. "It had to be healing."

"Yeah…we seem…better."

"So, you're not the reason he's still here."

I pressed my lips together and grimaced. "Yeah, about that…"

He set the mug down, extra slow. "What?"

I told him about Serge's flash drive and his theory.

Dad covered his mouth with his hand. "He really thinks his dad killed him."

"He's sure of it."

"What a life this kid led."

"Yeah," I said, wishing I'd been bigger and smarter enough to see the truth behind Serge's shadow and mirror tricks. "I should be okay. If I get the drive—"

"What's in it?"

"I don't know, but he thinks it'll get Reverend Popov convicted for his murder."

The chair squeaked as Dad leaned back. He folded his hands, rested them on his belly, and pressed his lips together. "All you have to do is get a flash drive and give it to Nancy?"

I nodded. "Yeah, it's at the school." I paused. "Bright daylight. Lots of adults and kids…"

"Don't oversell." He sighed. "Okay, if that's *all* you have to do."

"I swear."

"Go before I change my mind."

parked in the student lot. Serge had stayed home, but he'd given me the combination to his lock.

"You have to push the back wall a bit," he'd said, "but it's hidden in there."

"What's on it?"

"You'll see."

I got out of the car. The sun was bright but even the blue sky couldn't mitigate the ice-cold wind. I yanked my coat close and headed to the main entrance. The door was locked.

"Blood drive today."

I whirled around and grinned. "Craig."

"Hey." He wrapped his arms around me.

I buried my face in the warmth of his neck and inhaled the scent of him.

"I thought you were sick—you must be feeling better."

I nodded. My check rubbed against the soft fibres of his hoodie.

He pulled away, cupped my jaw in his hand. "I'm glad."

His lips touched mine. Cold skin, warm breath, wet mouth.

Wow, he tasted good.

Craig broke the kiss and smiled down at me. "Wanna go inside?"

I wrapped my arms around him. "No. I want to stay here, in this moment."

He laughed. "Let's go inside. It's freezing out here." Craig took my hand and led me to another entrance.

On the wall, white cardboard paper with large, red drops of blood directed donors to the blood bank.

"I should donate," I said.

"Yeah, but you're sick—or at least you were—"

"No, I'm better, now." I pulled him through the obstacle course of kids wandering the hall. "Besides, Nell's one of the organizers and I should say 'hey.'"

We moved past the windows that bordered the library and the main office. The hallway opened into the front foyer of the school. And there was Nell, sitting at a white cloth covered table.

I let go of Craig's hand and deked around the lineup of students and teachers waiting to give blood. "Hey."

Nell looked up. Her eyes brightened. Jumping to her feet and stretching across the table, she grabbed me in a bear hug. "OhmyGod." The words came out in one syllable.

I leaned back and stared at her soldier-style jacket and marine-green cargos. "What's with the dictator getup? Your first year as blood drive organizer and you go all despot in your clothes?"

"Don't knock it. The military design gives respect. Besides, we have to do good—this is the first year the blood bank's allowed students to organize and run the drive." She looked around. "Isn't it great? We've had a lineup since this morning."

I didn't point out the crowd was mostly boys and Nell was showing some really sweet cleavage.

Her eyes searched mine. Pulling me to one side, away from the crowd, she asked, "Are you okay?"

"Yeah."

Her gaze jumped over my right shoulder—probably to Craig—then came back to me. "So...you've been awfully quiet about a certain polo captain..."

"Some things shouldn't be put in text—"

Her gaze assessed me. Then she grinned. "That good?"

"I'm no longer single."

She did a tiny jig. "*Awesome*," she whispered. Her smile froze. The happiness on her face sank like a sunset, taking colour and light from her skin. "What about"—she glanced around—"you-know-who."

"Not so good." Reality sobered me. "I need to get to his locker and get something for him."

She gripped my hand. "Can I help?"

I shook my head. "No—there's lots to talk about, but I don't have time."

"Okay." She let go. "After school."

"Maybe."

She grabbed my hand. "No maybes. Definitely."

I grinned. "Okay. Definitely."

Nell pushed the sleeves of her jacket over her forearms. "It's too bad he's gone," she said. "He was one of the few people in this town with type AB blood."

I thought about the red liquid spilling from Serge and spreading out on the floor. "Yeah, it's too bad."

"More than too bad." A smile that held no humour lifted the side of her mouth. "He wasn't good for much, but that was one thing he was necessary for."

An unfamiliar spike of protection—for Serge—impaled my heart and I had to fight the urge to snap at Nell.

My instinctive reaction must have shown on my face because she said, "Wow. We really do have a lot to talk about."

The smell of bacon overwhelmed me.

Her face darkened with worry and she reached out to me. "Jeez. You okay?"

"It's such a long story," I said. I took a breath and let the air decompress the tight feeling in my chest. "So long and complicated."

"We'll go to your house after school," she said. "And you'll tell me everything."

I nodded.

Her gaze flicked past me. Her smile showed the dimples on her cheeks. "Your *boyfriend's* coming."

And there was a complication I hadn't anticipated. How was I going to get away from him and get to Serge's locker? I moulded to Craig's body as he slid his arm around my waist.

"Cute couple," said Nell.

I tilted my head back and met his gaze. "Did you donate blood?"

"Not yet."

"We might as well do it now, while we're here."

He shrugged. "Okay, sure."

"Great." I stepped back. "I'm just going to—uh—run to the bathroom."

Nell rolled her eyes at my awkward attempt to be smooth.

Craig's eyes narrowed. "You okay?"

"Um-hmm. Just gotta do...girl stuff." Wow. I am *so* lame. James Bond has nothing to worry about when it comes to me taking over his spy job.

My friends glanced at each other.

"See you in a bit," said Craig.

I ducked away. First job: get the flash drive from Serge's locker. Second job: figure out how I'm going to do ghost work while having a boyfriend. I sped past the auditorium and hung a left. The biology class was off this hallway, and the smell of formaldehyde seeped under the crack in the orange door and filled my mind with images of frozen frogs, dead baby pigs, and lidless cow eyes.

At the end of the hall, I turned right. The corridor was mostly deserted, with just a couple kids sitting by their lockers, eating lunches from cloth bags. I headed to the end of the hallway, where Serge's locker stood. As I drew closer, my steps faltered.

Dang.

The door was open and the locker was definitely empty.

Of course the school would have cleaned out his stuff and sent it to his parents.

I was going to head back to the blood drive when a familiar face turned the corner.

"Nancy?"

She was in uniform—the puke-beige colour that seemed to wash out every complexion but hers. Nancy glanced at the principal who was standing by her and then said to me, "Hey, honey. We need to talk."

"Oh, I *so* don't like your tone." I stepped toward her. She smelled of currants and roses, lotus blossoms and vanilla. I took her hand.

It was cold.

Her hands are *never* cold.

"Nancy?"

"Honey, I thought you were sick." Her eyes slid sideways to Principal Milton Larry, who was doing a weird stand-shuffle thing. His face was squished together like he had diarrhea and was trying not to have an accident. "The school said your dad phoned you in."

"Um, yeah, but I was feeling better, so…"

She nodded in acknowledgment. "Which is why we couldn't reach you at home."

In my stomach, fear scurried on insectile legs and made the hair on my arms rise. "What's going on?"

"I tried you on your cell—"

Dropping her hand, I yanked my phone out of my coat. "It's dead." Ice lodged in my gut. "I *know* I charged—"

"Get to the point, Nancy," said the principal.

My eyes slid from the black screen of my phone to Principal Larry, to Nancy.

"I need you to come to the station with me."

I loved Nancy, trusted her, but her tone made me step back. "Why?"

She glanced over my shoulder.

I turned.

The kids at the locker were staring.

"Nancy?"

"Mikhail Popov got an email—"

I blinked. "What?"

She licked her lips and lifted her hand, palm-up.

"Did you send him email and pretend to be his son?" asked Principal Larry. He leaned in towards me, and the saggy skin of his neck wobbled.

"*What?*" I jerked back, partly from shock, mostly because the principal wore cheap cologne that made my nose burn.

Nancy shot him a dirty look. "Honey, I know it's not you, but the email address is listed as yours, and you need to come with me."

I backpedalled. "Where's my dad?"

"He's meeting us at the station." Nancy's blue eyes held mine. "You don't have to say anything, Maggie. I know you didn't send Mikhail that message, but we still need to talk."

"But if you did," said Principal Larry in his high-pitched whine, "you'll be expelled. This school doesn't find pranks like that funny, young lady."

"Kiss my ass," I snapped. "Serge bullied and harassed me, shoved me into lockers and destroyed my property, but he got to stay in school. But the *rumour* of me sending an email and you're ready to kick me out. Aren't you the tough educator?"

His lips pruned together; his skin flushed beet red. "Listen here—"

Nancy restrained the principal by putting her hand on shoulder. "Can it, Milton. She's fine." The sheriff beckoned me to come to her. "Let's go to the station and get this sorted, okay?"

I took a hesitant step forward.

She gripped my hand and said, "It'll be fine. Promise."

Yeah. Right.

ead Falls didn't have much in the way of crime, and the police station looked more like a reject from a '70s cop show than a modern
facility. There were no glass buildings or high-tech security passcodes
here. Instead, the station was a box with a main counter that ran the
length of the room, with four scarred wood desks, almond-coloured
metal cabinets, and the smell of stale coffee.

"Have a seat by my desk," said Nancy, "and we'll figure this out."

"Okay."

She took off her brown coat and hung it on the rack. Unholstering
her gun, she stuck it in the top drawer of her desk.

"Can I use the bathroom?"

"Sure." She nodded towards the white door. "Go ahead."

"Do you need to watch me or—"

"No. You're not a suspect. I was only placating Milton." A smiled
ghosted her eyes. "I'll talk him down from suspending you for telling
him to kiss your ass."

I rolled my eyes. "He deserved it."

"I know."

I left the main area. The bathroom was a white toilet, rusted sink, and
handrails. I flipped on the lights. A few seconds later, the overhead fan
hummed to life. Nice and loud. Good. I closed my eyes and thought of
Serge. When I opened my eyes, he stood in front of me...with no shirt on.

Or pants.

"Are you kidding?" I hissed.

"What?" He scratched his chest. "I was lounging." He ran his hand
through his hair and gave me a worried grin. "I thought vegging would
leave me less freaked about what's going on, but truth is..."

"Yeah," I sighed. "Listen, can you put on some clothes? You're
distracting?"

"Yeah?" A slow smile spread across his face.

"Not that kind of distracting, genius."

He shrugged.

I blinked and he was dressed in a red sweater, sneakers, and jeans.
"So?"

"When we used the computer, did you send any email?"

His eyebrows furrowed. "You're kidding, right?"

"No. Your dad got some email signed from you—"

The blood rushed from his face. "Sorry, Maggie."

"You—" I glanced at the door and lowered my voice. "*You emailed your dad.*"

"Not on purpose! I was just thinking about all the things I'd never said to him but wished I had."

I groaned.

"You didn't tell me that would happen—"

"Holy crap. You were using the computer to talk to my dad. How did it not occur to you—?"

"Maggie." A sharp rapping sounded at the door. "Honey, are you okay?"

"Uh, yeah, Nancy. Almost done." I moved to the toilet and pressed the cold metal lever. Then I went to the sink and let the water run for a bit. Glancing at Serge, I said, "Stay with me. I have no idea what's going on, but I might need you to give me answers to Nancy's questions."

A smile flashed across his face, lighting his features. "Bet you never thought you'd say that about me."

I caught myself grinning at him. "Bet you never thought you'd *want* to stay to help me." I opened the door and stepped out.

"Were you talking to someone?"

"Just the air."

The wrinkles on her forehead didn't smooth out.

"Nancy, you know I didn't send the email."

She sighed and the muscles on her face relaxed. "I know, sweetie." She led me to her desk.

I sank into the black plastic chair.

Serge hopped on the desk.

"Mikhail's making a big stink—claiming harassment, and"—she blew out a breath and sounded like a bull about to charge—"he's being an idiot." She looked at me. "But you didn't make things easier for yourself."

"Me?" It came out as a squawk.

"Kid, you've led the charge to get him to give his son a proper burial—"

"Which he still hasn't done. Flippin' Serge's been sitting on ice."

"That's because we can't release the body until the investigation's done."

"You know that's just an excuse for them."

"Doesn't matter. You're a thorn in their side and you had an altercation with the reverend."

"The dead should be respected in principle. It's about transitions and moving on. You can't ignore that."

"And you happened to be there when Debbie-Anne's trailer exploded."

I raised my hands. "How's that—"

"She told me you were asking about Serge." Nancy glanced at the deputy standing by the file cabinet. She rose and went around the end of the desk. Folding her arms, she leaned against its side.

Basically, she sat on—through—Serge.

His arms spread out behind her and made her look like a four-armed goddess.

"Well," he said and poked his head through her chest. "This is a little weird."

"You think he murdered his kid."

I lifted my gaze to Nancy's face and tried to concentrate.

Serge pulled back, then poked his head through again. "Hey, if I concentrate, could I see her blood vessels? 'Cause right now, when I stick my head inside her, all I see is dark."

I ignored him.

"Let me try again." He disappeared.

"Fact is, I think he did it, too."

Serge's head exploded out of her chest. He craned his neck to look up at her. "Excellent deduction, Sherlock!" Shooting me a pointed look, he said, "She's hot but she's no genius."

Dad always complained about the amount of spirits that lingered at our house. I think it was practice for this moment right here: when the juxtaposition between ludicrous and intense intersected in the image of a ghost, cop, smart-aleck remarks, and me, pretending I saw nothing but Nancy.

"Tell her to arrest him," said Serge.

"Arrest him," I told Nancy.

"I can't." She stood.

"Almost." Serge gave her a wistful look. "I'm sure I almost saw her blood vessels." He froze for a moment. His face slackened, his eyes went blank. A couple seconds later, light crept back into his features, a human computer shut down and restarted. His spine straightened. He stared at me, then jerked his head in Nancy's direction.

Dead or alive, a man's hormones never stop. I sighed and started an internal count down: 5...4...3...2...

"What do I want to see organs for?"

He stuck his tongue out in what I could only assume was intense concentration.

Then he closed his eyes and flung his hand out in her direction. "Come on." His eyelids snapped open. "Give me boobs."

Seriously, if he wasn't dead, I'd be tempted to kill him. "Why can't you arrest Mr. Popov?" I stood and, as stealthily as possible, pushed Serge off the desk.

His limbs flew out in a perfect belly-flop position and he landed on the floor.

Nancy grimaced. "Evidence."

"But he was beating his kid."

Her scowl deepened and made her forehead pucker. "Do you know what his wife said to me when I asked her about it?"

"That he was a bad kid and they did the best they could." I grimaced. "She said the same thing to me, more or less."

Nancy let her breath out in a slow, long hiss. "That family." She scrubbed her forehead with the back of her hand. "I never liked that kid, but the more I know the parents—"

"The more you understand him."

She looked at me. "Yeah."

"I didn't send that email, Nancy."

"I know, honey. I have to find out who did. Our technology's basic. I can tell it came from your computer, but figuring out who really sent the email and hid behind your IP—"

The front door crashed open.

We whirled.

Dad stormed in. "What the—Nancy, what's going on?" His head swivelled from me to his girlfriend.

I edged out of his view. "I'll let you talk to him first," I said. "You can calm him down better than me." Better for her to deal with him when he was like this. She had a Taser.

Nancy moved to him. "Come here, babe. Let me explain."

"All I got from Don was something about Popov, and Maggie in jail—"

"She's not in jail."

"Since I'm not in jail—" I jerked my thumb toward the door. "Can I go home? You know where to find me."

"We need to talk, sweetie."

Oh, I did *not* like the way she said that. It was a mix of mom and cop, and that couldn't be good.

"Meet me at home?"

She watched me for a minute, then nodded.

"Be there, Magdalene," said Dad. "Because you and I need to have a *long* talk."

Crap. Just what I was afraid of.

CHAPTER TWENTY-THREE

Serge climbed in the passenger seat.

I adjusted my chair and pulled on the belt. The weather, like my luck, had changed. Dark clouds dirtied the sky. "What did you say in the email?"

He reached for the seatbelt, caught himself, and flashed me a grin. "Guess I don't need that." His hand fell to his thigh. Scrunching his face together, he said, "I just got stuff off my chest."

"Like what?" I put my key in the ignition and the car roared to life.

"Like how much I hate him and what a douche-bag I think he is."

The clouds chose that moment to empty their chests of water. Rain pelted the windshield and made the glass fog.

"Here's our problem," he said, spreading his hands.

I glanced at him, incredulous. "*Here* is our problem? Like everything's been so smooth 'till now?"

"There's stuff in there"—he put his hands on his knees—"stuff you wouldn't know...unless I told you."

"Great," I muttered. "Your maniac father thinks you confided in me."

"He won't think that."

"Because why? He'll decide he knows the truth: his dead son's haunting my bedroom and confessing his life's experiences to me?"

There was a brief silence. "Okay, maybe he'll think I confided in you."

"What did you tell me?" I glanced from the rain-darkened road to him.

Serge closed his eyes. "That he had affairs."

I almost swung us into the ditch. "Are you kidding me? Holier-than-Thou Popov was screwing around on his wife?"

"For years. Ever since I was a kid."

"But this town's so small. How did he keep that quiet?"

"Lots of conferences in big cities."

"Wow." My hand slid along the leathered bumps of the steering wheel. "Your family was really screwed—"

"Tell me about it."

We came to traffic light. My foot let up on the accelerator as green gave way to orange. "Unbelievable. He was always going on about God and religion, and being such—"

"A pompous ass."

"And the *whole* time—"

"Welcome to my life," he murmured.

Silence filled the car.

The factors of his life piled on me, one jagged brick after another. "No wonder you were such a bastard."

He laughed. Then he looked at me and regret dimmed the light in his blue eyes. "You have no idea how sorry I am about that."

"I do. Don't worry about it."

"I do worry."

"Well. Stop. It would be different if you were dead and gone, just some jackass who screwed with my life. But you're not." I smiled at him and pulled the car into the intersection. "You're still here. And you're sorry. I believe that. And since I believe it—" I shrugged. "We both need to move on."

"Some of us more than others."

I grinned. "You said it. Not me."

The Golden Chicken Market sign appeared on the horizon. "I need some junk food."

The doorbell chimed as we walked into the store. I headed to the chocolate aisle. Serge followed. I jerked to a stop as a shopping cart turned into the aisle and the person pushing it came into view.

Ice invaded my veins. "Mrs. Popov."

Beside me, Serge blanched. His skin tightened, leaving his jaw and cheekbones standing out in sharp relief.

Mrs. Popov looked at me, but it was like she was looking through me.

"Maggie."

"*Mom.*"

The anguish in Serge's voice twisted my heart.

"Ask her how she's doing," he said.

He gripped my shoulder—hard—and instinct said he was holding on for strength, and not to hurt me.

"Ask her. She's alone with him."

I ran my fingers over my shoulder, to let him know I understood. "Mrs. Popov, how are you doing?"

Her unfocused gaze remained on me...I think.

"Funny you should ask."

I winced. "I didn't write that email—"

The fog cleared from her eyes. She blinked. "What email?"

"Oh, uh, I thought you knew—that Mr. Popov had told you."

She brushed the hair from her temple towards her bun. The bracelet she wore caught the overhead lights and clicked against the metal of her watch. "Mikhail handles all my needs. He's a good provider."

Angry lines cut Serge's face into diagonal slats. "She sounds like a robot. She always does." He stepped toward her. Serge towered over his mother. He glared down at her. "Tell the truth. How much is he beating you?"

You liar. I knew he was beating her!

He flushed red but said, "Ask her. Ask her if it's worse because I'm not around anymore?"

My tongue clung to the roof of my mouth. I wanted to say something, to *really* confront her, but she seemed so fragile, I didn't have a clue how to broach the topic.

Serge rounded on me. "Ask her—make her tell you."

"Um." My hands did a chicken dance, fluttering to her then flapping back and hiding themselves in my back pockets. "Are you really okay? Losing a child is a hard thing—especially when he's so young."

Her gaze grew unfocused again. "He's in a good place."

Serge snorted.

"You don't know it—you wouldn't. But I know he's in heaven looking down on me."

Yeah. Right. At this moment, her son was glaring at her like a disgruntled ogre.

"Uh—"

"You don't like my family," she said. "You think you're better than us—"

"Whoa, *what?*"

"I saw the way you watched us"—her face contorted—"judging us that night at the pool."

"Me judging you—that's nice. Your husband—"

"Is a man called of God."

The venom in her voice made me recoil.

"He has a hard life, a higher calling, and it is up to me to support him—"

"He *beat* your son—"

"*No.* He disciplined him." Her mouth worked from one side to the other; her hands grasped the air. "Serge was difficult, and there are—were—things you don't know about him. Mikhail did his best with him. He did his best with both of us. Serge was a bad—he couldn't help it, but..." She trailed off.

My breath hissed through my teeth.

"And I will protect my family." She drew herself up. "From the evil that comes our way—even when it cloaks itself in lamb's clothing."

Wow, I wanted to punch her. "I'm not the evil—your husband is. And you are, for never standing up to him. Your son is *dead*, Mrs. Popov and it's your fault."

She flinched as though I'd hit her. Curling her bony fingers around the cart handle, she jerked the carrier away. "We'll all pay for our sins."

I jumped back, pressing myself against the shelf of cereal as she wrenched the cart around me. My hand went to my stomach, where the muscles cramped and shook. "She's crazy."

"Don't say that!" Serge's words sparked with fury. "It's not her fault. It's his—he's the one who did it all."

I didn't say anything—I don't know enough about abuse to understand the psychology of pain and violence, but I couldn't forgive Mrs.

Popov for not protecting Serge. She could say what she wanted about him being difficult, but there was a point where he was nothing more than a toddler, a baby, who needed love and compassion, not fists and harsh words.

"She's a victim too," he said. Desperation stretched thin the words, made them more plea than a statement.

"I'm...sure—"

"She is."

His gaze searched mine, looking for comfort? Agreement?

"Something's wrong," he said. "She looks different."

I frowned. "Different? How?"

"I don't know, but something's wrong. Her outline...it's all...edgy."

"Edgy?"

"Can't you see it?"

I shook my head. "She looks normal to me."

"You gotta talk to Nancy—get her to put my mom under protective detail."

I pushed away from the shelves. My legs felt like I had no bones in them and my feet seemed stuck to the floor. "I—" *I want her to burn.* "Let me process this and—"

"It's not her fault—"

It is!

He winced and clutched his head as my words exploded in his mind. "Don't yell!"

I took a breath, held it for a one-two count, then released it. *She had a choice—you were her son.*

You don't understand.

I don't want to. I stalked down the chocolate aisle.

You're supposed to help me.

Yeah—you, not her. She doesn't deserve anything. She's your mother. She should have stuck by you. Instead, she abandoned you—

Are we talking about my mother or yours?

His words, softly spoken in my head, reverberated down my spine and hit their mark.

"We're more similar than you want to believe," he said, "but my mom didn't have a choice. You don't get my dad. *None of us* had a choice." He stopped. His gaze softened. The smell of vanilla scented the air. "Maybe she didn't either."

My chest was tight, brittle. The topmost layer of my skin tingled with icy overlay. A hard stone of emotion stuck in my throat. *Go home. I'll meet you later.*

"Maggie—"

Go.

His mouth fell into a soft line. Serge took a step back and blipped from my sight.

I put my hand on the shelf and bent over, trying to get air back into my lungs.

"Maggie?"

Turning to my left, keeping my head down, I peered at the scuffed, black shoes. "Hey, Jason."

His wrinkled face came into view. "You okay?"

"Yeah, just having a little trouble breathing."

"You want me to call your dad?"

He had a high voice, but he was a soft-spoken man, and the pitch seemed to suit not only his personality, but his small, slight body.

"No, just give me a sec."

"Saw what happened between you and Lydia Popov."

"Great." The town should have the news by six o'clock.

"She's never been anything but Mikhail's puppet."

I stood and took a breath.

Jason straightened to his full height of four feet, ten inches. "I heard they're going to have the funeral."

"They have to—the body can't stay on ice forever."

"No." He waved his right hand as though sweeping away the words. "A real funeral. Public."

"Oh." I blinked. That didn't sound right.

Jason's brown-white eyebrows pulled together. "You okay?"

"Um, yeah—"

He took my hand and pulled me toward the freezers. "Come on. Go out back. There are benches. Sit for a second."

"No—" I leaned back, pushing my weight to my heels and trying to stop our forward momentum. Easier said than done. Years of stacking cans and lifting boxes of lettuce had made Jason strong.

"Amber's out there—"

I stopped pulling. The sudden drop in opposing force set me catapulting to him. I stumbled but regained my balance.

"—she can keep you company." He grimaced. "She had a run in with Lydia too."

"Oh, okay. Thanks." I pushed through the swinging doors that separated the employee area from the store. Flickering lights overhead gave the dank space a slaughterhouse vibe. At the sink, a grim-faced man in black rubber boots hosed down a deli-meat blade. Beside me, boxes of limp lettuce tottered on their skiffs.

"She's over there." Jason nodded towards the exit sign.

"Thanks." I flashed a smile and headed outside. A cool wind tickled its way down my neck. Blinking, I looked around and saw Amber sitting on a wooden crate.

"Hey."

"Hey." I walked over.

"What are you doing here?"

"Came for cookies. Then I ran into Serge's mom—"

Her oval face crimped together. "She's horrible. Can't stand anyone to be happy."

I sat on the crate beside her and pulled my sleeves over my cold fingers. "Like Serge?"

She snorted. "Like anyone."

"Yeah, but...Serge. You seem kinda conflicted."

Amber gave me a blank look.

"He was your boyfriend."

She shrugged and took a swig of orange juice. "He wasn't really 'anyone's' if you know what I mean. He cheated on me all the time."

"Why did you stay with him?"

A shadow passed over her face, turning her brown eyes to the colour of mud, darkening her cheeks, and turned her mouth flat. She shrugged. "Dunno. It was easy, I guess. Who wants to be single?"

"Yeah, but you're pretty and nice. You could have had anyone you wanted."

Again, the shadow passed over her.

"Didn't you ever love him?"

She stared at me. "Why do you care?"

"Because he's dead and no one else seems to care."

"I care."

The way she said it was like his death had inconvenienced her.

"He was never really a man, you know?" She took another drink. Her eyes went unfocused. "He tried, but he couldn't measure up."

"Measure up to whom?"

She blinked. "To anyone."

"You said that too fast."

"What?"

"Too fast. You're talking too fast. Who didn't he measure up to?" The sudden image of Craig flashed into my mind. "Who did you really want?"

"Not him."

"What's really going on? When Serge was alive, you were his shadow. Now, he's dead and you have nothing to say about it."

"I'm too sick for your Nancy Drew act, Maggie." She dug into her pocket and pulled out a handful of pills.

I grabbed her wrist. "What are you taking?"

She wrenched free. "They're just vitamins!" Tossing them down her throat, she downed the last of her orange juice.

"Were you cheating on him, too?"

She snorted. "No." She lifted her gaze from the empty bottle to me. I saw the sincerity in her eyes.

"Never cheated on him. He's gone"—her voice turned heavy—"and I'm free." She tossed the plastic container into the recycling bucket and stood. "I gotta get back to work." Amber turned and moved to the door. Looking over her shoulders, she said, "From one girl to another: stay away from the Popovs."

CHAPTER TWENTY-FOUR

The tires crunched the wind-blown leaves as the car braked to a stop. The wind had picked up. Branches of trees creaked in the wind, rubbed against each other, and sent yellow, orange, and brown leaves scuttling down the street. I pulled my jacket closer and jogged to the front door. Buddha greeted me as I stepped inside.

"Hey, Mutt." I rubbed the underside of his jaw. "Bet you're hungry."

"I miss that."

I glanced at Serge. "Being rubbed under the chin?"

A smile brought light to his face. "No. Hunger."

I shrugged out of my jacket. The lingering smell of last night's leftovers sprinkled the air. Dad obviously wasn't home, yet. Up to me to make dinner.

"I miss hot dogs and hamburgers. And steak." His expression grew wistful. "I really miss steak."

"Can't help you—never been a steak person." I kicked off my shoes and headed into the kitchen.

"How can you not like steak?"

"I don't like the taste—"

He shot me a look like I'd just threatened to kill his dog. "Have you ever had steak?"

I rolled my eyes. "Yeah, and it's not to my taste. However—" I picked Buddha's metal bowl off the floor and scooped a cup of dry kibble inside. Then I went to the fridge and pulled out a can of soft dog food. "He enjoys steak and lucky for him, that's what he's getting tonight." I scooped some into the bowl, mixed it all together and set it in front of my dog. "Stay. Sit."

Buddha dropped to his haunches.

"Good boy. Okay, go ahead."

His large head dived into the bowl.

"My turn," I said. I opened the freezer and peered at the array of pre-packaged meals.

Serge looked over my shoulder.

Weird. I could fell heat coming off his body.

"You can't be serious," he said. "You can't eat that."

"Watch me." I grabbed pre-made lasagne and turned. "Oh, wait. That's all you can do."

He made a face. "Don't be a jerk. Put it back."

"And do what? Starve? I can't cook."

"Sure, you can." He leaned on the counter and stuck his head into the cupboard.

Tried to.

His forehead smacked into the wood. "Ow!" He rubbed his hairline.

"Still working on the whole solid-gas thing?"

"I was practising while you were gone. You must make me nervous."

I snorted. "Talk about the worm turning."

He continued to rub his head. "Find some rice, onions, soy sauce, and an egg."

"Because—"

"I'm going to teach you how to make fried rice."

I closed the fridge door with a muffled *thump*. "*Get out*— you cook?"

"Since I was small."

Knowledge of his home life rushed back to me. "Oh. Uh, I thought your mom—"

"She wasn't always able to"—he swallowed hard, kept his profile to me—"sometimes she couldn't help."

I watched him for a second.

He dropped his hand to his side and jerked his chin toward the cupboard. "We gonna do this?"

"Oh." I started out of my reverie. "Yeah, right. What do we need?"

He repeated the list.

I had just grabbed the soy sauce from the fridge when Buddha scampered down the hall. A few seconds later, the door opened.

"Dad?"

"Yeah." His voice sounded up the steps.

"Nancy with you?"

Nothing.

"Dad?" I heard his footsteps as he came into the kitchen.

"No," he said, "she's coming later." He came to me and gave me a kiss on my cheek. "What's with the groceries on the counter?"

"Serge is going to teach me how to make fried rice."

Dad moved to one of the stools. "This, I have to see." He waved his hand at the chairs. "Anything occupied?"

"No." I frowned. "Actually, there hasn't been anyone…" I turned to Serge. "Since you."

"Anyone?" He repeated.

"Since you came, there haven't been other spirits in the house."

He considered this. "Is that good or bad?"

"I don't know," I said. "You tell me. Have you done anything to keep them away?"

He shook his head. "I'm still trying to figure out why I don't fall through the floors."

"What did he say?" asked Dad.

"He doesn't know." I turned to Serge. "You stay on the floor because you expect to stay on it."

"So if I wanted to sink through—" He began to vanish into the floorboards. Serge yelped and hopped on to the lino.

"What do I do with these?" I held up the soy sauce.

"First things first."

"Need any help?" asked Dad. "Or can I just enjoy this historic moment?"

"Enjoy it," I said. "And have a fire extinguisher ready."

He reached for the bowl of grapes and popped one in his mouth. "Will do."

Fifteen minutes later, the rice was boiling in the pot and the vegetables sat ready.

"What did Nancy have to say?" I asked Dad.

"She's getting suspicious."

"Why? Of what?"

"Of both of us." Dad sighed. "You're not acting like a normal kid and I'm not reacting like a normal parent."

"What are you going to do?"

He shook his head. "Your gifts aren't mine to talk about...she and I aren't *there* yet—"

"You're worried if you tell her, she'll bail."

Dad pressed his lips together.

I sat beside him. "Sorry."

He grabbed my shoulder and squeezed. "Not your problem, kiddo." He gave me a crooked grin. "Not a bad place to be, having a girlfriend and wondering about taking it to the next level."

"He should just tell her," said Serge. "If she can't handle it, why keep going?"

I rolled my eyes. "Dating advice from Serge—'cause you're such an expert."

"What did he say?" asked Dad.

"Nothing."

"Tell him." Serge made a shooing gesture.

"No."

"Tell me." Dad leaned forward.

"No."

Dad pulled out his cell phone. "Look, Serge, tap into the note section and tell me."

I glanced at the ghost. "He looks like he's constipated—"

"Shut up." Serge resumed concentrating.

I popped a grape into my mouth, "—it's not going to work."

Dad's cell beeped.

Serge's face smoothed out. "Showed you."

I ate another grape. "How about that? You used the force within."

He rolled his eyes. "I'm stuck with Yoda."

"Not Yoda." The scent of veggies and starch filled the air and made my stomach growl. I moved to the stove to check the rice. "I'm not much for talking backwards."

Serge's eyes went wide. "He never—" He groaned. "Of all the mediums in the world, why you?"

I grinned. "Just lucky I guess."

Dad laughed. Lifting the phone and turning it around so I could see the screen, he said, "Everything he's saying is texting to me." His gaze roved the room.

"He's by the fridge."

"Oh—yeah, she's no Yoda. Although when she was first born, she was just as wrinkly as—"

"Change of topic, please." I turned off the stove and looked at Serge. "Now what? I think the rice is done."

"Are you sure?"

"How am I supposed to be sure? I boiled it for fifteen minutes. Isn't that enough?"

"Man, I really hope you find a guy who can cook or else you'll die of starvation."

"Shut up."

"I tell her the same thing, Serge."

"You, too. Shut it."

Dad grinned.

"Take the rice off the element and get a frying pan—" Serge looked at me. "You know what a frying pan is, right? Round and flat, with a handle—"

"I was thinking a frying pan was your face."

"Really? Sarcasm when I'm trying to be helpful."

I sighed and grabbed the pan.

"Drizzle a teaspoon of oil and let it heat up."

I did. "Uh, listen, Serge—"

"The way you're talking's making the hair on the back of my neck stand up. I'm dead. Should that really happen?"

"Death is life: subjective."

Dad glanced at me. "What's with the tone?"

"Uh—" I glanced from one guy to the other.

"Just say it," Serge snapped. "You're creeping me out."

"I have to talk to you about Amber."

"Whoa." Dad, his gaze on the phone, stood. He looked up and wiggled the cell. "That's my cue to leave."

"Wha—"

"My phone just went dead."

"Sorry," said Serge. "Must be reactive."

"I'll be in the living room." Dad slid the phone into his chinos. Then he nodded at the stove. "Your oil's going to burn."

"Turn down the heat, Maggie."

I did.

"Now," Serge said as Dad moved out of the kitchen, "add in the onions and garlic. Don't let it sit—move it around on the pan or it'll burn."

The vegetables hit the heat and began to sizzle. The tangy scent of onions melded with the garlic. My stomach didn't just growl. It roared. I ignored it. "Amber."

"What about her?"

"What was really going on with you guys?"

"Dating stuff." He moved past me. "Watch you don't burn it."

I pushed the veggies in a circle. "It was more than that—there was something seriously screwed about your relationship."

He sat on a stool and laughed, but not a happy laugh. "Why does that surprise you?"

"It doesn't—"

"Are the onions translucent?"

I blinked. "What?"

He waved his hand at the pan. "The onions. Translucent. It's a change in colour—"

"I know what it is. I'm just surprised you know, too."

"High end porn." He gave me a sad grin. "It's a real vocabulary booster." He nodded at the pan. "Add the egg."

I cracked the shell and poured the contents onto the hot face. The albumin of the egg bubbled and frothed.

"Scramble it—push it around so you're not just frying it, but scrambling it as well."

I did. "Was she cheating on you?"

He didn't say anything.

There was a *feeling* to the silence, and it scratched against my skin like a wool blanket.

"No," he said finally. "She wasn't cheating on me."

"You're lying." The blanket feeling intensified, made me feel as though it was binding me.

"Nope." He looked me in the eye. "Not lying."

Insight flashed into my mind. "Then I'm asking the wrong question."

His jaw rippled, his mouth tightened.

"How could you not cheat on Amber but still be with—" My eyes widened. "Were you dating Amber? Really dating or was this some weird set up?"

He blinked and broke eye contact. "What a stupid question."

"Serge?"

"Of course we were—I was with her, wasn't I?"

I stared him down.

"No," he said quietly. "I wasn't dating her."

"Then why...why would you lie?"

He rubbed his nose and stared at the wall.

"*Holy.*" I almost dropped the spatula as the answer blinked into my awareness. "It's your dad, isn't it?"

Icy silence rolled from him, and his body turned tight, frozen.

"That's the *only* thing that makes sense. You wouldn't lie for any-one, but you'd do anything to protect your mom."

His mouth snapped together and his lips formed a thin, hard line.

"Oh, man." It came out as a whisper. "You guys were dating since junior high. What your dad did—that's illegal."

"Yeah," he ground out, "and gross."

"Did you ever—with her—"

"That's disgusting, Maggie! You'd think I'd want—" His face con-torted with distaste.

"No, no." I waved the spatula like a white flag. "I just wondered if you'd been dating and he took her—"

Serge snorted. "No. She was always his."

"But the morning after you were killed, she said you had a video."

"Yeah," he said with a smile that held no humour. "For a seemingly weak chick, she knows how to take care of herself, doesn't she? There was never a video." His eyebrows bunched together then pulled apart. "It wasn't always bad between us. We used to talk, Amber and me. She'd come into the church to help her mom and I'd be there— y'know checking up on my mom. But when *he* saw her... He sighed. "She asked me out and at first, I thought everything was okay. But she never wanted to do anything physical—not even kiss. I figured it was because of her mom, but then I walked in on her and him..."

"Gross."

He forced a smile. "It's fine. I cut a deal. I wouldn't tell. He'd lay off with the things he said to Mom and he'd leave me alone."

"But you and Amber were together since junior high."

"So?"

"So, why would your dad kill you? He had your silence. What's the point?"

"He hated me—"

"Yeah, but he'd hated you for seventeen years. Why now?"

He rubbed the back of his head. "I don't know why he decided to do it now. But he did it, Maggie. He killed me. I know it. Your egg's going to burn."

I spun around and scraped it off the pan.

"Add the rice." His voice sounded right behind me.

I looked over my shoulder and saw him a foot away.

He came closer and heat radiated off his body. "What's with the look?"

"What?"

"You got a look on your face."

"You're putting off heat."

He shrugged. "But I also seem solid."

"Yeah, no. Warmth is one thing, but you're *putting off heat.*"

"You don't know why?"

"Not a clue."

"Could that be bad?"

"Could be good."

He snorted. "With my luck? I doubt it." He nodded at the bowl. "Add the rice, now, or else the egg'll just burn."

I did. "Did you threaten to out your dad and Amber, and that's why you got back on the team?"

"Yeah."

"Maybe that's why he killed you. He thought it was just a matter of time before you told someone."

Serge shook his head. "I'd never do that to my mom. Not that it matters, now. All that stuff was on the flash drive. When you were at the cop shop, did you give it to Nancy?"

"No..." I took a breath.

His head tilted to the side, his eyebrows drew together.

"The school had already given your family your stuff."

He closed his eyes. "That was my one shot at getting him."

I turned as a knock sounded behind me.

"I don't want to interrupt—" Dad's head swivelled, left to right.

"He's by the stove."

"Oh, okay." Dad reached into his pocket. "Nancy gave me a copy of the email—I don't know if you and Serge talked about this—" His gaze scanned the area around the stove. "But there's some pretty spicy stuff in here...I'm guessing"—he directed his comment to where he thought Serge stood—"this was you."

"Yeah, sorry. Oh—" He closed his eyes.

Dad's phone beeped. He took it out and read the screen.

"I didn't know it would send to him," Serge said. "I was just thinking how great it would be to tell him off."

Dad sighed. "Unfortunately, it looks like Maggie or I sent it."

"I know. I'm really sorry." He turned to me. "Add the soy sauce and stir the rice."

I did. "I can't believe she had to bring me in."

"They're not going to let this go," said Dad. "Popov came in after you left, screaming about charges and slander."

"He can't charge me with slander," I said.

"I know." Dad sat down and put the phone face up on the counter. "Slander is saying defamatory things. It would have to be libel because the accusations were written."

"I wasn't looking for a clarification on legal charges." Turning off the stove, I moved the pot to a cold element. "I meant I wasn't home. I couldn't have sent it."

"I don't think that will stop Popov." His fingers flicked at the page, bending and creasing the corners. "Serge, what you said in this letter—"

"It's all true."

Dad looked at the phone and swore.

I took out two bowls and dished the rice into them.

"Maggie, do you know everything Serge said?"

"No." I handed him a bowl and reached for the letter. "Does it get worse?"

Dad winced. "Depends on your definition."

I scanned the email. "Details of abuse, Amber, and you say he was stealing from the church." I looked at Serge. "Can any of this be proved?"

"I wish." Both Dad and Serge spoke.

"Amber loves him," said Serge. "She'll never tell."

"Toss me a fork and a pop, would you?" said Dad.

I grabbed the utensil. "Catch."

Dad flinched and crossed his arms in front of his face. "Don't even joke about that."

"Wuss."

I gave him the fork, then headed to the fridge. "Well, that explains the water polo game. I saw Mr. Popov with two straws but Mrs. Popov never had a drink. Plus, Amber and the reverend were together. I saw them coming out of the hallway." Cold air blasted me as I opened the door. I scanned the shelves of milk, orange juice, and leftovers, looking for pop. It was on the bottom shelf.

"Wow, Maggie, this is good. I'll even bet I won't get food poisoning this time."

I rolled my eyes. "I thought we'd agreed we wouldn't talk about that incident."

"You're cooking," said Dad. "Can I help it if poisoning's at the front of my mind?"

As I reached for a can of Coke, the puzzle piece fell into place, and I froze. I slowly closed the door and faced the two men. The memory of the night of the game came rushing back. Amber. Popov with two straws.

Serge caught my gaze. His arms, crossed at his chest, slowly dropped.

Dad looked up and stopped mid-chew. "What?"

"I think we can prove it."

They both frowned. "How?"

I moved to Serge, touched his arm. "I'm sorry"—my gaze moved to my dad—"but I think Amber's pregnant."

CHAPTER TWENTY-FIVE

Serge's face went ashen. "Pregnant? Are you sure?"

Dad followed the ghost's side of the conversation on his cell.

"Amber said she was sick—maybe it's morning sickness. She said she was taking vitamins to feel better, but what if they were for the baby?"

Dad's face wrinkled. "That's pretty fluffy."

I took a breath and met Serge's gaze. "She was drinking orange juice."

"Now, I'm even more confused." Dad's cell beeped and he looked down. "Oh." He looked up. "She never drank OJ. And this is important because…"

"Folic acid's important for the fetus."

Dad's eyes narrowed.

"I saw it on an ad."

"So…no personal exploration on the topic."

"Geez, give me some credit."

The cell beeped.

Serge's jaw dropped and he spun around. "Sorry, Mr. Johnson. I was just thinking it."

The doorbell rang.

Dad stood, his body stiff. "Don't think that about her. *Ever.*" He moved with deliberate care and went down the stairs.

"What did you think?"

Serge groaned.

"Seriously."

"I just wondered how you'd be in bed."

I laughed. "Yeah, my dad wants me to be the second coming of Mary: give him grandchildren but do it through immaculate conception."

He walked to the counter and stood, rubbing his chin with the back of his hand.

"What?"

He did a half-turn to me, then spun back to his sentry position. "It's just—"

"What?"

"Your dad." He sighed and his shoulders dropped. "He was actually being nice to me. I screw up even when I'm dead."

"Whoa, slow the horses down before you fall off the cliff. He's fine."

"I said something grossly inappropriate to his kid."

"Wow. Really? You're feeling remorse?"

"You know—" He sank onto the stool. "Ever since I exploded, I've been feeling...calmer. I don't understand half the crap going on, but I don't feel as angry." His blue eyes fixed on mine. "I thought, maybe, this was my chance to sort of redeem myself...maybe get early parole from hell or something."

"I think you're putting a lot of pressure on a simple statement. Trust me, Dad's not going to hold it against you. And you're not going to hell."

"It's not your dad I'm worried about—well, it is, a little." He took a breath that shuddered his chest. "You're good people, Maggie. And when you were being nice, I thought...maybe, maybe I could be nice. Be good. But now—" He ran a hand through his hair. "If I can't even keep it together for you guys, what's going to happen on the other side?"

"I still think you're over-thinking."

"You don't know," he said. "No one's ever come back."

"Probably because if I got the answers, it would take the point out of life."

"I'm dead. I don't need a point to my—"

"Hey Maggie." Dad's voice sounded down the hallway. "Nancy's here."

"We'll finish this later," I said.

A couple of seconds later, they came into the kitchen.

"How are you doing, sweetie?" Nancy wrapped me in her embrace.

"Good. I didn't write that email."

"I know." She smiled, but it left her face as quickly as it came. Tiredness lined her eyes, made her skin sallow.

"Hard day?"

"Mikhail Popov's an idiot."

Dad's phone beeped. "Sorry, should charge that sucker." He grabbed the cell and, after shutting if off, plugged it into the outlet.

Serge gave me a sheepish shrug.

"We need to talk." She took off her leather jacket and draped it on a chair by the table. Fluffing the cowl of her mint-green mohair sweater, she said, "What do you think happened?"

"Uh—I think someone else did it—" I wracked my brain, trying to remember any buzzwords from the cop shows I watched. "Maybe someone bounced it off another router or...stuff and used my IP address to hide behind."

Her clear blue eyes seemed to bore into me.

"Maybe." She crossed her arms over her chest.

I adopted a relaxed pose by leaning against the counter by the stove and sticking my hands in my jeans. "What else could it be?"

She said nothing.

Seriously, it felt like her eyes were drilling into my skull and rooting for information. No wonder she'd had one of the highest conviction rates when she'd worked in Vancouver. Nancy was the perfect mix of Buddhist patience and drill-sergeant resolve. The urge to confess my misdeeds pushed against my voice box.

She turned to dad and smiled. "How about some tea?"

"Sure." His relief in the change of subject—however brief—showed in his too-quick response.

Nancy's infrared gaze zeroed in on him.

"Are you hungry?" asked Dad. "Maggie cooked some rice."

"Maggie *cooked*?"

That was the proverbial smoking gun, proof positive I must be up to something bad.

Her eyebrows were low over her eyes, and I could barely see her pupils.

"I'm trying to be more helpful."

"Uh huh." She said it like she was debating if she should put me in cuffs or Taser me and *then* cuff me.

Dad's phone beeped.

"Shoot. I really gotta stop doing that," muttered Serge.

"Wasn't that off?" Nancy asked.

"Must need a new battery," said Dad.

"Why? Because it works too well?" she shot back.

"Why don't we sit?" I moved from the stove and went to the table.

The chair scrapped against the floor. I brushed the cushion and sat. "I can't tell you what happened."

Serge dropped into the seat next to me.

So did Nancy.

"Well," he said, spreading his arms wide, "this is awkward and a little too familiar." He gave me a goofy grin. "You think she's psychically attracted to me?"

I coughed to cover up my laugh.

"You know what Pete told me when he retired as the head of the department?" she asked.

I shook my head.

"He told me to watch you because you had a knack for catching trouble."

"Trouble was the name of Mrs. Potterly's cat, and she was always getting lost—the cat, not Mrs. Potterly. Although at the end—"

"Maggie—"

Nancy's voice went dead quiet—the kind of soft tone I was sure preceded her shutting off video surveillance in the interrogation room.

"—do I strike you as an idiot?"

"No, ma'am." I glanced at Dad.

He stood behind her, a pensive look on his face.

"I've got a murdered kid and a man getting messages from his dead son—messages that implicate him in serious offences."

"Yes, ma'am."

"Does this seem like something I'd take lightly?"

"No, ma'am."

"Does this moment strike you as a moment for levity?"

"No, ma'am, but Trouble really was—no, ma'am."

Serge flinched. "Whoa. That's a jump in her energy—like getting zapped by static." He shifted and rose from the table. "She's ticked and afraid. Not a good combo." Serge walked to where Dad stood.

Nancy leaned in. "What is going on?"

My breath turned to ice. Then, I opted for truth-as-misdirection. "I think Amber's pregnant and Mr. Popov's the dad."

Her eyes widened. "How do *you* know this?"

"I saw her today, drinking orange juice and taking vitamins. She hates orange juice."

"And the email?"

Dad's gaze and mine met.

Nancy swivelled from me to him. "Who's protecting who?"

"We protect each other," said Dad.

"She's spiking again," said Serge.

How are you doing that? I projected the question to him.

"Not a clue," he said. "I just sense it in her."

What kind of fear?

He frowned. "There are types?"

Can you tell what she's afraid of?

"How do I do that?"

Concentrate.

He closed his eyes.

Hurry.

"Not helping."

Nancy stood, slow.

"I sense pain in the fear," said Serge, his eyes scrunched together.

What does that mean?

"How am I supposed to know?" he asked irritably. "You're the resident Deadhead."

The shrill ring of her cell jarred us.

She yanked it out. "Nancy." She listened; her face went white. "I gotta go."

"Nancy?"

She pushed back, sped for the stairs. Then she skidded to a stop. "This isn't over." She pointed her index finger at me, then Dad. "And you two better decide what your story is."

The next day, the reason for her sudden departure was scrawled on the wall posts of the social networking sites. The words "Amber tried to kill herself" glowed from the screen of my cell, black words encased in a blue bubble. I made eye contact with Dad from my spot at the kitchen table. "We need to go to the hospital."

Dad folded his arms and shook his head. "No."

"Dad—"

"No, Maggie. Firstly, they wouldn't let us in. We're not family and she'll be under psychiatric watch. Secondly, you weren't her friend. You have no reason to go."

"But I have information!"

He stared at me. "What's your source?"

"I get it—"

"No! You obviously don't get it."

I flinched at his tone.

Dad pointed out the window. "Kids are dying, Maggie. Popov *murdered* his son. What do you think you're going to do?"

"I don't know! But you're the one who told me this ability was a gift, not a curse—that I was supposed to embrace it."

"That was before, when you were dealing with long-dead ghosts or spirits from halfway across the world. Now, you're in the middle of a murder investigation." Dad put his hands on my shoulders.

His fingers, cold on my shirt, tightened and bit into my skin.

"Honey, I can't risk it. I can't risk *you*."

"What am I supposed to do with the information I have?" My voice pitched hysterically.

He yanked me into a hug, his arms strong, his body shaking. "I don't know, my darling girl, but it ends now. It has to."

Serge sat on the table but said nothing.

"When you were born," Dad said, "You needed a lot of attention and care and your mom—" He stopped and swallowed. "She wasn't ready for a child."

I took his hand. "I know."

"It was just me and you needed me, all the time. As you grew older, you needed me even more to help you figure out this talent, to guide you to your path and support your gift." He looked up and gave me a bittersweet smile. "You're so grown up now, but you're still so young to me. I—the past few years, it's gotten better. You go out, you have friends." He squeezed my fingers. "You have a boyfriend. I don't want to take that away from you."

"Are you sure we can't trust Nancy—"

"If Nancy can't accept your gift, she'll *fear* you and people notice that. You have one more year," he said. "Then you can leave this town and go to university."

"There won't be a 'then' if you don't tell her. She'll leave. Nancy's straightforward and upright. She's not into greys or shadows. If you don't tell her, she'll walk out the door." I gripped his hand. "Dad, you love her. You can't let her go."

"I can," he said quietly. "You're my daughter."

"Don't." Visions of my dad, alone and lonely, made my throat clog and brought tears to my eyes. "You can't keep sacrificing—"

"I'm a dad. It's what we do." He gently pushed me away. "Go to your room. The decision's been made."

"But—"

Serge came up behind me. His heat warmed my back. The scent of rain surrounded him. "He's right, Maggie. This ends here."

"What about you?" I turned and made eye contact. "You planning on living in limbo for eternity?"

He shrugged. "The world is full of mediums. I'll find someone else."

My voice box bobbed. "This isn't fair—"

"There's a difference between fair and right, and this is it."

I looked at Dad, then Serge.

The ghost put his hand on my shoulder. "Relax. You did all you could."

Logic said they were right. Common sense said to go with what they advised, and protect myself.

"This isn't a failure," said Dad. "Maybe you weren't supposed to save Serge, maybe the point was to *try.*"

I sighed. "Fine. You're right. I won't do it anymore. Let someone else find proof of Mikhail's guilt." I glanced at Serge. "You can hang around as long as you like. You don't have to go looking for another medium righ—"

The radio by the toaster clicked on.

I froze. "Serge, was that—"

"*Maggie.*" The whisper rose from the speakers, a trembling melody of fear and warning, and plucked at my terror with the exquisite skill of a violin master.

Serge's gaze slid to the radio. "What the—?"

"*Maggie.*"

The ghost took a step back.

"Honey? Dad reached for me with one hand and grabbed his beeping cell with the other. Glancing at the screen, he asked Serge, "Can you hear it?"

"You can't?"

"All I hear is static."

"*Maggie.*" The Voice sounded as though it was weeping.

"Dad—" I grabbed at my chest. "It feels like there's something on my ribs."

"Just take a breath."

"I...can't." I bent over. "My heart hurts."

"*He's coming. For you, Maggie. He comes for you.*"

My fingers and toes turned to ice. Tremors wracked my body. "Breathe. I can't—" The words came in panicked, guttural gasps. I dropped to my knees.

Dad followed me down. His pupils had dilated so much, only a small ring of brown bordered the black circles. "Serge! Can't you do something?"

"I don't—Maggie. What do I do?"

"*It's too late. He's coming. He's coming.*"

Dad stumbled to his feet, lunged for the radio, and ripped the cord from the socket.

Blessed silence swept into the room.

The pain in my chest lessened. I took a breath that seared my lungs. "Thanks—"

The radio clicked back on. "*Maggie.*" The voice paused. Then, it took up its mournful keening, again. "*Oh, Maggie.*"

My heart constricted. The muscles twisted, contorted until it felt as if the organ was being turned inside out. Sweat pushed out from my skin, not in drops, but in sheets of salty water that poured onto the floor. The weight on my chest spread to my back and my kidneys. Invisible hands reached into my torso, grabbed and wrenched my stomach. They yanked my intestines, tried to pull them through my skin and out of my body. I vomited on the floor, crying, retching, unable to breathe, and sure I was about to die.

"Serge! Do something! Help my daughter!"

Serge fit his body over mine, pushed his mouth to my ear, and pulled the sweat-slicked hair off my forehead. "Maggie, help me. I don't know what to do. Tell me how to help!"

"I—" There was no air, no exhalation on which to carry the words. I was trying to talk and inhale at the same time. The pain luminesced in my veins, the agonizing burn lit my brain and made my sight blur. "—I don't know—"

"Okay, okay, I can do this. I can help." Serge tightened his hold. "Feel me breathing. Take my breath."

Dark spots flickered in my vision, punctuated by sharp pinpricks of colour. My heart crashed against my chest. The voice may have still been on the radio, but now it was also in my head, reverberating, softly crying, wailing my name.

"*Maggie. Oh, Maggie.*"

"Maggie, I can hear him—"

Oxygen deprivation made Dad's voice sound `like it came from a tunnel.

"—I can hear Serge. Do what he says. Take his breath."

"*He wants you.*"

Serge grabbed my hand, unclenched my fingers and put them against his belly. "Feel the breath. Imagine it going into you."

I bore down and fought the convulsions wracking my body. Clutching at Serge, trying to get his blurry image to pull into focus, I pretended he was a lifeline, a tube through which oxygen flowed from his fingers and torso into my skin and diffused through my veins.

Tendrils, bubbly sensations—more pins and needles then effervescent fizz—prickled my fingers and spread their cool foam through my flesh. I gurgled, gasping for breath and choking on hysteria.

"Slow."

I let Serge's voice guide me.

"*It's too late. He's coming.*"

"Just take it slow. Breathe like it's your air, not mine."

I inhaled. The weight lifted but didn't disappear. The tremors lessened but didn't evaporate, and I knew—*I knew*—the only thing that would take the pain from me. "I won't quit," I gasped the words to the voice echoing in my head and vibrating the radio speakers. "I won't quit. I'll stay. I'll transition Serge."

The sudden stop of pain rushed through my body like a hurricane wind, skyrocketed my blood pressure, and pushed air into my lungs with the force of a fighter jet's engines. I clawed at my throat and lungs, fighting the urge to rip at my skin.

Serge pushed me back against the fridge, propped me up by the door. "Don't fight it. Just breathe."

Dad's face hovered behind him. His lips repeated the instructions. "Just breathe."

I took a breath, a second, and a third. Clarity of vision returned. The thrumming roar in my ears dimmed. My veins stopped glowing.

"Maggie."

I looked at Dad.

Tension turned the edges of his lips white. He squinted as if staring into a bright light. Gripping me by the shoulder, he said, "Just breathe, baby." His voice cracked. "Just keep breathing. Let Serge help you."

I nodded. Keeping one hand on Serge's wrist and my other hand pressed against his stomach, I focused on his breath, held to the rhythm of his inhalations and exhalations because it was the only thing keeping my body from exploding.

"I'm here," he said. "Now and forever. We'll take care of this, right?" Serge smiled through his tears. "I promise—I swear, I'll protect you. I won't let that voice get you. I won't let my dad hurt you."

Help Serge or be killed by the poltergeist. Help Serge and possibly be killed by his psychotic father.

What a set of options.

CHAPTER TWENTY-SIX

I hate hospitals. For a chick who deals in death and blood, I shouldn't freak at that smell—but that antiseptic-human waste-overcooked food smell always makes me gag. I stepped inside and the automatic doors swished closed. Pale-white fluorescents bathed the lobby in light that seemed starved, hungry as it sucked the colour out of the green and pink surroundings.

A nurse in blue scrubs with multi-coloured fish stood at the counter, behind a wall of Plexiglas. She looked up as we came in.

"I'm looking for Amber Sinclair," I said. "I'm a friend."

"She's not allowed to see visitors."

"She's in ICU?" asked Dad. "I'm sorry. Of course, we'll go. We thought we'd support Amber's Mom—" He glanced at me. "As a parent..."

The mask of professionalism loosened, slipped from the nurse's face. Her brown eyes softened, so did her mouth. "No, it's not that—" She tilted her head and gave me a gentle smile. "When kids try to harm themselves, we put them in the psychiatric ward. We need to make sure they don't hurt themselves again. I wish I could help, but we have to protect the patient's privacy. And the family's. Unless they give permission to have visitors, there's nothing we can do."

I nodded. "Oh, of course."

"Can we see her mom?" Dad asked.

"I promise, I won't try to sneak in or anything," I said.

The nurse smiled. "Those doors are kept locked. You can't sneak in."

"Right."

She shook her head. "I'm sorry. That area is restricted." She took a clipboard off the counter. "I wish I could help."

"Are you going to see her?" I asked. "Maybe if Amber's mom gives you permission...?"

She hesitated. "I have to do rounds. I can't guarantee—"

"It's okay." I rushed the words. "I'll wait." Glancing at the entrances that banked the left and right sides of the check-in kiosk, I asked, "Which door will you come from?"

"The left."

Dad caught my gaze, and I knew he guessed what I was trying to do.

"I—the ward isn't on the main floor, is it?" He faked the perfect combination of curiosity and concern. "Those poor patients, having everyone walk by their doors—"

"It's on the seventh floor," she said. "Privacy is everything."

Dad smiled. "Isn't it, though?"

We moved away from the pink counters with their white tops.

"Did Serge come?" Dad glanced over his shoulder and watched the nurse.

"Would you?"

"Point taken." Reaching into his pocket, he pulled out a loonie. "There's a vending machine by the doors. I suddenly feel thirsty." He moved as the nurse left the kiosk. He smiled, softly chatting, holding his loonie like a pass card.

When she got to the door, the nurse scanned her card into the reader. Dad—such a gentleman—held the door open for her. She smiled and left. He let it close, waving for me with the other hand, and kept his gaze on the nurse through the door's narrow window.

"I need to let it close in a little more," he whispered. "Can you grab it at the bottom?"

Bending, I did as instructed.

He left, moved to the vending machine. The coin rattled down the tube and a pop followed with a dull *schunk*. Popping the tab, he took a sip and gazed through the window. "Okay, she's gone. Go and be careful. We've never been in a psych ward."

"Not for a lack of my trying to get you committed."

"So funny."

"I try."

"Try harder and be sensitive to the environment, this time."

"Will do."

He looked down at me. "Are you going to be okay? Some of these people will be legitimately mentally ill, but some..."

"I know. I'll be fine. The dead hardly linger in hospitals. They're sick and tired and death is a comfort, a release. I don't think anyone will be there."

"Maybe," he muttered. He pressed his finger to the middle of his forehead, to the spot between his eyes. "Maggie. You glow when you touch Serge, people are trying to kill themselves, and other ghosts don't want to be around you. Doesn't that strike you as odd?"

"Well, when you put it like that..."

He rolled his eyes. "Go. And be careful. If they catch you, I'll deny all knowledge of you and your operation."

"That's what I love best about you. The way you always have my back."

"Go before I change my mind."

I gave him a quick kiss on the cheek and left. The white hallway was quiet and empty. At the end of the corridor I saw a set of cream-coloured elevator doors. I took a second to pull my hand over my sleeve and pushed the 'up' button. When the cab arrived, it opened to reveal '70s fake wood paneling and large, white posters, admonishing visitors to wash their hands. The ride on the elevator didn't take long but with each passing floor, my anxiety rose. I could talk big and tough, but when it came down to it, I was praying Nancy didn't freak. The bell chimed and the doors slid open.

There was nothing in the barren hallway, no posters or signs, hand sanitizers or people. Instead, a lone desk stood by a set of double doors that had windows on their upper half. The kidney-shaped desk was pink on the bottom, with a white surface.

"No sharp edges," I muttered. "Just in case."

"What are you doing here?"

I yelped as I stumbled back.

Nancy stood by the open door.

I saw a bubble-gum pink hallway beyond, empty, sterile. "Hey."
I lifted my hand in a wave and tried to look casual, which made me
look like a dork.

"And I ask again—" She stepped forward. The door slipped from
her fingers and slid closed on its hydraulic hinges. "What are you
doing here?"

"I wanted to talk to Amber's mom, and you," I said. "Especially you."

She pressed her lips together. The lines of her body went frozen, stiff.

"Uh—maybe I should talk to Amber's mom, first."

"What do you want with May?"

I shrugged. "Her daughter tried to kill herself. I thought she might
want some comfort."

Nancy's eyes narrowed to slits. "Shouldn't you want to talk to
Amber?"

"I thought they'd have her sedated."

She grunted.

"So…?"

"You gonna tell me what's going on between you, your dad, and
this case?"

"I will if you let me see Mrs. Sinclair."

"How about if I arrest you for coming to this floor?"

"Dad wants to tell you what's going on"—the words came out in
a torrent—"only, he's afraid of what it'll mean for me and you, and
the relationship between all of us. I want to tell you but he's freaked."
I took a shallow breath. "He loves you, Nancy, you know that."

"I love boa constrictors," she said. "That doesn't mean I trust them."

"Please. Let me see Amber and Mrs. Sinclair, and then I'll do my
best to make Dad talk to you."

She sighed. "It's not my place to give that kind of permission. They
need privacy—"

"It's all over the social networks," I said. "And what people don't
know, they're making up. Someone has to quell the rumours at school."

She cursed. "Professionally, I can't care about that. As a person—"
She stopped as May came through the doors.

May turned hollow eyes to me, then looked back, down the hall-way to where her daughter lay.

"They gave her something to sleep," she said. "She was...upset."

"I'm sorry this happened." I stepped closer, but gave the older woman space.

"I've just been standing here—" Her fingers knotted and bunched at her chest. "What was going on that I didn't see this? She was a trial but the past few years..."

I didn't say anything.

"They made me hold onto her jewellery." She opened her palm to show me the gold necklace, earrings, and her bracelet. Mrs. Sinclair turned to face to me. "What do I do with them?" she said, the dull-ness of her tone edged by barely contained hysteria. "I don't want to lose them. Sometimes they make me leave the room. What if someone takes them when I'm gone." She took a sharp shallow breath. "I can't keep carrying them around—"

"What about your purse? Can we keep them in there?"

"What if they fall out? What if something happens? If I can't see them, I can't protect her!"

"Ma'am, are we talking about the jewellery or your daughter?" Gently, I put my hands around hers. The icy cold of her skin ripped the heat from my body. Frozen tingles spread up my arms to my elbows. "Why don't we find you a chair?"

Her body bowed in half.

Awkwardly, I put my arm around her.

She fell against my chest, and for all her voluptuous curves, she felt fragile, a crystal figurine too easily broken.

"How could she do this?" It was a half-sob-half-moan. "How could she *do* this!" Mrs. Sinclair reeled back, clapped her hand to her mouth. "Oh! Not that I'm angry—" Tears rushed down her cheeks.

"I know, ma'am."

She sniffled, her mouth trembled. Her auburn curls caught in the flow of her tears and stuck to her face. Still bowed like a hunchback, she looked at her daughter. "Whatever it was, we could have gotten over it. I would have done *anything*."

"She'll wake soon," I said, grateful that I could utter the truth of that statement. "You can talk then." A pleather and pressed wood chair stood by the door. "Until then, why don't you sit?"

She nodded and stumbled for the seat. Grabbing my hand, she said, "Thank you." Her fingers slid from my grip, leaving the jewellery in my hands. Her wounded gaze returned to the hallway. "Thank God the reverend will be here soon."

The hair on my arms and the back of my neck rose as though exposed to electricity. "Sorry?"

"Reverend Popov." She sniffed, took a breath, and seemed to calm down. "He'll make it better."

I froze. Nancy's expression went so stony, she could have been made of granite.

"I phoned him as soon as I got the news, but he's in Tender Flats. He left immediately, but it's a three-hour drive and the roads are…" She seemed to realize she was on the verge of babbling.

She looked up at me. "I know you and his son had problems."

"Had."

"He's a good man. Caring and attentive—he's been so good to me and my daughter."

I nodded. What else could I do? But the blood rushed in my veins and made my heart slam against my chest. What was this woman going to do when she found out that Amber's current condition probably had a lot to do with the pregnancy the pastor was responsible for?

"Especially Amber. He's been so sweet to her."

She didn't know the half of it.

Mrs. Sinclair clutched her stomach. "He'll make it right. He always does."

Yeah, right. I felt heat on the back of my neck and turned. Serge.

Sadness darkened his eyes. "I couldn't stay away. We didn't get along, but this…" He shook his head. "This is no good." His gaze lingered on May. He took a step toward her.

I thought back to what Bruce had said about Serge and an older woman. *Serge?*

He looked my way.

You and May—

A frown wrinkled his forehead.

Bruce said he thought you were sleeping with—

"That's disgusting. You think I did Amber's mom?" He made a face. "No, I guess I deserved that." He sighed. "I never—I saw her a couple of times. I wanted to tell her about Amber and who she was really sleeping with but in the end..." He took a breath. "It was enough that he was breaking my mom's heart. I didn't need to destroy someone else's mom just to get revenge." His gaze flicked to the door. "Maybe I should've. Maybe then—"

I can't believe she did it.

He sighed. "Believe me, it was always in her...when she and my dad got together, she stopped talking about it." Serge's expression went bleak. "Of course, she stopped talking to me, period. But still..." He frowned at my hands. "Why do you have my mother's jewellery?"

This is Amber's.

He shook his head. "No. That bracelet."

I looked down at the item.

"He bought it for her on their honeymoon. It was a gift of his love, so she says. She's never taken it off. He wouldn't let her. It's proof of their commitment—he says," Serge finished with a contemptuous twist of his mouth.

So, why would she?

"She wouldn't." His face slackened. "He made her. He made her take it off. She wasn't going to be his wife anymore."

You think he was going to divorce your mom?

"Maybe not legally, but if he gave Amber the bracelet..."

I frowned and glared at the linoleum floor. Her baby's daddy wanted her...so why had she tried to kill herself? Guilt over Mrs. Popov? Amber seemed too self-serving for that.

"Do you see that?"

I lifted my gaze and turned it to the bed.

"That fuzz."

Fuzz?

"There's fuzz." He cocked his head. "Like poplar fluff. It's floating."

I looked through the window in the door, into the hallway, but saw nothing. My eyebrows pulled together. That sounded familiar. *Where had I heard that? A ghost.* I squeezed my eyes shut, trying to remember.

"Maggie?"

My eyes snapped open.

Mrs. Sinclair was staring at me. "Honey, are you okay?"

"Um, yeah."

"Can you remember?" asked Serge. "About the fuzz."

Then I realized my mistake. I'd come to the hospital believing what I'd been told about Amber. Psychic gifts—mine, anyway—work a lot like electricity. If I don't flip the switch and concentrate, I don't sense anything. I took a breath and tuned in. *Oh, man.*

Fuzz.

"Maggie?" Mrs. Sinclair rose. "Honey, what's with that look on your face? You've seen a ghost?"

Nope. Just remembered one. My eyes slid to Serge.

"What's the fluff?"

Leftovers.

He frowned. "What?"

She didn't try to kill herself. Someone tried to kill her.

CHAPTER TWENTY-SEVEN

"What do you mean someone tried to kill her?"

Dad hissed the question as we walked away from the main doors. Nancy stood in the entranceway, her arms folded across her chest.

"There was cottony fluff floating around her." I looked over at my shoulder at the cop. "Uh, listen, I may have bartered the visit with the understanding you'd spill your guts to her."

Dad jittered to a stop, the skin on his face tightening. He glared at me. "You did not."

"I did."

"Maggie!"

"Look, it's either you spill our family secret or the formless voice on the radio kills me! Take your pick."

"What a choice." He sighed. "Why fluff?"

I shrugged. "Why not fluff? I don't understand why certain things appear, but if there's fluff, someone tried to kill her."

"Come on." Dad threw his arm around my shoulder. "Let's go home. We'll eat and figure out how to spend our lonely, boring nights once word of your gift spreads and we're ostracized from the town."

"Oh, our nights'll be busy. I'm going to sell my story to a cable network and get a reality show where I read cards and explain why psychics can't win the lottery."

He gave me a half grin.

"Nancy will be fine. After a good night's sleep, you'll see. It'll get better in the morning."

But it didn't get better.

Three days later, it got infinitely worse.

CHAPTER TWENTY-EIGHT

"Something's wrong," said Serge.

"You'll have to be more specific."

He paced from one end of my room to the other. "Bad. Something bad will happen."

"That's not more specific. It's just more words."

"Don't you feel it?" He turned worried eyes to me.

"What does it feel like?"

"Like there's a monster in my closet and the door's creaking open."

"Crap." I flipped off the TV. "Let's go see what's going on." I crawled off the bed and pulled my hoodie over my head.

"How?"

"We're going for a drive." Dad was sleeping, so I left a note on the table for him. After making sure Ebony and Buddha had enough water and treats for the night, we got in the car and I started the engine.

"How will this help?" Serge reached for his seatbelt.

I didn't bother to point out the futility of his action. "You'll feel a strong pull to go in one direction. If we drive around long enough, you'll take us where we need to go."

He nodded.

I backed the car out of the garage and headed east. We drove in silence. I looped around our neighbourhood, branching out farther and farther, but Serge said nothing.

"Aren't you feeling anything?" I asked.

"Miserable." He hunched in the seat. "I feel miserable."

"Stop thinking about how you feel and start thinking about how the feeling feels."

"What?"

"You're thinking about how the feeling makes you feel. Stop it."

"Being dead is very confusing."

"So's being alive. Just concentrate on the feeling, okay?"

In the dark, he nodded.

I figured it would take a while for him to figure out the difference between the two emotions, so I headed to the Tin Shack to grab a shake. There was a short lineup of cars and two lengths in front of me, I saw Craig's vehicle.

"You really love him, don't you?"

I started. "What?"

"Captain Polo."

"Oh. You saw the car, too?"

He nodded. "That and your aura went pink."

"What colour was it before?"

He shrugged. "I couldn't see it before."

"Oh."

"So. Do you?"

"I dunno...I guess." I glanced at Serge then pulled the car forward. "He's the first guy who actually paid attention to me."

Serge grunted.

"Why don't you like him?"

"There's something wrong with the guy. I know it. I feel it."

"Like that 'something bad' feeling?"

"He's not..." His eyebrows pulled together in frustration. "He's not what he seems. I just know it. And he's creepy. Always watching me."

I snorted. "No kidding, Sherlock. Everyone was always watching you—who wanted to be in your way when your firsts started flying?"

The dashboard light lit up his wince. "Still...he's no good, Maggie. Trust me."

We both froze and looked at each other.

"Never thought I'd say that to you," he said.

"Never thought I'd consider it."

"Are you, really?"

I pursed my lips. "I can't discount it. You're on the other side, which means you've got information I don't. But I don't think you're right. You and Craig hated each other."

"He watched Amber," Serge said quietly. "Always subtle, always out of the corner of his eye, but she was always in his sights."

My heart clenched. "He doesn't care about her. Not that way."

"Are you sure?"

The clench became a full-fisted twist. The truck in front of me pulled ahead. I moved to the order window and asked for a chocolate shake. "I don't want to talk about this," I said when the window closed and the cashier moved away. "You don't have any right to tell me anything." The words and my tone came out harsher than I intended and I expected him to push back.

Instead, he softly said, "I know."

Two silent minutes later, we were back on the road and driving.

"Feel anything, now?"

"No."

"Are you trying to concentrate?"

"I'm going to implode if I try any harder. It's a weird feeling, okay? And it makes me feel like vomiting."

"Ghosts can't vomit."

"They're not supposed to put off heat, either."

I couldn't argue that. "This isn't going to work unless you start being objective. Whatever it is, it can't hurt you. Trust me, you're dead."

He laughed softly.

I realized I'd never heard him laugh. It was a nice sound, deep and lovely, and it made me sad to think it had taken us so many years to get to this moment.

"I'm trying, promise."

But ten minutes of driving, we were still in the psychic boonies. So, I followed a hunch.

I drove toward his home.

"Whoa." His eyes widened and he gripped the dashboard. "Maggie, turn around."

"Why? Is the feeling getting fainter?"

He shook his head. "I'm going to hurl. Turn around."

"Can't. This is the right direction."

He squirmed in his seat and whimpered.

"It'll be okay. I promise." I glanced at him, waited for him to meet my eyes. Then I said, "Trust me" and turned back to the road.

His breathing slowed—a little—and I continued to drive. As we got closer, though, his panic increased. Serge gripped the door handle with one hand and with the other, began rapping his knuckles against the console.

"I'm okay," he said in answer to my unspoken question. "I am. I'm okay."

It sounded more like a mantra than an assurance.

I reached out to grab his hand. His fingers were stiff and ice cold and his palm was clammy, sweating.

We drove another two blocks before he suddenly yelled, "Pull over!" His head snapped back. "Maggie, *please*."

"Okay, okay. I will." I moved the car to the side.

"No! No! Go into a driveway. Now!"

The hysteria in his voice made panic spike in my body. I swerved into the first driveway I saw.

"Douse the lights."

I did.

We sat in silence. My heart pounded and his breath came out in rapid, shallow pants. "Why are we sitting here?"

"Something's coming."

A few seconds later, I heard the hum of a car coming down the road. Both Serge and I turned and watched out the back window. The car drove by.

My lungs froze. "Craig's car."

I looked at Serge.

"I don't know why, but he's dangerous," he said tightly, his gaze still on the street.

I put my hand to his cheek. "You did good. I won't make you go any further." Twisting back into my seat, I put the car into reverse and parked it on the side street. I unbuckled my seat belt. "Stay here."

There was a momentary pause then he gave a soft chuckle.

"I'll be back in a few minutes."

"No. Let's go home. Something's wrong with this whole thing."

The ulcer forming in my stomach confirmed his words but I still said, "You don't know that for sure."

"Why's he driving to my house? Did Craig ever act like he liked you until after the murder?"

"No, but—"

"Your dad's dating the town cop—you're ground zero for information about Amber. Don't you find it weird?"

"You think it was Craig and not your dad who killed you?"

He shook his head. "No, but something's weird and he's suddenly all over you? It's not right."

"Thanks a lot." I pushed out of the car.

"Maggie, I didn't mean it like—"

"Just stay here. I'll be back." I slammed the door and took off down the street. There was a full moon and, coupled with the streetlights, the path before me was illuminated. I jogged. My breath came out in foggy puffs that curled into the air and disappeared into the black sky.

I tried to stay focused on the task. Whatever was going on, the psychic side couldn't hurt me. After all, I was doing what The Voice wanted. I had some protection, but I still needed to stay on guard. Easier said than done. Serge had pissed me off.

He was wrong.

So why had his words hit the bull's eye?

Because part of what he'd said had merit, said a small voice inside me. Because Craig really hadn't done much to start a relationship until Serge's death. Because all we seemed to talk about was the murder.

Man. Someone please tell me I hadn't hooked up with some guy who only wanted me 'cause he got off on murder and disaster and was living out some bloodlust fantasy through me.

I turned down the street. Serge's house was four doors on the left. I took a few steps then hit a wall. Or maybe it hit me. All I know was something hard and solid slammed my body. I hurtled backwards. My head smacked the grass of someone's lawn, the rest of my body caught the cement driveway.

I groaned, coughed, and rolled over. Every part of my body hurt, my ears were ringing, and my head throbbed. I pushed my hands against the grass and winced as the cuts and abrasions mixed with dirt. Stumbling to my feet, I checked out the area, but saw nothing.

Okay, *what* was going on?

I crossed the street, shuffling because I was too sore to walk and because I wanted to go slow in case I hit any other invisible walls. Hanging a left as I stepped onto the curb, I moved to Serge's house.

And bounced off an invisible shield.

I heard a boom, like the burst of a sonic jet. Then a high-pitched keening rose into the air.

My heart jerked, every hair follicle on my body rose. Instinct pushed me behind a parked car and my freaked-out body, in survival mode, didn't register any pain.

The wail grew in intensity, volume. Then its tone changed.

From despair, I heard anger. Rage. A high undertone of violence throbbed in the scream. I slapped my hands over my ears and cowered under the minivan's bumper.

"Maggie."

My eyes snapped open. Serge crouched in front of me, but he looked terrible. Sweat poured off his face, and he clutched his stomach.

"We gotta get out of here." He wheezed the words. Serge dropped to all fours, groaning.

"What's wrong with you?"

"I—I don't know." His body went surfboard straight, rigid and tight. The skin on his face went leathery. His mouth pulled back in a rictus grin. His eyes, wide and frightened, stared into mine.

My skin crawled as though I was being swarmed by a billion insects. "Come on, I've got to get you up." I grabbed at him, but he couldn't bend. My sweat-slicked hands slid on his clothing. I started crying. *Come on, Come on, Maggie. Man up and help him.* I slid my hands under his armpits, locked my fingers across his chest and heaved.

Man, he was heavy.

Serge made a snuffling sound, and I knew he was crying.

"It'll be okay, it'll be okay." I was almost straight upright; I glanced over at his house. The walls and roof bowed, the edges blurring like a painting with too much water poured on it. It stretched and warped, and the colours changed, like reverse negative. Bright purple, too-lime green.

And black smoke.

It spewed from the windows, exploded out of the chimney.

The front door opened.

Fear locked me into place.

A figure stepped out. The night was dark, too dark to make out faces, but I knew that frame. Had worshipped that walk.

Craig.

His head snapped in my direction, like he was honing in on me.

I dropped to my knees, cushioned Serge's head on my thighs. "This is bad. This is so bad."

"Leave me. I'm dead. What could happen?" He wheezed the words.

"Can you try to bend? Move?"

"No."

"Can you handle the pain? Try to stand?"

He winced. "Yeah. Sure."

The tears streamed down my face. I knew he was lying.

Either way we were dead.

"Go! Go!" He tried to push me away but I wouldn't move. He was sobbing, now. "Just go. Don't be killed because of me."

I went to all fours, peered around the wheel of the vehicle. Craig was gone. "It's fine. I think I can drag you."

"I always knew you were an idiot. Totally stupid. Deadhead."

"Nice try." I hooked my arms under his armpits. "I'm not going to get huffy and stomp away."

He clutched my hands. "You should. I'm already dead. This is a second death and it's killing me."

I swallowed the boulder-sized stone of fear. "Let's go."

The wailing suddenly stopped. I looked at the house.

"It stopped," said Serge. "Why did it stop?"

"I don't know but it doesn't make me feel good."

He took a breath. "The pain, I mean, it stopped." Serge twisted to his feet.

I let go. "Let's get out of here."

I turned and found Craig standing behind me.

CHAPTER TWENTY-NINE

"Are you totally insane?" asked Craig.

"Uh—"

"Kick him in the balls," said Serge. "Kick him and run."

Craig's eyes slid to Serge. "I wouldn't suggest that."

The hair on my arms rose. I gulped for air.

"Whoa." Serge stepped back.

My thoughts exactly.

"Both of you," said Craig. "We're going now."

Serge's chest puffed out. "I'm not—"

The wailing began again.

"Go! Now!" Craig pushed me and at the same time, spun and ran in the opposite direction of the house.

I sprinted down the street.

Serge kept up, but when the keening increased in volume, he stumbled and fell.

Craig doubled back.

So did I.

I grabbed one arm, Craig grabbed the other, and we dragged Serge down the street.

"I'm going to die," moaned Serge. "I'm going to die all over again."

"Probably," Craig said through gritted teeth.

"But he's already—"

"We'll never make it." Craig pivoted.

"Make it where?"

"There." He pointed at an abandoned house. "Drag him there." Craig put his arm around Serge and resumed carrying him.

The wailing grew closer.

Serge slumped forward.

"Hurry, Maggie!"

I was too freaked to argue, too terrified to pull rank or ask what he was doing. We dragged Serge through the broken-down wooden fence and onto the middle of the lawn.

"Keep him upright!" Craig let go.

My legs buckled under Serge's weight, but I held him steady.

Craig dug into his jacket and pulled out a small vial. He uncorked the top and moved in a circle around us, chanting.

It sounded like Latin, but I didn't dare question him. There was something in the way he moved, an authority in his voice that said whatever was coming at us, he was the guy to take it on.

A powder fell to the ground from the vial. As he spoke, it began to glow, black, blue, then a bright, pure white. Its brilliance shot upwards, contained us in a vertical cylinder.

He corked the vial and stepped inside the circle. Grabbing hold of Serge, he quietly said, "Don't let him out. Don't step out the circle."

I nodded and swallowed, but my throat was desert dry and my voice box felt like it was stuck.

"I'll explain it all, later. Right now, you need to trust me."

The night went silent.

Deep in my bones, where the marrow and cells were born, fear was also birthed. My terror was deep, primal. I wanted to vomit and my legs barely kept me up.

The scream came immediately in front of us, loud, high, and full of murderous intent.

Instinctively, I took a step back.

Craig reached out, grabbed the front of my shirt and yanked me forward. "Stay still."

A heavy, loud thump sounded. The luminescence of the tunnel obscured my view of the thing. But I could make out large, bat-like wings and red eyes. I was panting, now, rapid, shallow breaths. "What is it?"

"You don't want to know," Craig said, his expression grim, his tone flat.

"Is it human?"

He paused. "It used to be."

And that frightened me more than if he'd said "no" or "yes."

"It wants Serge?"

"Badly."

"But he's dead."

"There are levels to death," he said. "And with each level, there are...challenges."

"What does that mean?"

"Hell is nothing compared to what this thing will do to him."

Beside me, Serge stirred, moaned.

Craig let go of the ghost.

Serge sagged against me. He groaned and tried to rise.

Craig made a fist, and clocked Serge on the back of his head. Then he grabbed hold of the ghost once more. He glanced at me. "It's better for him if he's unconscious."

A bright circle of white exploded in front of me and radiated out. The thing was hitting the shield.

A howl of frustration rose, a high, keening shriek.

"It's trying to get in." Craig yelled to be heard above the creature's screams. He looked at me. "You'll have to hold him."

"Okay."

He held my gaze. "You'll be fine—but if this gets him..."

I swallowed and nodded.

"No matter what, you can't let go."

"I won't."

Craig turned. "I have to go out there. The spell won't hold it for much longer."

"It won't hurt me. Will it hurt you?"

He laughed. "Oh, yeah. This is going to hurt."

A glow lit his eyes, one I'd never seen before. It turned his brown eyes to amber, throbbed with electricity, and I got the distinct feeling I was no longer looking at a seventeen-year-old boy.

"Stay here." His voice rumbled like a lion's roar. He dropped his messenger bag and stepped out of the circle.

I shivered. Whatever he was, instinct said the creature had met its match.

Either Craig pushed the thing into the column or vice-versa because bright flashes of light pulsed in the milky screen of the tunnel, blue and green, black and red.

I gripped Serge, held him tighter as he moved.

Consciousness returned to him. He put his hand to his forehead and groaned.

I tried to imitate what Craig had done. Pulling my fingers into a fist, I slammed him in the back of the head.

"Ow!" He grabbed my hand. "Holy crap, Maggie. Why are you hitting me?" He winced and rubbed his head with his other hand. "That hurts." He looked around, taking in the tunnel and the particles of light that moved skyward.

"Craig knocked you out. He said—"

"Where is he?" Serge stepped away and wobbled on his feet.

"Out there. Fighting that thing."

"What thing?" He frowned. "Why don't I hurt anymore?"

I thought. "Maybe it only has so much energy. It can't fight Craig and hunt you at the same time."

"What is it?"

"No idea…it used to be human."

"*Used to be?*"

"Yeah."

"Geez."

"Yeah."

Light continued to crash into the force field.

"Wish I could tell who was winning," said Serge.

Me too.

A bestial cry rent the night.

I heard the crush of bone, the soft, squishing sound of blood and organs.

"Maggie," said Serge. "I think we just found out who won."

The force field dropped.

CHAPTER THIRTY

Cold air blasted my face. The night was lit up like a spotlight, though what illuminated the earth, I didn't know. Craig lay a few feet from me. Bright red blood poured from him and sunk into the ground.

I registered it, but couldn't process the rising agony and disbelief because standing over him was the freakiest thing I'd ever seen.

It had to have been twenty feet. Standing upright, it had legs like a goat. The arms, instead of ending in hooves, each with four-inch talons. Its body was black, pebbled like a snake, and it had wide leathery wings.

There were no eyes, only empty sockets that glowed red. It screamed.

I slapped my hands over my ears. The sound drove me to my knees.

Saliva dripped from its fangs. It howled again.

Serge fell beside me. Blood ran from his ears.

I grabbed and pulled him into my arms, trying to shield him with my body.

The thing howled once more.

My stomach dropped. It wasn't just screaming. It was calling. Calling for Serge.

"Maggie."

I could barely hear Serge above the creature's scream.

The Thing stopped screaming. It sniffed the air with its pug nose, then dropped on all fours. It began to circle, but from the winding trail it took, I knew it didn't know where we were.

"It can't see," I whispered to Serge. "Stay quiet. As long as you're quiet, we'll be fine."

He mouthed the word "go."

I shook my head.

He tried to push me away.

I held him steady and shook my head again. "Me and you." I mouthed the words.

He started crying.

I pulled him closer.

The creature's long pointed ears perked like a bloodhound and rotated in our direction. Growling low in its throat, it crouched on its haunches and waited.

Don't cry.

It moved in the opposite direction, snuffling the ground. The scent of it—burnt rubber and sulphur—assaulted my nose.

Leave me. I deserve this.

No!

Maggie, go!

I didn't say anything. He tried to break out of the field but the close proximity to the creature had weakened him, and I was able to hold tight. *We stand together.*

He looked at me and everything he needed to say was in the tears that streamed down his cheeks.

Another voice sounded in my head: Craig's. *Stay still, both of you.*

We froze and looked at each other.

You think I'm bleeding for the fun of it? There has to be a blood sacrifice. Neither of you move.

Are you okay? I asked.

If I lose too much blood it won't be good. Talking to you is taking my concentration.

I got the message: shut up.

The creature howled and the trees shook.

Serge jerked back.

My heart slammed against my ribs.

Serge, said Craig, *call to it.*

The ghost met my gaze. I shrugged.

"Uh, here kitty." Serge frowned. "Who am I kidding? Hey, Ugly! You want a piece of me? Try your best!"

The Thing screamed, high, piercing, and pounded towards Serge.

"Geez, Serge. He said call to it not challenge the thing's masculinity."

Stand in my blood.

Aware of the demon-seed thing pounding its way to us, saliva dripping from its fangs and spraying the night air, and too freaked out to be squeamish, I grabbed Serge's hand and did as commanded.

The thing rushed closer and the air carried the scent of its mouldering breath.

"Grab my hand," Craig whispered.

We did. Light exploded from the contact, mushroomed out like a nuclear cloud, and sped to the thing.

The creature howled in pain, brought its claws in front of its face. It couldn't stop its momentum and ran into the cloud of light.

The force field obliterated it, seared its body and left nothing but floating ash.

Sudden silence descended. The night grew dark again. Leaves rustled in the stillness.

Beside us, Craig stirred. His blood reversed flow and seeped back into his body. The bruises and mangled pulp of his nose knit together.

I crouched closer to him, but Serge pulled me back.

"Do you see that?" he whispered. He nodded in Craig's direction. "He's got leather wings."

My heart stuttered. "Like the creature's?" I squinted towards my boyfriend.

Serge shook his head. "No...but similar."

What was going on? "Come on, let's see if he needs help."

Serge held me fast. "He doesn't—don't you see her?"

"No," I said irritably. "I don't." What I did see was Craig rising to a sitting position.

My ears twitched as he began to talk. My skin went ice cold. "That's not English."

Serge stood and pulled me up with him. "It's ancient Egyptian."

I heard the frustration and anxiety in his voice as he asked, "How do I *know* that?"

"Can you understand what he's saying? Who's he talking to?"

"There's a woman in white. They're talking about what just happened. I think." Worry tinged his words. "I don't understand all the words but it's not good."

"Great."

"He's saying that they should have told her—you. I think they're talking about you." He paused. "Craig says they could have killed you—you should have known and he should have been given the update on the..." He shook his head. "I don't know—I can hear the word but I can't repeat it—the thing. He should have been told about the thing. She's saying the plan had to unfold as it should or—" He stopped.

"Serge?"

"—or I'd fail the test," he finished quietly.

Test?

Craig jumped to his feet.

I blinked.

This guy could *not* be human. No one could have lost that much blood and hop around like a rabbit. I calmed my frantic pulse and tried to tap into the conversation. But it didn't work. All I felt was frustration and anger...and a whack-load of terror.

Serge had gone quiet, which meant no help.

I closed my eyes. Instead of trying to see *and* hear them, I just concentrated on hearing.

"You knew he would pass. This was unnecessary," said Craig. His voice rumbled, thrummed as though a dark band of electricity ran through his body. In my mind's eye, he seemed bigger, a gigantic creature of lava and leather, fire and iron.

"No, we theorized he would pass. Until he was willing to sacrifice himself to protect Magdalene, we could do nothing."

The female had a soothing voice, the kind I'd imagined perfect mothers have when they rock their kids to sleep.

"How did the—"

Craig said the creature's name and I knew what Serge meant about hearing but not understanding. It *sounded* like a mix between "bellabok" and "Nybbialas" but there were "r" and "ph" sounds and my braid couldn't sort the syllables. I got the gist, though: ancient evil.

"It shouldn't have been released from its cage."

"Because we cannot foresee every action of human, we cannot prevent their energies from loosening the gates between their realm and hell."

"The plan should have changed as their actions changed," said Craig.

"You know that cannot—"

"She almost died! And Serge—he barely made it! As it is, the"—he spoke the creature's name—"will be back."

Instinctively, I grabbed the ghost's hand. My eyes snapped open. "How do I protect him?"

Craig's head whipped in my direction.

I blinked and squinted, unsure of what I was seeing. It seemed as though there were images superimposed on images. There was his human form, but something else—the shadow of wings blocked the view of barren trees and moonlight—mixed with the sense of a giant who had stuffed himself into a human form fifteen sizes too small.

I stepped back, but I held my courage. "Where does Serge have to make it?"

"Come on," he said. The red glow dimmed from his eyes, turned them from ruby-amber back to brown. "Let's go home and I'll tell you about it."

"Tell me about what—what *are* you?"

The shadows left him as he walked to the car, turned him fully human. "A ferrier." He glanced back at me. "I transport the dead."

CHAPTER THIRTY-ONE

I came through the front door and headed into the kitchen. Buddha lay on the couch, his fur glossy and smooth under the ceiling lights. Dad stood by the stove, stirring a pot. The smell of garlic and onion, thyme and basil scented the moist air.

"Hey," I said.

He turned. Three faint lines wrinkled his brow. He glanced from me to Craig.

"This is my boyfriend, Craig. He's a ferrier."

Dad's frown deepened. "You shoe horses?"

"That's a farrier," he said and slid into a chair by the counter. "Change the 'a' to an 'e' and you've got me."

"It's a convenient title since he ferries the dead," I clarified, my voice one pitch short of hysteria.

"Oh." Dad's brow smoothed out, and he turned back to the pot. "I always thought that was a reaper."

"Those guys separate the soul from the body." Craig rose and made his way over to the stove. "I take spirits across the bridge—over the river Styx." He shrugged. "Or wherever they need to go." He leaned over the pot. "Spaghetti?"

"Yeah, I thought cooking would soothe me but the sauce seems..."

"Thin?"

Dad nodded.

I went from contained hysteria to all-out freak. "Are you *kidding* me? He's transports the freaking dead and you're talking about *sauce*?"

Dad gave Craig an "I'm Sorry My Daughter's Such a Drama Queen" look and said, "Maggie you transition the dead all the time. Why are you surprised that there are others like you?"

That stopped me. I sighed and slid onto a stool. Serge appeared beside me.

"It needs oregano," said Craig as he sniffed the sauce.

Dad handed him the spoon.

Craig tasted the marinara. Steam rose from the pot and filled the kitchen with humid air. "And thyme. Maybe a dash of salt."

"When you're done," I said, "perhaps you'd be good enough to explain what happened tonight with me and Serge and that thing."

"What thing?" asked Dad.

"The thing that tried to eat us."

The wooden spoon clattered to the stove and splatters of red sauce marred the stove. "Something tried to eat you?"

"I thought it would be easier to explain it with your dad here," said Craig.

"Something tried to eat you?" Dad asked again, his voice faint. "Like an escaped lion?"

"More like Satan's escaped pet monster," I said.

He blinked and stared at the spaghetti sauce as though it held the answers he sought.

"Is it coming back?" asked Serge.

"Yes, but not for a while," said Craig.

"Yes but not for—wait, is Serge talking?" Dad's head bobbled from one direction to the other. "Let me get my cell."

"Sorry." Craig strode to Serge and grabbed his arm. Blue light emanated from my boyfriend's palm and radiated out in a circle.

"What the—hey, Serge." Dad froze in the middle of wiping his hands.

"You can see him?" I jerked my thumb in his direction.

Dad nodded.

"Way cool," said Serge.

"Hear him, too." Dad's phone beeped.

"Is that me?"

Dad looked down. "No. Nancy." He went down the stairs and unlocked the door. "She's coming over." He moved back to the table. "Talk fast before she gets here." He nodded at Serge. "Uh—we'll fix that before she gets here, right?"

Craig grinned.

Serge cleared his throat. A crimson flush rose from his neck to his hair. "About the way I behaved when I was alive—"

"Don't worry about it," said Dad, wiping his hands once more. "It's been talked through."

Serge swallowed and nodded.

"Okay. We can all see each other and hear each other." I fixed Craig with a stare. "Start talking. What are you and what is going on?"

"Big points: When someone dies, I take the soul—"

"Where?" asked Serge, worried.

"Where it needs to go."

"Like…heaven or hell."

"Sometimes," said Craig. "But sometimes it's Valhalla or limbo. It depends on the soul, on what their eternal cycle is. Some people die and go to heaven. Some die and are reborn."

Dad turned the heat down and stepped away from the pot. "This sounds like a conversation to have around a table. I'll get the coffee."

We sat and I said, "Okay. Ferriers. I thought death was death."

"Maggie," he gently chastised me. "Life isn't even life. It doesn't have one reality. How can you think death would have the same?"

"Of course life has one reality," I returned, affronted.

His dark eyebrows rose. "You think the reality of your life is the same as the reality of a woman living in Africa?"

"Well, no but—"

"There is no 'universal, one-fit' anything. Life is nothing but preparation for death. And death—the end of existence or even the strumming harps in heaven—are just two options on what waits on the other side." Craig put his hand to his chest. "I'm a ferrier. I come for the soul after a reaper separates it from the body."

"Does everyone get a ferrier and a reaper when they die?" asked Serge.

Craig made a face. "Yes and no."

"Well, that clears it up." Dad set the coffee pot in the middle of the table and handed the mugs out. He put a dark blue mug with gold moons in front of Serge.

"Thanks, Mr. Johnson, but I can't drink."

Dad paused, laughed. "Sorry. Force of habit."

"Yeah, you can," said Craig.

Serge's eyes widened. "I can?"

"For now—until I turn you back."

Serge jumped up and grabbed for the coffee.

"I should warn you," said Craig. "It won't taste quite the same."

Serge's hand hovered over the pot. "Bad?"

Craig shrugged. "Different."

I watched, part of me fascinated, most of me horrified that we were talking about coffee when a leathered-wing-thing had tried to eat my ghost for breakfast.

Serge poured his drink and took a swig. He held the liquid in his mouth, frowned, swallowed. The wrinkles disappeared from his face. "Not bad...different."

"How?" asked Dad.

"Maybe we can talk about this later," I said. "Right now, I need to know about that thing—and you, Craig. What about Dad's question: does everyone get a reaper and a ferrier?"

He nodded. "Yes, but death—think of it like this: death sends out a signal, and ferriers and reapers hone in on it. But this only works if the person knows they're dying, if they're aware of it. For those who don't or can't acknowledge death, they hone in on people like you, Maggie. And you transition them. Then we take over."

"To where?" I asked. "Where do the dead go?"

"The bridge."

He said it like he was confused I didn't know.

"Imagine the warm version of the North Pole or Antarctica. A place of white and blue, full of peace and solitude. That's where they end up." He mimed the words as he said, "There's a long bridge that connects that spot to The Beyond. The souls you transition are met by their ferriers, who take them across."

"Across to...where?" asked Serge. His fingers played with the handle of the mug.

Craig shrugged. "Wherever they're meant to go. Like I said, some souls will cross over to their image of heaven and that's it. Others will come back to earth and some…" He paused. "Some souls have made life decisions they will pay for in death."

"Like me?" whispered Serge.

Craig frowned. He glanced from me to Serge and back. "You mean about—no, that's not it."

I was still trying to wrap my head around everything he'd said. "You can cross over," I said. "From life to death."

He nodded. "Part of the job."

"How do your parents deal with this?" asked Dad. "I thought having Maggie was complicated, but…"

"They're Guardians. That's their job. They're not my biological parents," he added. "A ferrier has to be born into the world by an innocent—a woman who doesn't have a clue about what really happens after death."

"So…how did your parents get you?"

"I was abandoned." He glanced around the room and grinned. "It has to happen like that—we're purposely birthed by mothers who give us up. I was a private adoption—my biological mother was a sixteen-year-old girl who was sure she was doing the right thing." A soft smile crept across his lips. "And she did. Guardians raise ferriers, but they can't have their own children." He gave me a meaningful look and said, "Technically, they're co-workers. They're not supposed to fall in love or use their adopted son's car on Widow's Peak. Especially when they're giving him grief about wanting to date you."

Oh, so that explained his reaction that night. "So." My brain chugged like a too-slow steam engine, trying to keep up with the twist and turns of his story. "How long have you been a ferrier?"

"A few thousand years."

Dad choked on his coffee.

"You've been alive for over a thousand years?"

He smiled. "No. We have to be born and die and reborn."

"But you remember?"

The side of his mouth lifted. "Have to, if you're to be a ferrier."

"You're what—three thousand years old?" asked Serge. "Or, at least, you have the memory of three thousand years of living."

"With this world and this reality, I'm around five thousand years old. With everything else…" He closed his eyes and did the math. "Say, about ten-thousand years."

Ten thousand years. *This* reality. *This* world. The terror of our brains exploding from information overload kept us quiet about asking what he meant, and just how many worlds and realities were out there.

"So…when you have to ferry someone—you just blip in and out of existence?"

"Basically—"

And I thought my life was complicated.

"—but sometimes, we have to be around our charge…to watch over them before the moment of passing."

"That's why you came to Dead Falls," I said. "For Serge."

Craig's breath hissed through his teeth. His voice was heavy, laden as he said, "I didn't come for Serge."

The air around the table went suddenly cold. In the background, the sauce quietly bubbled.

Dad and I stared at each other. I tore my gaze from him and set it on Craig. "Who did you come for?"

"I came for Amber," he said. "She was to die." The intense light in his eyes dimmed to something softer, sadder. "She was to kill herself. Instead"—his gaze moved to Serge—"someone murdered you."

"That's why you were always around her, watching."

Craig nodded. "We're not allowed to change the course of events, but we can influence them…to some extent. I had seen the plan of her life"—his face tightened—"and the outcome of her decision. But when Serge died, those plans and consequences…things changed."

"What happens, now?"

He shrugged. "I don't know. We aren't allowed to see the full future. I only know as much as I need to work my cases. That's it."

"But that thing, tonight—"

He took a deep breath. "Horrific." He scrubbed his forehead with his hand.

"Why is it coming for Serge?"

"Because it blames him for its life."

Serge frowned.

The front door opened. Before any of us could react, Nancy was up the stairs. "Sorry about the—" The grin dropped from her mouth as her eyes lit on Serge. She yanked out her gun and pointed it at him. He bolted back and threw his hands up to protect himself.

I jumped up.

So did Craig.

"What's going on?"

"Put down the gun!"

"What!"

"*Put down the gun!*"

Dad got to Nancy first and clamped his hand on the cold muzzle. "He's already dead." He paused and repeated, "He's dead. You can't do anything."

She blinked and blinked again. "Holy crap." She dropped her shoulders and the gun descended. Nancy collapsed into a chair. She lifted her gaze. "Someone please explain what is going on."

CHAPTER THIRTY-TWO

Nancy was in the kitchen where Dad was trying to explain it all to her. Craig, Serge, and I had taken to the family room, where I needed explanations of my own. I sat on the couch, Serge to my right, and Craig took the coffee table. We made a triangle, our knees touching each other...it felt weird and sacred, all at once.

"I need an info dump. You have to explain this all to me because I don't understand how you can know our destiny, but not the future," I said.

Craig shrugged. "I'm like a social worker. I know enough about my cases and the people surrounding them to do my work, but I don't get to know everything."

"But would you"—I stopped, took a breath to calm the adrenaline rushing in my blood—"do you know about The Voice?"

He frowned.

"There's a voice, it comes to me. Not often, but—"

"It tried to kill her," said Serge. "When she wanted to stop helping me prove my father killed me—"

A shadow passed over Craig's face.

"—this voice came over the radio and stopped her heart."

Craig's eyes went wide. Turning to me, he asked, "What does it sound like?"

"It's female and it wails, keeps telling me 'he's coming for you.'"

"The 'he' is obvious," said Serge. "The great and pious reverend—"

Again the shadow blanketed Craig's face.

"—but why would it try to kill her?"

Craig shook his head. "I've never heard of this. Let me look into it, okay?"

I nodded.

He smiled and squeezed my hand.

"What about the wings?" asked Serge. "How can you have leather wings—that thing had leather wings and it was evil." He took a breath. "Shouldn't you have feather wings or something?"

Craig laughed. "Only humans think feathers mean good and leather means bad. Besides"—his grin crinkled his eyes—"they're scales, not leather."

Scales?

"You talk about humans like you're separate," said Serge, "but you're human aren't you?"

Craig nodded. "Just on a different plane. Not exactly more evolved, but certainly older."

"How old am I?" I asked.

"How old are you or how many lifetimes have you lived?"

"Both."

"You've lived two hundred lifetimes and you're somewhere close to two thousand years old." He glanced at Serge. "You, too."

Craig's gaze washed over me in a warm wave. "You're definitely *much* younger than me."

I cleared my throat. "What can you tell us—about the original plan, with me and Serge."

He ran his hand through his hair. "Amber was going to kill herself. She went to Mikhail, told him about the pregnancy. Originally, he cut her off, and distraught, she threw herself off the Lodgen Bridge. Instead"—he splayed his fingers—"Serge was murdered and Amber lives."

"I know that—what I mean is how was her death to impact us?"

Craig's eyes turned to Serge. "Something about her killing herself would make you click into the truth of your life—the futility of the decisions you'd made concerning your parents, Maggie, life. You took the flash drive to Nancy, had your dad arrested."

"Then Mom and I—"

Craig shook his head. "Your mom was diagnosed with cancer three months after his arrest. She passes away within six weeks, and you end up living with Nancy."

"What!"

Craig nodded. "And you take over where she leaves off. You become a cop, just like her. But the real key of your original destiny was Maggie. The two of you bond over Amber's death, your mom's sickness. You're the cop; she's a private investigator. Between her abilities and your access to the legal system, you guys put away a lot of criminals. The amount of murders and abuse you prevent—" He stopped, took a breath. "I don't know," he finished softly. "I don't know what this means for all the people you were supposed to save."

He was talking long-term future, I was still thinking about the immediate impact of Amber's death. "Serge and I become a team?"

"You've always been a team."

We both frowned and looked at each other.

Craig leaned in, resting his elbows on his knees, and folded his hands. "Your past lives—they've always been intertwined. Soul siblings—born in the same time and living in the same circles. You've always looked out for each other—protected each other."

I glanced at Serge. "What happened with this life?"

"Nothing. You scripted it this way."

My eyes went wide. "I wanted to be bullied by Serge."

"No—no, sorry." Craig puffed out a breath. "Let me see how I can explain this. A soul lives and if it chooses, reincarnates. But you have to be a certain soul age before you can do more than be reborn. That can take a lot of lifetimes—you have to be born into a variety of social classes and different bodies in order to understand what it means to be human.

My head was already hurting as I tried to figure this out.

"Serge wanted to be a guardian; so did you. In order to that, you have to go through the first level: Protector. That position can take several lifetimes to achieve and several more lifetimes to finish. And— well, you have to go through some rough things. You have to understand the hardships of life from a personal level, not just theoretical. It's part of the initiation."

"This sounds barbaric. Torturing us in life so we prove ourselves in death."

"It's not about torture, it's about connection. If you're going to watch over the most vulnerable, those at highest risk, you can't be some soul who lived in an ivory tower and never knew torment or pain." His mouth pulled to the side. "It's a war, Maggie, and souls are in danger. In this battle, your commanders always come from the frontline. And one of the strongest tools in your arsenal is forgiveness. It's powerful and it opens energies in your body, and you need those if you're going to be a protector."

I slowly nodded. "Okay, I think I get it."

"You weren't to be tortured—" He glanced at Serge. "You weren't supposed to turn out...like that. But it's the problem of a non-corporeal being living in a physical body. Until your soul gets older, you won't remember your past lives. You come to earth and it's like you're living with amnesia."

"What was I supposed to do?"

"Persevere and rise above your circumstances." Craig puffed out a breath. "You and Maggie are destined to be bonded for eternity. But to be protectors and guardians is to have the ultimate trust and confidence in your partner, the system, and yourself. To be partnered with her, you had to live a life of hell and come through the fire."

Serge frowned. "Why didn't Maggie have to do the same?"

"She did. The last lifetime."

He looked pained. "And she passed."

Craig nodded. "You were the protector of her. In this life, she was to protect you."

"But I failed," I said.

"No," said Serge. "I failed. I should have...I should have been stronger."

"No," said Craig. "You should have been weaker."

Serge frowned.

So did I.

"You misinterpreted strength," Craig clarified. "To have reached the goal, you needed to acknowledge you needed help and take it. You couldn't because you thought it was 'weak.'"

Serge looked away, his jaw worked up and down.

Craig put his hand on Serge's leg. "Look, you're fine. You passed—you were dead, but you learned the lesson of this life and that's all you needed to do."

"When we glowed, right?" I asked. "When we let go of the earthly bounds and psychically remembered our bonds, we glowed."

Craig nodded. "And when he was willing to sacrifice himself to protect you."

"Tell me more about being a protector—"

Footsteps coming down the stairs temporarily halted my words.

Nancy and Dad turned the corner. The cop's eyes locked on Serge.

He rose, slowly.

"Hank told me about what's been going on," she said, her voice strained. She closed her eyes. "I want to get very, very drunk."

Serge stood, silent. His fingers flexed open and closed.

He did that when he was nervous, scared, and I wondered how I knew that. Was the knowledge of my past lives breaking through into this life or was it just my subconscious creating a hypothesis from his tight stance and the pinched sides of his mouth?

"You and I have a history," he said. "A bad one. And I owe you—" He swallowed. "I owe you an apology, but I know my words will never make up for what I did and the pain I caused. I was a pain to you, to—well—everyone." He looked at Craig. "And, had things turned out differently—" His Adam's apple bobbed. "I think I would have owed you my life and my happiness." The muscles at the base of his jaw rippled. "I'm sorry—" His voice was husky.

Nancy took a step toward him. "This is the kind of freaky I can't explain and I don't know…" She put her hand to her forehead. "I think I'm in shock." She swallowed and her hands moved to her waist. Her fingers played with the handle of her gun. "But there's an opportunity here, one I don't intend to pass up." Nancy took a breath that stretched the buttons of her shirt.

"I'm sorry, too." She took a shuddering breath. "You were *such* a pain. So is your dad. The rules and laws didn't give me enough room to do what was right." Her face crumpled. "And I went with what was easy: I made you the bad guy when the truth was, we were both bad. I should have tried harder for you, Serge, and for that, I'll never forgive myself."

He shook his head, his mouth trembling, and his eyes glassy. Embarrassed, he swiped at his face. Serge stepped to her. His fingers shaking, he extended a handshake.

The scene was eerily quiet. Serge made no sound.

She took his fingers, pulled him into a hug.

He held his body tight, as though he couldn't believe what was going on, as though he expected her to push him away at any moment.

Nancy must have sensed it too, because she tightened her hold and whispered, "I'm sorry. Please forgive me."

He froze, stone still.

"I'm so glad Craig turned you solid," she continued, "because I have a chance to hold you, tell you how much sorrow I feel." She paused. "To tell you I forgive you."

He melted into her. The lines of his body went soft, slightly blurry.

She held him tighter and whispered, "I hope you forgive yourself...and me."

He sobbed, never making a sound. Then he began to glow. Purple, blue, then white, the aura washed out from him like a wave and warmed my face and skin.

Dad tiptoed to me, sat down, and took my hand. He leaned in and whispered, "Is this what you see every time you help a ghost? The colours?"

I shook my head and looked at Craig.

"You'll see them, now." His gaze remained on Serge. His sigh dropped his shoulders and relaxed his chest. "This is good."

He said it quietly, but the conviction and relief in his tone caught me. "What?"

"Serge couldn't move on—he couldn't be a protector until he'd let go of the pain of this life. You can't hold on to your mistakes or to the mistakes of others. They become chains that weigh you down and eventually drag you under."

Nancy pulled away from Serge but kept her hands on his shoulders. "Honey"—she maintained eye contact—"there's something I need to tell you."

Her tone signalled terrible news and I rose, went to him. Taking Serge's hand, I said, "What is it?"

She took a deep, sad breath. "It's your mom."

Serge glanced at Craig. "She's sick, right?"

Craig frowned and rose slowly to his feet.

Nancy waited until he'd reached us. "No. I'm sorry honey…" Then she quietly said, "She killed herself tonight."

Serge's legs buckled.

Craig and I grabbed him.

"Killed—no, you're wrong."

Craig slung Serge's arm over his shoulder. "I—are you sure? She committed suicide?"

Nancy nodded. "There isn't any doubt."

"Something's wrong," Craig said as he helped Serge to the couch. "She…I didn't expect this."

"I thought you couldn't see the future."

"I can't—"

Serge slid to the cushion.

"—but I know probabilities. There's something wrong. I need to look into it." He straightened and looked at Nancy. "Are you positive?"

The sheriff grimaced. "She…left proof."

Geez. I didn't even want to think about what that meant.

"I'll be back." He turned to Serge. "I have to make you non-corporal, again."

He nodded.

Craig closed his eyes. A beam of light engulfed Serge. When it cleared, I could still see him, but I knew I was the only one. Craig took my hand, held it for a minute.

A bead of light—red-copper—rapidly grew from his chest, expanding vertically until it was a thick line dividing his left from right. Then it expanded outward.

In a blink, he was gone.

"I really need to get drunk. Or eat enough sugar to put myself into a diabetic coma. My brain's going to explode," said Nancy, rubbing her forehead. "Serge's dead but sitting in the family room, Craig's some kind of supernatural guardian, and Lydia Popov just took her life—"

"She didn't." Serge's voice was rough, gravely. "I don't care what kind of evidence you have, my mom wouldn't kill herself. She's super religious and suicide—"

Nancy's phone beeped. She looked down at the screen. "Honey, I'm sorry, but—"

"No! Even if she did it, *he's* still responsible. He beat me and he terrorized her. He must have forced her to do it." Anger twisted his features. "Because he wants Amber and her baby. He couldn't have them and my mother. So he made her kill herself."

Pity was in Dad's eyes. "I'm sorry, Serge," he said.

"Yeah," he muttered. "Me, too." Slowly, rising as though the movement brought him physical pain, he said, "I'm going to go upstairs and rest."

"Do you want some company?" I asked.

He shook his head. "No, I think I want to be alone for a while." He turned and moved away from me.

CHAPTER THIRTY-THREE

That night was spent with Dad and I trying to explain my abilities to Nancy. The next morning, I was in Nell's art deco bedroom, lying on a quilt of red, black, and white squares, and telling her everything. Her eyes, already wide, grew rounder as I talked. By the time I got to the attempted murder on Amber, I was so worried Nell's eyeballs would fall out, I tried to peddle back but she threatened me with bodily harm if I didn't finish, so I continued with The Thing, Craig, The Voice, Nancy finding out, and the mysterious woman only Serge and my boyfriend seemed able to see. When I was done, I settled back on her king-sized pillows and waited. And waited.

She sat cross-legged, her pink silk pyjamas clinging to her curves, glass of soda in hand, and her mouth opened so wide I could have fit an accent pillow inside.

"Are you going to say something?" I asked.

She continued to stare.

"Nell," I said, irritated. "I can see the dead but I can't read minds. What do you think?"

Her mouth closed with a *snap*. "I don't. You've managed to blow my mind." Her head swivelled left then right. "In fact, I'm looking for pieces of my brain. I'm sure they're scattered on the floor or sticking to the walls."

I grabbed a gingersnap cookie from the white saucer on her black night table. "Hurry and gather, because I need answers."

She blinked, long and slow. "Craig's ten thousand years old?"

"Give or take a millennium."

"How do you think he is in bed?"

"Geez! Nell!"

"Gimme a break." She uncrossed her legs. "I'm trying to focus on the things I can comprehend and slowly moving my way up." She rolled to her stomach and set her glass down on the floor. Flipping her hair back, she said, "A ferrier?"

I nodded.

"Carries the dead from…well, one place to another."

Another nod.

A faint frown puckered her forehead. "You'd think a guy who's lived through history would do better in social studies."

"*Nell*, I'm begging—pleading—please focus on the problem."

"Problems," she corrected. "You're facing multiple crises—" She cocked her head. "Crisie? What's the plural of crisis?"

"You," I said and reached for another cookie. It cracked against my teeth and the scents of ginger spice filled my nostrils.

"Do you think The Creature and The Voice are related?"

I shook my head. "No. The Creature wants Serge. The Voice wants me."

"You're a real dynamic team," she said drily. "Remind me not to hang out with you after sunset."

I tossed the cookie crumbs at her. "Shut up."

"Seriously, though…"

I waited for a brilliant plan of attack.

She scanned the ceiling.

I took a swig of tea.

"You're sure you don't know how Craig is in bed?"

I slapped her with a crimson-coloured accent pillow that was embroidered with dragons.

She laughed. "I can't believe I ever envied you. Just your past twenty-four hours will keep me in therapy for years."

"More like institutionalized if you ever told anyone."

Nell's smile faded, her expression sobered. "What a life you live."

"Yeah, but it's the only one I got, so…"

She sighed. "So, the issues at hand." She rolled on to her back. "Are we sure Lydia Popov killed herself?" Her eyes met mine. "Is it possible that Mr. Husband of the Year did it?"

My mouth twisted to the side. "Possible, but Nancy seemed pretty sure she killed herself."

"How?"

"Oh. I don't know. She just said Mrs. Popov suicided."

"Whoa," breathed Nell. "How's Serge?"

"Hiding in my room and not talking to anyone."

A humourless smile slanted her lips. "I never thought I'd say this, but poor guy."

"Tell me about it."

Nell grabbed her drink and crawled over to me. She reached across my lap for a cookie and flopped on the pillow to my left. "It's weird, don't you think, that she'd kill herself? Isn't that a big bible no-no? And she's a pastor's wife."

I shrugged. "Craig seemed surprised by it, too."

"That's saying something."

"You know what else he was surprised—well, not surprised, but—" I turned to face my friend. "When Nancy and Serge were talking, he insisted his dad had murdered him, but Craig...he seemed hesitant." I sat back. "Craig knows who really killed Serge and I don't think it was his dad."

Nell brushed the crumbs from her top. "No one else had motive."

I snorted. "Uh, it's pre-death Serge. Half the town had a motive. Still, his dad seems the one with the biggest reason to murder."

Her pixie features contorted. "Maybe, but if you think about it... Popov was screwing Amber since she was in grade nine." Her face slackened. "Holy crap, that's so gross." She shook her head. "But she's been sleeping with him for four years. Why would he kill his son, now?"

"Because Amber was pregnant."

"So?"

"So..." So, what? "Okay." I pressed my fingers to my temple. "Let's think this through. Originally, Popov was supposed to reject Amber and the baby. She'd kill herself and that act would spur Serge to take what he knew about his dad to the cops." My eyes widened as I realized what I was saying. I grabbed Nell's wrist. "Serge's moral compass."

"What?"

"Look, he was a sleaze ball, but the death of Amber and her unborn child would galvanize him—"

"Which means…?" Nell asked doubtfully.

"Which means he has a moral compass. When Popov made the decision to accept the pregnancy, he knew Serge had to die."

Nell frowned. "Why?"

"Because there's one person Serge loves and protects. His mom." I leaned forward and drew my knees to my chest. "I think it was one thing for Serge to look the other way with the affair but if there was a baby born, it would have humiliated his mother."

"Why? She probably already knows what's going on between her husband and Amber—"

"Yeah, but that's behind closed doors. Now, she'll have to *see* it every day."

"Oh. You think he would have gone to the police because of the baby?"

I sighed. "Yes—maybe. This is what I know: he loves his mom, he'd do anything to protect and care for her, his father's having an affair—"

"Lydia excused the affair for years. I don't see how a baby—" She stopped. Her eyes went wide.

"What?"

"Remember the blood drive?"

"Yeah."

"Well…I was doing some background checking—"

She wasn't making eye contact with me. "You were snooping."

Nell blushed. "I was—but with the murder, I thought knowing the family's medical background might come in handy."

"And?"

"And Serge is AB, RH-. Both his parents are blood type O."

I gave her a blank look.

"This is why you shouldn't have skipped the bio classes on genealogy. Popov wasn't Serge's biological dad."

"*What?*" Memory blazed into my mind. "That's why he always called Serge *her* son and made all those weird comments about morality." I shot Nell a dirty glare. "Why didn't you say this before?"

"Honestly, I didn't think it mattered. Either Popov always knew Serge wasn't his or he'd found out just before his kid was killed—"

"Uh, duh, yeah. You don't think that's a motive?"

Her cheeks turned scarlet. "I thought it'd make more sense to kill Lydia, not Serge. Besides, with the way he treated his kid, I figured he'd always known."

I sat back. "Yeah, that's true."

"And anyway, you said it wasn't Popov who killed Serge."

I fidgeted, the sensation that I was missing something obvious crawled along my skin and scuttled along my brain. "I know, but Craig's expression—it wasn't that he totally discounted Serge's assertion, it just seemed like there was more to it."

We went quiet. The only sound was the wind outside sending the tree branches scrapping against the window.

"What if Popov set up the murder?" asked Nell.

"But who—" And the answer came to me. It made the blood rush to the outmost layers of my skin then race back to my heart and left my flesh tingling. I turned to my friend. "I know who killed him."

Her eyes turned glassy. "It was Mrs. Popov, wasn't it?"

I nodded slowly. "I think so. Serge can't remember the night, can't remember who killed him, but if it had been his dad, he'd have known. He hates his father. Serge blocked the memory because—"

"She was the one person he loved."

I was so horrified, I couldn't even think of a good enough curse. "I should have seen it, sooner. His relationship with his mother—she was bonded to her husband, not her son. The kid's the product of an affair or something that happened before they got married. She's always been ashamed of him—"

"—and Popov never lets her forget it. He throws it and her son in her face all the time." Nell's face darkened.

"Whenever Serge talked about her, he was in the protector's role. His mom never looked out for him. He looked out for her."

"Amber gets pregnant. Popov decides to keep the girl and the kid, but now Serge has to die."

"And once he's dead, everyone thinks the baby's his. Popov's in the clear."

"I hate this guy," said Nell. "I *super* hate this guy." She traced the rim of the glass with her index finger. "But how would he get Lydia to kill her son? She's a screw-up but isn't offing your children a Godly no-no?"

I shrugged. "In abusive relationship, maybe the abuser has the power of God over the victim."

Nell breathed out. "In this case, Popov was definitely Lydia's God."

I stumbled to my feet. "I have to tell Nancy—" I looked at her, stricken. "Do I have to tell Serge?"

A tear tracked its way down her cheek. Slowly, she nodded.

I closed my eyes, turned away. He'd been so afraid he was going to hell. My knowledge was about to put him there.

CHAPTER THIRTY-FOUR

When I got home, I found everyone in the family room. Buddha was on the floor by Dad's feet. Ebony was curled on Serge's lap.

"Hey." I dropped my jacket on the couch arm. "Uh, I need to talk to Serge about..." I moved to him and gently sank to the chair. The furnace breathed to life and the drone of heated air filled the room.

He scratched the cat's forehead.

"Um, how are you doing?"

The urge to say something sarcastic passed like lightning across his face. "I'm okay."

Dad's phone beeped. He looked down then gestured to the television. "I thought he might want to watch the football game with me." Setting down the cell, he asked, "What did you want to talk to Serge about? Should I leave?"

I shook my head. Reaching over, I took the ghost's hand. "I have a theory about your mom's death but I need your help." I paused. "And I need you to stay calm."

Wary, he nodded.

"Amber is pregnant. Had you lived, what would you have done when you found out?"

"Gone to the cops," he said.

Ebony preened, stretched her front legs and purred.

Serge smiled and rubbed her forehead.

"Why?" I asked.

"If he wanted to screw her, fine, but no way am I changing diapers and pretending his kid's mine."

Oh. I hadn't thought of that. "Is that the only reason?"

"What do you mean?"

Dad tracked the conversation on his cell.

"Your mom—would you have outed him for her?"

"Of course." He said it as though I was the world's biggest idiot. "She'd have been humiliated. It's one thing for him to sneak around but to have that kid in her face…"

"That's what I thought," I sighed.

Dad moved to us. "What's going on?"

I looked at Serge. "Give me the cat."

"What? Why?"

"Because if you blow up, I don't want her hurt."

"I'm not going to—"

"Give me Ebony."

"Maggie—"

"Hand her over."

He scowled but did as I asked. I gave her furry head a kiss and set her down.

"Maggie?" asked Dad.

"Serge—and this is only a question—" I held up my hands in a surrender gesture. "Is it possible that your mom may have been the one—" He looked at me, earnest and focused, and the words stuck in my throat. I blinked back the tears of sympathy and pity. "Is it possible that she is responsible for your death."

His breath left his body in a forceful *whoosh*.

I tensed.

Serge's head dropped to his chest.

After a few seconds, I tentatively reached out and touched his knee.

"I wondered why I couldn't remember the murder," he said dully. "It seemed so obvious that he did it, and so stupid that I couldn't…" He lifted his head and swallowed. His eyes were bleak as he said, "It's the only thing that makes sense, isn't it?" His lips compressed into a tight line. "But I can't believe it. She was my mom—she'd never—"

Dad looked up from his cell and we exchanged glances.

Serge rose to his feet. "She wouldn't." His jaw worked up and down. "He killed me. He killed her, too and I can prove it."

I frowned. "How?"

"The flash drive. It's documentation of abuse. Somewhere there are hospital records that will back it up."

"But your dad took it—"

"Yeah, I still know how to get into the house." He stretched out his hand. "Please, Maggie. Help me prove my mom didn't do this to me or herself."

Dad gave me a small nod.

I grabbed my jacket. "Let's go."

CHAPTER THIRTY-FIVE

Serge had been quiet from the moment we got in the car, and five seconds ago he started crying. I glanced over and gave him a thirty second count. "Serge?"

"I remember."

"Remember?"

"The night I died." He laughed, the sound hollow. "You know how she got me?"

I peeked at him from the corner of my eye.

"She told me we had to talk but she didn't want to do it in the house. So we drove and she"—his voice cracked—"she said she was going to leave him." The tears came in a rush, drowned his conversation.

I reached over, took his hand, and let him cry.

"I told her we could just start driving that night, but she said no. She wanted to do it right, not sneak off." He swallowed. "M—Mom took me to the mill. She had bought a bottle of tequila. Said it was proof of her emancipation. She'd drink coffee, alcohol—whatever she wanted."

"She got you drunk."

He shook his head. "I only remember taking a swig, maybe two."

"She must have put something in the alcohol. When you were knocked out, she—" I stopped, not wanting to put into detail that she'd probably poured the drink down his throat, pulled off his shirt. I felt sick at the idea of her undressing her son and leaving him to choke to death on his vomit.

I pulled to the curb two blocks from the Popov's house. Staring at the otherworldly fireworks in the sky, I said, "You can't go near it."

Serge tilted his head and peered through the windshield. "Maybe it's not the house."

I shot him an incredulous look. "There are geysers of neon green and electric purple lights streaming from the ground to the sky, and you don't think your house is involved?"

He craned his neck down and the wash of otherworldly lumines-cence painted his face. "Maybe it's someone else's place."

I twisted my gaze from him and looked to the sky. The colours, warped and winding, coiled their way upward as black shadows dart-ed around them. Fear and revulsion snaked in my belly. "Oh, yeah," I said sarcastically. "That's totally not your house."

"I'm just sayin—"

"I don't know what those things are, but I don't think they're here to sell us cookies."

His jaw went rigid.

"Serge, you can't go any further."

"How are you going to find the drive?"

"I dunno, but it's bible night at the church. Your dad—"

"Don't call him that."

"—won't be home for a while." I pulled the key out of the ignition and opened the door. "Stay here. Okay?"

Stone-faced, he nodded. "There's a key by the back door, in a flower pot. You'll know it because the roses are dead and all that's left are the thorns and crooked branches. The flash drive is green with a silver top."

The cold metal of the door bit my fingers as I slammed it shut. Dead leaves chased dust down the darkened street. I flipped the col-lar of my jacket up started jogging to the house. The acrid, burning stench of rotten eggs, rubber, plastic, and brimstone, left the air putrid.

Half a block away, I stopped. Getting the flash drive was a great idea. Walking into a den of evil spirits and being eaten alive was not. I hesitated and took a step back. Nausea hit, hard and fast, and drove me to my knees.

I may have wanted to turn back, but the forces that ruled my gift had decided differently. Lucky me. I groaned and pulled myself to my feet. A step forward and the sick feeling vanished. Still, I didn't move, too worried by what I saw to rush in.

Maybe it was a force field, maybe it was a boundary the spirits couldn't cross, I wasn't sure. The houses on either side of the Popovs stood straight, quiet. Mr. and Mrs. Popovs' house on the other hand...a photo-negative effect was in place, turning the house a sick, stark white that flickered and sparked against the too-black sky. The lines and air around the house bent and swayed, making the residence seem liquid, blurred paints mixing together and running down the drain. Keening shadows blipped in and out of sight, flew in manic circles around the columns of electric green and purple. The smell of rot and decomposition made my nose burn.

Crap, we were so screwed.

The wind rushed at me. It ran its smooth tongue down my skin, licked the sweat from my temple. I stumbled forward. My foot stuttered against the asphalt. I pushed ahead, raced along the sidewalk.

The air this close to the house was mouldering, fetid. Lightning crackled and thunder boomed. I jogged up the driveway, taking shallow breaths, and headed to the back door before common sense and terror could force me to go the other way. Light emanated from the kitchen windows, but the illumination was courtesy of darker forces and not the utility company. Yellow and soiled, it slid along the stucco walls and puddled on the patio floor. I spotted the planter, dug into the dry dirt, and yanked out the key.

I unlocked the door and found the house cluttered with four spirits. One was skinny—the kind of emaciated only long-term drug use could bring—with an oily comb-over. The second man was short and wiry. These guys worried me but the other two—one in a pale blue Oxford shirt and beige khakis and a California tan, the other with the benign face of an indulgent grandfather, suspenders, and white hair— terrified me. The gaping hole in the floor didn't do anything to put me at ease, either. Smoke poured out of it and from its fathomless depths, the black shadows rose.

I shoved the key in my pocket and left the door open. I turned and peered down the wide hallway.

"Who do you think she is?" asked the grandfather with a cozy rumble of a voice.

The preppy guy looked up. Leaning against granite countertop, he drawled, "Not sure. You want her?"

Grandfather shook his head. "She's too old." Lust infused his face with corrupted light. "If she was in elementary—" He licked his lips and shivered.

The wiry guy moaned his agreement. "They're so tender at that age."

My skin crawled. Pushing down the hallway, I wondered about the most likely place for the flash drive. If I'd been anywhere else, I would have psychically honed in on the device, but I worried that using my abilities would light me up like a Christmas tree at Rockefeller Centre and bring the spirits on me. I knew what they'd done when they lived, and I feared to think of what they were capable of dead.

I moved past the white-stained wooden staircase. Water pooled on the floor and the steps, the transparent sheen marred by cloudy red and the scent of copper. So that's how Lydia Popov had killed herself: in the tub. I continued to move. Black specks floated in the oily air and clung to my skin, clothing. The ash seemed to originate from a room with the door partially open. Taking a deep breath, trying to calm the frantic *clickety-clack* of my stampeding heart, I stepped in.

It was Mr. Popov's study, the walls lined with bookshelves and a desk in the middle. There was a fireplace with a chair and a small table in front of it. On a cushion was a tablet and an empty brandy snifter. Plugged into the electronic device was Serge's flash drive.

I shivered, chilled by the vision of Mikhail Popov, warmed by a fire and lounging in his armchair, drinking liquor, and casually reading the chronology of his destruction of his family. My fingers closed over the tablet and drive. I sped for the front door.

I wrenched it open and found a dark figure looming. Lightning ripped the sky and electric silver brilliance lit up Mikhail Popov's face. His expression slackened in surprise and shock. His gaze bounced to the tablet in my hand, and his lean features twisted into a feral snarl. Before he could move, I slammed the door and raced for the back exit. My feet pounded the hardwood. I saw the open door ahead, the rippling shadows of the wind-swept barren trees beyond.

The preppy guy and the grandfather exchanged wolfish grins. "This might be fun," said the older man.

"High school girls were always my favourite," said Preppy Man. Electricity buzzed from his fingers and forked light hit the door.

My exit slammed shut. The lock shot into place. I skidded to a stop. The hot breath of Mr. Popov heated my skin. Then his hand closed around the back of my neck. He slammed my head into the door. The contact made a sick sound, like watermelon breaking on a cement floor. I bounced off. The tablet dropped from my hand.

"Stupid bitch!" He smashed my head into the wood, again.

I shoved against him, aimed my elbow for his stomach. He grunted, stumbled back. I whirled around. The room spun, my head throbbed, and I tasted the metallic-sweet tang of my blood.

The four spirits stood in a horseshoe around us; the black shadows floated behind them.

I put my fists up. Mr. Popov smiled.

"Get her!"

"Hit her! Hit her hard!"

"Do it! *Do it!*"

Mr. Popov wiped his mouth with the back of his hand. "I've been waiting for this. *Praying* for it."

I flinched. "Don't you—don't you *dare* call God into this!"

He smiled, made a fist. His knuckles connected with my jaw. Sparks of colour showered my vision. "You know your problem? Your father never disciplined you. If he had, maybe you'd have better reflexes."

He hit me again.

The sharp, piercing agony of pain mixed with my terror and rage. I rocked back, fell into the wall.

Preppy Man cheered.

Grandfather's hand disappeared down the front of his pants.

I stepped forward and drove my knee into Mr. Popov's crotch.

His face blanched. He dropped to his knees and vomited.

"Discipline that, you bastard." Bringing all the force and weight I could manage, I drove my knee into the underside of his jaw.

The pointed crack of his teeth snapping together met his guttural groan.

His vomit stained my jeans.

"That wasn't fair," growled Grandfather.

"Get her," snarled Preppy Man.

Grandfather shook his head like a wet dog. Insectile pincers emerged from his mouth, splitting his lips and ripping his flesh. A large, bony collar with ridges and spikes grew from his neck.

Preppy Man shivered. The sculpted lines of his body loosened, blurred. His flesh sagged like melting candle wax as he transformed into a thick, pink wormlike creature. The bristly hair covering the squashed, segmented ridges trembled.

The druggie's body lengthened and thinned as he morphed into a cancerous black snake that had huge chunks of its flesh ripped off.

The wiry man shuddered. His skin rippled and bulged as though something crawled underneath. A fissure split open from his wrist to his elbow, and millions of insects came writhing out, their mandibles clicking, the hiss of their need in the air.

In unison, they stepped to Mr. Popov. Then they stepped *inside* him, pouring into his mouth, his ears and nose, and burrowing into his skin. His screams came out a muffled moan as his body trembled, jittered.

I lunged for the tablet, wrenched the flash drive out, shoved it in my jeans, and grabbed for the lock. Whatever the spirits had done, they'd done well. The knob remained cemented in place. The black shadows swept past me. Their heat burned my eyes and seared my skin.

I pivoted.

Mr. Popov was still on the ground, doing his snaky dance.

I gave him a wide berth, tried to avoid the smoky pit, and rushed for the front door.

His iron grip clamped on my ankle, and with a jerk he brought me to ground.

I used my arms to break my fall.

He dragged me close.

The fog from the hole slithered to me. Oh, man. That wasn't smoke, anymore. It was hundreds of scuttling hands. I twisted my head away. They grabbed my hair. The fog pulled me to the pit. Mr. Popov pulled me to him. The contact from concentrated evil twisted my insides, left me roiling with nausea, and covered me with a thick, suffocating energy full of perverted images.

The beings fought for control, pulled me taut. I hovered on the knife's edge of destruction and screamed at the excruciating pain of my shoulder dislocating from its socket.

"Maggie!"

Through the revolting haze of the demented aura, I saw the tops of Serge's sneakers. An explosion of white light blasted from him. The creatures squealed and recoiled. Serge grabbed me by the arm and I shrieked in pain.

"I'll apologize later! Look away!" He shoved my head to his chest.

Another foundation-shaking explosion rocked the house. Splinters and fragments flew into the room as the door detonated. Serge hauled me out.

Shifting from certain-death to possible-survival, my body pumped painkillers and adrenaline into my system. The knee-buckling agony disappeared. We ran. "How did you make everything explode?"

"I don't know," he said through gritted teeth. "We'll figure it out later." Half a block away, he turned and said, "You're not going to like this," and then, without waiting for me to ask "Like, what?" He grabbed my wrist with one hand, my shoulder with the other, and snapped my arm back into place.

The shock took the strength from my legs.

He caught me.

I fought the urge to pass out and swallowed back my nausea. "I thought I was immune to spirits."

"We'll work on your superpowers right after we get to safety."

Together, we raced back to my car and dived inside. I stuck the key in the ignition and waited for the horror-movie moment when the car wouldn't start, but it roared to life and I blew out my pent-up breath.

I threw the gearshift into drive and peeled away from the curb.

Serge looked back. His face blanched of colour. Twisting back, he stared at me with terror-filled eyes. "Oh God, Maggie. They're coming for us."

CHAPTER THIRTY-SIX

The car lurched down the feeder streets as we raced for Parsons Avenue. I kept my eyes on the twists and turns ahead. Serge kept a running commentary of what was going on behind us. Flopping down and looking at me, he said, "I wish you had a faster car."

Mr. Popov's high beams flashed in my rear-view mirror. "I'm doing my best but this isn't exactly a Daytona-approved race vehicle." My foot stamped on the accelerator hard enough to push my foot through the bottom of the car. I dug into my jacket pocket and yanked out my cell. The screen was smashed. I pressed the power button. "No!"

"What?"

I tossed the phone at him. "It's out of power."

He fumbled and caught it.

I pumped the brakes and took a hard left on Claxton. The tires squealed but the car held its ground. My fingers, numb from fear and adrenaline, lost hold of the wheel. It spun back to its original position. I grabbed it with one hand and flipped the heat on with the other. Dusty air hissed through the vents, but if it held any warmth, I didn't feel it.

My mind was focused on one of the big problems of living in a small town: late at night, everyone's home. The streets were bare, save the gravel and leaves. If I wanted help, I'd have to pull to the curb and get out. Between Mr. Popov and his band of merry men, I'd make it to the front door…if I was lucky. I took a right on Sierra and did the next best thing. As the car hurtled along the avenue, heading for the bridge, I laid on the horn and made as much noise as possible. If it didn't get people going to their doors and looking out, surely *someone* would call the police and I'd get back up.

The lamplights zipped past, the rows of dark houses—the sleepy rise of their roofs against the backdrop of night—blurred as the needle of the speedometer tipped to 75 km/hr. Ahead, the metal rafters of the bridge came into view.

I heard the roar of the car behind me.

Mr. Popov rammed his vehicle into mine.

My car lurched forward.

He hit me again, this time on the right side of my bumper.

Serge and I spun in a nausea-inducing circle. The world smeared into a sickening blotch of monochromatic colour. I clutched the wheel. The car bounced off the cement posts of the bridge, and the screech of metal grinding against the bridge girders shrieked in my ears. When the momentum stopped, I found us facing north on Sierra. I needed to turn the car around and head in the opposite direction. The only problem: Mr. Popov's car blocked the road.

I put my arm on the passenger seat, threw the car into reverse and sped down the road.

"Maggie, he's gaining!"

"I know! It's a lot harder to drive backwards than you'd think." The car wouldn't—couldn't—go any faster. "You're electricity," I yelled. "Can't you do something?"

Serge put his hands through the dashboard. Lightning forks of red light shot out of the hood. The car raced away.

Serge tried to give juice to the phone, but the cell remained black.

Panic turned me into a moron. I found myself yelling, "We're almost there!" as though Serge was incapable of seeing that for himself.

Popov's car was suddenly blocking the way.

I hit my brakes. "How's that possible?"

Before Serge could respond, his father slammed his car into mine. I was going too fast to correct the trajectory of the vehicle. The car careened to the railing. I mashed the brakes, but Mr. Popov was behind in a bigger, stronger vehicle and pushing me towards the edge.

"Put down your window, Maggie! Put it down!"

Why, I wanted to scream, *why*? But then the car was smashing through the railing in a hair-raising, sickening *crunch* of bent beams and broken rivets, and I was plunging to the dark water beneath. Then

I realized why he was telling me to roll down the window: it would be my only way to escape the vehicle—if I survived the impact.

The car jolted to a stop. I slammed—face-first—into the wheel. The wood cracked my skull. I tasted blood and heard the celery-cracking sound of cartilage breaking. Pulling myself away, moaning in pain, I realized we were hanging at a ninety-degree angle. "What the—"

I turned painfully to Serge.

He rose on his knees, his eyes glued to the back of the car, and tilting to the side, pushed his head out the window.

I fumbled for the seatbelt and released myself from the harness.

His face returned to view. Eyes wide, he said, "It's Craig."

I twisted around. A torso almost as wide as the back windshield, lean and cut, with green-black scales whose edges glowed red. A pointed tail flicked into my vision. It moved with serpentine grace to my door, opened it.

"Maggie."

His voice—though it sounded as though it was a hundred voices combined—rumbled and vibrated through my bones.

"Lean out."

I didn't want to die. Didn't want to plunge into ice-cold water. But this version of Craig, massive and imposing, with a tail whose circumference was the size of my entire body, terrified me.

"It's fine."

I heard the rumbling gentleness in his words.

"Trust me."

"It's okay," Serge said. "Lean out. He'll catch you."

I unclenched my fingers from the headrest and put my right foot on the driver's railing. Taking a breath, I gripped the side of the car's frame. Wind whipped around my face, its scent cold and tart with the smell of decaying leaves and algae from the water below. I leaned out and got a full view of Craig.

He wasn't massive. He was *gigantic*. Wide didn't describe him—his thigh must have been the circumference of a big rig. His legs ended in hooves. Muscle rippled on muscle. His wings seemed to block the night, and though they were scales, the wind made them flutter like feathers. Red-orange eyes glowed at me. His tail curled around my waist and pulled me to his chest.

"Serge?" He asked.

The ghost appeared on top of the car. "I think I can get myself to the bridge."

"Are you sure?"

He shook his head.

Craig held out his hand.

Serge took it, careful to avoid the six-inch claws.

Craig let go of the car. It plunged into the inky water and a geyser shot up as it hit the surface. With one beat of his enormous wings, he brought us back to the bridge.

Popov swivelled and pointed at Craig. "Your pet protected you, but that won't happen again." His voice was a mix of the demons and himself.

"What is he talking about? Can he see you or is that the dead talking?"

"He sees me, but trust me"—Craig's voice rumbled—"that isn't a good thing."

I glanced over to where Serge stood clutching the edge of the broken rail. "Can he see his son?"

Craig's glowing eyes turned the ghost's way. "Not yet."

"Finish her," Reverend Popov's words hissed, sizzled. He gave me a predator's smile and in the voice of the preppy man responded to himself with, "I will."

The sound of his voice made me feel as though someone had shoved a hot skewer into my eardrums. I slapped my hands over my ears, trying to stem the burning, piercing sensation.

"Do it now." The legion of spirits looked over at Craig. "Stay out of this, Ferrier." Popov's tongue flicked out. Skinny, triple-forked, and with sharp barbs on its end, it undulated as though scenting the air.

Craig loomed over me.

The reverend's flicked his tongue out again. "She lives or dies by herself."

Craig gave him an evil smile. "As you wish." A red-orange ball of light appeared in his palm. Fast and ruthless, before I had time to figure out what he was doing, he launched the light at Mr. Popov.

He screamed—*howled*—as the demons shot out of his body.

Craig's tail snaked out and grabbed the men. They bellowed in pain at his touch. "Let's get you home, shall we?" He looked at me. "This is yours to handle." Then he disappeared.

Mr. Popov blinked and glancing around, stared through Serge. "Where—?" His gaze honed in on me. "You," he snarled. "You were in my house. With the drive." He took a menacing step towards me. "Give it back and I'll let you live."

"No." I held my ground. "You're evil. You killed your son—"

"His whore of a mother did that."

"You put her up to it."

He smiled. "She's always been a good wife." Then he rushed me.

I spun and dived out of his way, but he caught me by the hip and dragged me to the ground. My chin smashed into the road. The hard metal girding sliced my skin and drove pain through my bones.

He grabbed me by the hair, yanked my head back.

Instinct said he was going to strangle me.

I twisted around.

"Hit him in the crotch! Punch his solar plexus!"

There was too much movement, too much action for me to be able to follow Serge's commands. I reached up, clawed at anything solid I could find. My fingers found the soft wet of his eyes. I gouged my nails into them.

Popov howled.

I tore myself away. There was nowhere to run. Nowhere to hide. Where was the police? Had *no one* phoned in the noise? How was I going to fight a guy twice my size? I put my head down and charged him. Driving into his stomach with my shoulder, I brought him to ground. His head hit the road with a sickening *thunk* and he lay still.

Serge ran to me. "Is that it?"

"It can't be," I gasped. "It can't be that easy." I bent over Popov. Big mistake.

His eyes snapped open. He grabbed me around the neck and started squeezing. I clawed at his hand, but his grip was iron-tight. He rolled and suddenly, I was on my back, the cold hardness of the metal seeping past my clothing. Mr. Popov straddled my chest and squeezed harder. My head throbbed, my lungs burned. Sparks of light exploded in front of my eyes. I kicked, trying to drive my knees into his back but the lack of oxygen left me weak, helpless.

Serge loomed over Popov. "I hope this works." He took a breath. He drew his hand back, opened his fingers and shoved his palm between his dad's shoulder blades.

His fingers poked through the older man's chest. Mr. Popov jerked, his eyes widened. "What the—"

Blood rushed into my head, a pounding, throbbing, painful rhythm. I shoved him back and stuttered to my feet.

Serge pulled his hand out.

Popov spun around. He fell on his butt and crab-walked backwards. His mouth gaped open and closed. "What—" He clutched at his chest. Then he turned, fumbled to his feet and ran.

"Get him, Maggie."

Serge didn't need to encourage me—I was already on my feet and chasing the minister. My raw throat burned, I had the migraine from hell, and my lungs felt bathed in acid, but I was going to get him, make him pay for what he'd done. I came abreast of him and shoulder checked him into the beam of the bridge.

He ricocheted off the girder and fell against the railing. Popov jerked and scuttled backwards. His feet slipped and he pitched over the side.

Instinct made me grab him.

Craig appeared beside me, in human form, and caught hold of the reverend as he began to slip from my grasp. "We have to let go," he said. "He's not to live past tonight."

I jerked. "What? No. He has to account for what he did to Serge."

"Let him go."

Mr. Popov's terror-filled eyes met mine. "Don't! Don't let me die."

Maybe it was the lack of oxygen or the fight between instinct and justice that left my mind muddled. "No—that's killing him. I can't just—isn't that vengeance? Shouldn't we—"

"Maggie." Craig's voice was quiet. "This life was for you to decide if you wanted to be a protector—"

"I do—but—"

"This is the frontline stuff I was telling you about. There is the human legal system and there is justice. You need to decide which you'll follow."

Mr. Popov and I exchanged a long look.

"Serge," I said. "This is your call. I'll do what you want."

The reverend's eyes widened. "Why are you calling him?"

"You don't want to drop him?" Serge peered over the edge to the water below.

"I'm—I'm not sure." I clutched at the older man's arm. "It feels wrong to me."

"Then don't do it." He looked at Craig. "Turn me solid. Let me talk to him."

The ferrier did.

When the reverend saw Serge, he jerked and bucked, his eyes white with terror. He babbled, incoherent.

Serge came behind me, grabbed the reverend's arms. "Let go, Maggie."

I did.

"Get out of the way."

I ducked under his elbow and moved into Craig's embrace.

"I—I—it wasn't me." Terror pitched his voice high. "Your mother killed you. Son—"

Serge laughed, the sound held no humour. "There was a day when all I wanted was for you to call me that."

"She was unbalanced—ill."

"Did you tell her to kill me?"

"No—no." He wheezed like he was trying to laugh through a closed throat. "I told her to take care of it—you—but she got it wrong. It was her. Why would I kill you?"

"Amber was pregnant."

"So? It wouldn't have changed anything." The air was thick with his lie.

"Did you kill my mother?"

Reverend Popov shook his head with such force I thought it would snap. "No, no, no! She did that! She did that, alone! I swear it!"

"You didn't tell her to."

"Suicide is against God's law."

"So is beating your family."

He flinched. "I've made mistakes. Forgive me—I'll do my time. I won't put in an innocent plea. I'll tell the police everything—don't kill me!"

Serge pulled his father to him, grabbed him by the shirtfront.

The reverend's feet found the bridge's solid ground and he laughed, relieved. "I knew you couldn't—"

"You tortured me," said Serge, his face set into quiet lines, his voice solemn. "It's not about forgiveness, anymore."

The older man's smile trembled, fell.

"I was a child. All I wanted was your love, your acceptance. Instead, you beat me, burned me, and locked me in closets. Every day I was alive, you murdered me a little at a time." Serge pulled the reverend close, until they were nose-to-nose. "I asked Craig to turn me solid because I wanted you to see me. I want the last thing you'll ever see to be the face of justice." His fingers tightened, then Serge shoved him off the bridge.

CHAPTER THIRTY-SEVEN

Popov plunged towards the water, but he seemed to fall in slow motion. The world went quiet. He must have been screaming, but there was silence, the quiet *hush* of the physical and metaphysical world touching each other. The minister hit the water. A column of dark liquid rushed past him, swallowed his body.

One, two. On my third breath the water exploded, turning a violent purple colour. Popov shot out of the water, fast and hard. His mouth contorted in a soundless scream. His body came level with us and he hung there, suspended by what, I didn't know. His eyes rolled in terror, foam sprayed from his mouth.

"What's going on?"

Craig touched my shoulder. "Here's part of it."

Fog and mist covered the bridge. The guttural, high-pitched squeals of Mr. Popov left my ears throbbing. I scanned his body, but I still couldn't see what held him.

From the mist, a woman appeared. Tall, with lush, blue-black skin and clothed in a white ancient Grecian robe, she seemed to glide to us.

"You've done well," she said in a deep voice.

I leaned towards Serge. "Is she—?"

He nodded.

"I know you're all angry," she said. Giving Craig a small smile, she touched his cheek. "But to be a protector and to be a guardian is to exist at a higher level. The danger is real, the chances of failure, high." She turned from him and cupped my face.

Her touch was warm, healing. Peace flowed from her into me, and the sense that everything had worked out as it should, that I was right where I needed to be, thrummed through my system. "As you get older, the memories of your past lives come back to you. One day you'll understand why I needed to be cruel."

"Are you the woman from the radio?" I asked.

Her eyes clouded, sadness pulled down her full mouth. "No, my darling, I am not, but you will find her soon enough."

I wanted to be worried, I wanted to ask a million questions, but her peace flooded me, left me languid. The sense that I was going to walk through fire but not be burned, that though the future was scary, I was not to *fear* it, left my tongue motionless in my mouth.

She let go of me and turned to Serge. "Come, my darling. Come to me."

He moved into her embrace.

"Such a hard life," she murmured as she held him. "So much worse than you'd scripted before this birth. Rest easy, my love. Your pain is gone. The memories can no longer hurt you."

He melted into her. Their forms blurred and for a moment, he glowed neon-white. She gave him a final squeeze then let go, and turned to Mr. Popov.

"Mikhail, oh my little one, the choices you had, the decisions you made. I'm so sorry this was the life you chose. You had such...potential." She sighed and sounded full of sorrow as she said, "Come, now, we must take care of you before you transition."

A low hum, like electricity running through wires, vibrated in the air. Tentacles shot from the water, snaked around Popov's arms and legs. He began to scream, to *howl*.

His cry ripped through me, made me feel like vomiting.

He continued to scream, though I could see nothing but the arms holding him. Serge, however, must have, because his face was a mask of revulsion and fascination.

"Serge?"

He took my hand.

There was a blinding light and then I saw what he saw: Popov over a boiling lake of lava. Scrawny, emaciated creatures with green skin and large black eyes scurried along his body. Instead of mouths, they had large, gaping holes, wounds from which multiple, pointed tongues emerged and licked his skin. Popov's flesh peeled back, layer by layer, exposing unprotected nerves. Everywhere they touched, a blistering wound was left.

"What are they—?"

"They are Serge's memories of abuse, his pain and humiliation, his yearning for his father's love, and his confusion at his rejection," said the woman.

Serge blinked, his jaw worked up and down. He looked at me with glassy eyes.

I put my arm around him and pulled him close.

He smiled down at me.

"Everything we do to others imprints on their souls and at death, we must account for these decisions. We must live through all the joy and pain we've caused." She watched Mr. Popov writhe. "For him, there will only be pain."

"What about my mother?" asked Serge. "Why isn't she here to make him pay?"

The woman took his hand. "She couldn't be here."

"Because she killed herself—?"

"No, my darling, because she's chosen something else."

I didn't like the way she spoke the words. There was sadness in her voice, resignation and a hint of anger.

Her eyes found mine. "We all have choices. In life and in death." She turned back to Mr. Popov. "Craig, I don't think we'll be needing your services. I believe we know where Mikhail will spend his eternity."

"Wait," I said, "I thought everyone transitions—is reborn."

"Hera is right," said Craig. "We have choices in life and death. We make reality based on what we believe." He nodded to the pastor. "He believes in eternal hellfire and damnation, in swift, cruel, unrelenting punishment. He will spend his eternity like this, living in Serge's pain." Craig paused. "Not everyone gets a ferrier. Not everyone sees the light."

The police cruiser's lights retreated down the trail. The cops had cordoned off the broken section of the bridge, taken my statements, and listened to Craig's version of events. Divers were still dragging the water for Mr. Popov's body.

Nancy came to me, her jacket open despite the cold night, her cheeks red from the wind. "The official report will back up everything you say—uh—everything physical you say." She patted my knee as Craig walked over. "Can you tell me what really happened?" she asked.

I glanced at my boyfriend and said, "He died."

She hesitated.

"You don't want to know more," said Craig. "Not right now."

She and Dad exchanged looks, and she nodded.

"What about me surviving the bridge plunge? How do we explain that?"

She shrugged. "Most people have a hard time remembering their trauma." She glanced at the evidence bag clipped to the board in her hands. "If you have holes in your memory, no one will question it. This flash drive will give us all we need about Popov." She hesitated and glanced around. "Serge—?"

"I'm standing beside you."

Her cell beeped. She looked down and turned in his direction. "We found journals your mother kept. She admitted to trying to kill Amber. But her suicide, you were partially right. Her phone shows a call from Mikhail an hour before she died. The call lasted a half-hour... he probably talked her into it." Nancy looked at us. "If Mikhail had survived—"

"Yeah, I know. You would have prosecuted him." Serge folded his arms across his chest. He walked to the broken railing and looked down. "With a good lawyer, time in jail during the prosecution, and good behaviour while incarcerated, he would have been out in five, maybe fifteen years."

Nancy read his words, her mouth pulled back in a grimace. She looked up at me, her gaze direct. "About what happened to Mikhail tonight...tell me he suffered."

"For eternity."

She nodded, satisfied.

"Let's go home," said Dad. "With the Popovs out of the way, we can finally get Serge buried, properly."

"I have a couple of things to wrap up," said Nancy.

"Dad." I handed him the coffee. "Why don't you help her? I need to talk to Craig, alone."

The lines of his mouth hardened, but he sighed and climbed out. "Don't think this gets you off the hook. I'm in a weird state between being ecstatic you're alive, wanting to do some kind of spirit quest to kick the ass of whatever thing decided this was your destiny, wanting to know all the gory details, and being terrified of what you'll tell me." He pointed his finger at me. "When we get home, you're telling me *everything*." He handed me his cell. "Try not to drain the battery on this one."

"Drain the battery?" asked Craig.

"My phone—it won't hold a charge."

"I know why that's happening," said Craig.

We waited.

"It's the combined energy between me, Serge, and Maggie. It's shorting out the battery."

"Great," Dad muttered. "What is she supposed to do if she needs help?"

"It only happens when we're together, and if she's in trouble—" He shrugged. "I may be ten thousand years old, but I still have some game."

Dad gave him a paternal glare. "And if you need help?"

"Maggie's here. Serge will be around, too. If we're incapacitated, the force will come."

I blinked. So did Dad. "I'm going to need visual aides to understand all of this," he muttered. "Forces or not, stay safe. All of you."

I scooted to the edge of the seat and flung my arms around him. "I love you, Daddy."

"I love you too, Maggie." Tears clogged his words.

I pulled back at looked at my ghostly friend. "Serge," I said, "You too. Give me some time with Craig."

He frowned. "What? I know why you don't want your dad and Nancy to know certain things, but—"

Dad and Nancy looked at their phones.

"—because," I said. "You shouldn't hear what I'm about to say, not if I'm wrong."

His eyes narrowed. "Wrong about what?"

I sighed. "Serge, please. Trust me."

"Fine." He scowled and walked away. So did Dad and Nancy.

Craig climbed into the seat next to me. "What didn't you want Serge to hear?"

"When we were at his house and attacked by the creature—" I took a breath. "That thing was his mother, wasn't it?" I twisted in my chair to face him. "When I'd asked you what it was, you said it blamed Serge for its life, but the only person whose life really connected with him was his mom."

A long, heavy sigh left his lips. "Yeah."

I slumped in my chair. "This guy can't catch a break. He's tormented by his father in life and in death, his mother tries to kill him because she blames him for the way her life turned out." I paused. "She's not gone, is she?"

"No."

"Will she come back for him?"

"Yes. For her to have transformed into—" He sighed. "There is no accountability in her, no responsibility. Her hatred, her complete inability to see her mistakes...Serge will be in danger." He took my hand and his fingers were strong, warm, as they wrapped around mine.

I laid my head on his shoulder and looked over to where Serge stood.

He looked at me.

I smiled and waved him over.

He grinned and came toward us.

"I never thought we'd be friends, but it's more than that," I said. "I feel the lifetime connections, the eternal bond." I looked up at my boyfriend. "He's important to me. I'll protect him." I felt Craig's warm breath on my hair as he kissed my head.

"I know," he said as Serge came into our circle. "And I will, too."

"What will you do?" asked the ghost.

"Protect you," I said.

He smiled as he crawled in between us and flung his arms around our shoulders. "Me, too," he said. "I'll protect you both." He looked into the dark night and chuckled. "Who'd have thought I'd have to die in order to start living?"

I smiled.

"Get ready," said Craig. "Life and death's about to get really interesting."

ACKNOWLEDGMENTS

Much thanks to my editor Catharina de Bakker for her support, enthusiasm, and edits on *Guardian*.